Fred faced us. He wore a stern expression as he stared. There was no way he or the women at his table could hear our conversation. Maybe he didn't like seeing me talk to the police. *Too bad.* I turned away.

"Who else does Isabelle donate to?" I kept my voice soft.

"Still working on that," Wanda said.

She'd been forthcoming about Isabelle's past. Maybe I could learn a bit more about the case, things I doubted Harris or Octavia would tell me.

"Wanda, what do you know about alibis?" I asked. "For people like Zeke, Wendy Corbett, and Isabelle?"

"Zeke and his lady love claim they were with each other. Maybe they were, maybe they weren't. Ms. Cooper lives alone. I'm afraid old Don's a problem, too. His wife was out of town. As was . . ." She glanced at the slim gold band on my ring finger.

"Yeah, as was Abe." Should I challenge her about suspecting me? No. I didn't think she was serious. I sure hoped she wasn't. "Sorry I asked . . ."

Books by Maddie Day

Country Store Mysteries
FLIPPED FOR MURDER
GRILLED FOR MURDER
WHEN THE GRITS HIT THE FAN
BISCUITS AND SLASHED BROWNS
DEATH OVER EASY
STRANGLED EGGS AND HAM
NACHO AVERAGE MURDER
CANDY SLAIN MURDER
NO GRATER CRIME
BATTER OFF DEAD
FOUR LEAF CLEAVER
DEEP FRIED DEATH
CHRISTMAS COCOA MURDER
(with Carlene O'Connor and Alex Erickson)
CHRISTMAS SCARF MURDER
(with Carlene O'Connor and Peggy Ehrhart)

Cozy Capers Book Group Mysteries
MURDER ON CAPE COD
MURDER AT THE TAFFY SHOP
MURDER AT THE LOBSTAH SHACK
MURDER IN A CAPE COTTAGE
MURDER AT A CAPE BOOKSTORE

Local Foods Mysteries
A TINE TO LIVE, A TINE TO DIE
'TIL DIRT DO US PART
FARMED AND DANGEROUS
MURDER MOST FOWL
MULCH ADO ABOUT MURDER

Cece Barton Mysteries
MURDER UNCORKED
CHRISTMAS MITTENS MURDER
(with Lee Hollis and Lynn Cahoon)

Published by Kensington Publishing Corp.

A Country Store Mystery

Deep Fried Death

MADDIE DAY

Kensington Publishing Corp.
www.kensingtonbooks.com

KENSINGTON BOOKS are published by

Kensington Publishing Corp.
119 West 40th Street
New York, NY 10018

Copyright © 2024 by Edith Maxwell

All rights reserved. No part of this book may be reproduced in any form or by any means without the prior written consent of the Publisher, excepting brief quotes used in reviews.

To the extent that the image or images on the cover of this book depict a person or persons, such person or persons are merely models, and are not intended to portray any character or characters featured in the book.

This book is a work of fiction. Names, characters, businesses, organizations, places, events, and incidents either are the product of the author's imagination or are used fictitiously. Any resemblance to actual persons, living or dead, events, or locales is entirely coincidental.

If you purchased this book without a cover you should be aware that this book is stolen property. It was reported as "unsold and destroyed" to the Publisher and neither the Author nor the Publisher has received any payment for this "stripped book."

All Kensington titles, imprints, and distributed lines are available at special quantity discounts for bulk purchases for sales promotion, premiums, fund-raising, educational, or institutional use.

Special book excerpts or customized printings can also be created to fit specific needs. For details, write or phone the office of the Kensington Sales Manager: Attn.: Sales Department. Kensington Publishing Corp., 119 West 40th Street, New York, NY 10018. Phone: 1-800-221-2647.

KENSINGTON and the KENSINGTON COZIES teapot logo Reg US Pat. & TM Off.

First Printing: January 2024
ISBN: 978-1-4967-4226-1

ISBN: 978-1-4967-4227-8 (ebook)

10 9 8 7 6 5 4 3 2 1

Printed in the United States of America

For my two brilliant and beautiful daughters-in-law, Alison Bliss Russell and Alexandra Santiago Llegus. Thank you for making my boys happy.

Acknowledgments

Apologies to the real Abe Martin Festival and "Nashcar" Outhouse Race in Nashville, Indiana. When I read about it, I couldn't resist staging a body in a fake outhouse. As far as I know, no murders have ever occurred during the Abe Martin celebrations.

Many thanks to Nashville Chief of Police Heather Burris, who seemed delighted to answer my many questions. I've modeled my Chief Haley Harris on her but kept Harris fictional, so I could make her say things and act in ways the real chief likely never would.

Once again I'm pleased to feature a recipe from Jane Deichler Carter. Her mother-in-law was Hoosier Rosemary Carter, an intrepid Quaker farmer, who passed along the apple dumplings recipe—albeit a bit scant on details—to Jane. Jane's husband Max Carter is the professor I refer to in the book. They are both also Quakers and delightful people, and Jane is a big fan of cozy mysteries. The no-fail pie crust recipe is in *From Julia Child's Kitchen* (1975).

I stole the name for the accountant mentioned in the book from my expert tax person, Ann O'Sullivan. Thank you to Hoosier Jeff Danielson for spring flora and fauna details. Thanks also to long-time grad-school friend Guta Ribeiro, who has returned to live in Bloomington, for other local touches.

Alert readers will notice the murder has nothing to do with deep-frying. We loved the title so much we had to use it.

My versions of the Indiana University women's (and men's) basketball teams, their playing records, and their personal lives are entirely fictional. As someone whose grandfather (Allan B. Maxwell) was captain of the IU basketball team in 1916, I would never cast aspersions on a Hoosier netter.

Gratitude, always, to Jennifer McKee, who relieves me from having to create my own social media graphics (mine wouldn't be pretty, just saying) and who helps me behind the scenes with all kinds of authorly tasks.

I've been blogging and hanging out with my talented Wicked Author pals—Barb Ross, Liz Mugavero, Julie Hennrikus, Sherry Harris, and Jessie Crockett—for eleven years. I couldn't have navigated this path without them. Readers, please find us at wickedauthors.com.

Thank you, always, to my agent, John Talbot, and to John Scognamiglio, Larissa Ackerman, and the rest of the amazing and hardworking crew at Kensington Publishing. I love my publishing home.

Blessings go out to all my (so many!) devoted fans of this series. You were thrilled by the news at the end of *Four Leaf Cleaver*, as was I, and I hope you enjoy this story just as much.

Finally, love and fierce hugs to my sons Allan and John David and their wives, Alison and Alex, to my sisters, Janet and Barbara, and to my Hugh. You are my world.

CHAPTER 1

Whoever thought a parking lot full of brightly painted outhouses was a good idea had too much time on their hands. What could possibly go wrong? Plenty.

"What did we get ourselves into?" I asked my co-chef Danna Beedle from the back seat of the pickup truck we'd borrowed as Turner Rao, my other full-time employee, drove the truck into the lot at the top of the hill.

"Hey, you're the one who filled out the application form," she said.

"It's good publicity for Pans 'N Pancakes," Turner added. "Now let's get this baby unloaded so we can all enjoy our Friday evening."

The baby he referred to was our themed rustic outhouse, which of course wasn't a real outhouse at all. Kitted out with two small window boxes planted with real geraniums, the outhouse rested on a four-wheel base. It had a Dutch door in the front and a wide handle on the back for pushing or pulling it. Inside was a bench seat and a steering lever. The top Dutch door had the classic crescent moon cut out of it, and my country store restaurant's logo of a grinning stack of pancakes holding a skillet was painted on the back.

This parking lot was on the highest hill in Nashville, the county seat for Brown County, Indiana. All the outhouses would race down the hill tomorrow morning, powered only by gravity, as part of the Abe Martin Festival. I didn't care if we won, but, as Turner pointed out, it was good publicity.

After we successfully slid the outhouse down the portable ramps Turner's dad had included in the truck loan, I glanced around for direction. Camilla Kalb stood not far away. She owned Cammie's Kitchen here in Nashville, a popular home-style eatery. Her entry resembled the restaurant, painted red and white with lace curtains at the fake windows. A cast-iron skillet hung from a hook on one side and a muffin tin on the other.

"I'll be right back," I told my team and headed her way.

"Hey, Camilla," I said. "Do you know who's in charge?"

She greeted me. "Zeke Martin is, Robbie, but he's being his usual pedantic self." She gestured across the lot. A man held a clipboard and was talking to a woman quite a bit shorter than he.

"Thanks. I'll check with him." I'd heard of Zeke, but I hadn't realized he was the one organizing the race.

"Good luck." She raised a penciled-on eyebrow.

I made my way past the Nashville Library outhouse, the walls of which held real books on shelves.

I passed the Step Up Thrift store outhouse and the South Lick Bikes entry, which had bike wheels in many sizes fixed to the sides. The Nashville Fire Department's was painted bright red.

I slowed, blinking, at the sight of the person standing next to the entry for Hickory Fine Art Gallery. What was Jim Shermer doing here?

"Jim?" I asked the man who had thrown over our budding romance a few years ago for a former lover, whom he was now married to. I no longer cared, being happily married, myself.

He turned, then took a step back. "Robbie Jordan." His gaze shifted anywhere but at my face, and he shoved his hands in the pockets of his khakis as if to hide an onset of nerves. Jim's eyes were as green as ever, but the dark red hair, now tied back in a thin ponytail, had mostly disappeared from his brow.

"I thought you were living in Indianapolis," I said.

"We, ah, moved back to Brown County."

"It looks like you work at an art gallery." I didn't get to Nashville that often. Even if I'd been browsing the shops, acquiring fine art wasn't something I made a practice of.

"I actually own it." He gestured at the outhouse walls, which were adorned with folk art in the style of Grandma Moses.

I blinked again. He owned the gallery?

He flipped his hands open. "It's more interesting than real estate law."

"I suppose. Is Octavia still with the state police?" I'd met the detective after the body of a murdered woman had been deposited in my restaurant. It

was during that case that she and Jim had reconnected in the fullest sense of the word.

"She is."

He glanced at my Pans 'N Pancakes t-shirt, my
daily uniform, albeit one that fit more snugly by
the day. It was a bit early for much of a baby bump,
but I could already feel my pregnant body growing
fuller.

A commotion drew my attention away. The
woman Zeke had been speaking to threw a hand in
the air and turned her back. Now that I was closer,
I could see it was Evermina Martin, the proprietor
of the new Miss South Lick Diner, a breakfast and
lunch restaurant in direct competition with my
own, or at least that was how she'd positioned it.
I'd heard she was also Zeke's ex-wife.

"Uh-oh," Jim murmured.

CHAPTER 2

Zeke Martin blustered his way toward us. In his forties, he looked trim in a blue polo shirt and linen Bermuda shorts. Unlike Jim's, his hairline was intact, his dark hair neatly styled. His features were anything but neatly arranged. He'd pressed his lips together and narrowed his eyes. The pale skin of his neck was mottled with red.

He opened his mouth. I didn't need anger in my life, not today, not ever.

I preempted him. "I'm Robbie Jordan. Where do you want the Pans 'N Pancakes entry?" I pointed behind me, vaguely in the direction of our outhouse.

He tapped his pen on the clipboard. "You were supposed to have it here at four o'clock."

"I run a business." I kept my cool. "We loaded up after we closed and cleaned the restaurant. We made it over here as soon as we could."

"It's only four thirty, Zeke," Jim said.

"As long as your outhouse is in the lot, you can

leave it anywhere." He checked off my entry on his list. "We'll line everybody up in the morning. But don't be here any later than eight. Race gets going at nine sharp."

"Do you have overnight security?" I asked.

Zeke performed a classic eye-and-head roll. "You think somebody's going to steal a makeshift outhouse on wheels?"

"It's a valid question. The business owners and organizations put a lot of work into these things." Jim gave me a tentative smile. "People might have plans for them afterward. Plus, there's a big prize at stake."

Yeah, the big pot of fame and fortune, which was no more than an aluminum Abe Martin outhouse trophy and a picture in the *Brown County Democrat.* I smiled back.

"The lot's entrance and exit will be roped off after everybody clears out. I'll see you both in the morning." Zeke strode away.

"Much ado about nothing, I'd say." Jim shook his head.

"Everybody has to have their fiefdom." I watched as Zeke gave the next entrants his officious treatment.

A movement near the Miss South Lick Diner outhouse nearby caught my attention. A woman I'd never seen before squatted and peered at the wheel. Her sleeveless top showed off tanned and toned biceps. She looked about my age and had dark hair that fell in that way that expertly cut and styled locks do. Maybe she was a friend of Evermina's.

I turned back to Jim. "If running a fun festival makes Zeke feel powerful, so be it. Do you know what he does for a living?"

"He's a commercial illustrator, but he fancies himself a fine artist. Judging from the work he's tried to convince me to sell, he either doesn't work very hard at it or doesn't have a lick of talent." He glanced behind me.

"Hey, Jimmy," a woman's voice said.

I turned, but not before I saw Jim cringe.

"Can you give me a hand, hon?" Evermina stroked the corner of her green outhouse with one hand as she set her other hand on a cocked hip. The name of her diner was lettered on the side of the outhouse. A sign mounted on the roof read, *Best Eats in South Lick*. The other woman had disappeared. "Hi there, Robbie. Do you know Jimmy?"

"I do," I said.

Her snug V-neck top was the same color as the outhouse. Evermina's tight jeans looked hot and uncomfortable to me, but they definitely showed off her curves. Her bouffant blond hair and heavily made-up eyes seemed out of the previous century and made her look as much of a caricature as the folksy comic strip guy the festival celebrated.

"Good luck tomorrow to you both," I said. "See you later, Jim."

He gave me a desperate look, which I ignored. Jim was an adult. He could handle Evermina's come-hither look—or he couldn't. It wasn't my problem. I didn't need to spend any more time with either of them.

I made my way back to my staff. Pans 'N Pancakes offered good eats in South Lick. We were a popular restaurant, and I was confident we could withstand competition from a new diner. As long as I got tomorrow's breakfast prep done.

CHAPTER 3

They weren't kidding when they called it "morning" sickness. I usually felt fine later in the day. But beginning at about four AM, I was just plain nauseous.

I'd gone early to the restaurant Saturday morning to get the first batches of biscuits cut and into the oven. I mixed up the pancake batter and started the first pots of coffee. Too bad the smell of the brewing java, an aroma I loved and usually inhaled on purpose, made me feel even sicker. Still, I had a business to run.

It was a stretch for Turner, Danna, and me to all be out on a weekend morning when Pans 'N Pancakes invariably had a line of hungry customers out the door. My fourth employee, Len Perlman, had arrived on time at six thirty, though, and Danna's mom, Mayor Corrine Beedle, had offered to help out until we returned after the race. She'd shown up at the appointed time, too.

Now, climbing out of my car in Nashville at seven

forty-five, I made sure to tuck a packet of saltines into my turquoise cross bag. I left my bike on the rack in the back for now. Before the race kicked off, I planned to ride down to the finish line to snap photos.

Evermina must not have had a backup crew in place. When I'd driven by the Miss South Lick Diner on my way out of town, the windows had been dark and the parking spaces in front of the retro metallic storefront were empty of cars.

I nibbled on a cracker as I found my way to our entry. Danna, who usually dressed in colorful vintage flair, today sported a store t-shirt and denim cutoffs. She'd braided her red-gold dreadlocks into two fat plaits tied with red ribbons matching her high-top tennies. All she needed was a set of fake freckles to complete the Sadie Hawkins look. She was today's star of the show, though. She'd volunteered to be our outhouse driver, riding inside and steering it to a win.

Turner held a takeout cup of coffee in one hand and thumbed his phone with the other. He also wore a Pans 'N Pancakes shirt, but with black sports pants and running shoes. His role in the race was pushing the outhouse off to a good start. He'd also volunteered to run alongside in case a problem arose.

"Hey, guys," I said. "You look great, Danna."

Danna peered at me. "Are you feeling okay, Robbie? You aren't usually so pale."

"Mornings are tough." I held up the cracker. "Have saltines, will travel."

"Good," she said.

A man with a big camera approached. "Photo for the *Democrat*, please."

"Danna, you get in the middle," I said. "We'll flank you."

She stuck a corncob pipe in her mouth and pulled a spatula out of her back pocket, holding it up and grinning. I set a hand on her shoulder and mustered a smile, while on her other side Turner pointed to the logo on his shirt.

The reporter snapped a couple of shots. "Thanks. Pans 'N Pancakes is in South Lick, I gather?"

"Yes. I'm the owner." I spelled all our names and told him of my staff's roles today.

He thanked us and hurried over to the next entrant.

"It's strange, Robbie," Turner said. "There's no sign of Zeke Martin. Everybody's milling around without direction."

"Seriously?" I asked. "Yesterday he was adamant about being here promptly at eight for a race that doesn't begin for another hour."

It was true. I scanned the lot and didn't spy Zeke anywhere. Wendy Corbett stood next to her Nashville Treasures outhouse, which was painted to resemble her folksy gift shop here in town. A tall woman nearing fifty, she cast her gaze right and left, as if searching.

Beyond her was Don O'Neill, my brother-in-law, with his green Shamrock Hardware outhouse. He always looked a little worried, the outer edges of his eyebrows drawn down. He had the same big brown eyes as my husband Abe. But where Abe's expression usually sparkled with warmth or humor,

Don's habitually appeared concerned, bordering on distraught. I wished Abe had been able to be here, but he'd taken his teen son Sean camping for the long weekend.

"I haven't seen—wait," Turner said. "There he is."

A whistle pierced the air. Zeke, dressed in the corniest of straw hats, rolled up jeans, and a plaid shirt under red suspenders, blew it again.

"Is he trying to be Abe Martin himself?" Danna asked.

"No idea," I said.

"Who was this Martin guy, anyway?" Turner asked. "Is Zeke related to him?"

"Not unless Zeke is fictional, too." I smiled at Turner. "Abe Martin was a Hoosier cartoon character drawn by an artist and journalist named Kin Hubbard more than a hundred years ago. Abe Martin, who ostensibly was from Brown County, dispensed folksy wisdom often mixed in with political commentary."

"Like, 'Now and then an innocent man is sent to the legislature,' for example." Danna spoke in her best twang.

"Or, 'Flattery won't hurt you if you don't swallow it,'" I added.

"I like this guy," Turner said.

The whistle trilled again.

"People," Zeke yelled. He waited a moment until the chatter subsided. "Please proceed to the starting line according to your entry number. We don't have all day."

"What's our number, Robbie?" Danna asked.

"Umm, it's, uh . . . hang on." I patted the pockets of my jeans shorts and came up with no piece of paper. Where had I stashed that thing? I snapped my fingers and fished it out of my bag. "We're fourteen."

"Out of how many?" Turner asked.

"Not sure. Twenty?"

Danna stood up tall and surveyed the lot from her six-foot vantage point, bobbing an index finger as she counted. "I'd say twenty's about right."

"We're not going to all fit in a single line across the road, are we?" Turner asked.

"I don't know." The whole event struck me as crazy, or at least mismanaged. Why didn't Zeke have any helpers to direct all of us? And once we did get to the start and the outhouses started rolling, they could crash into each other side by side, or one could bump into the one ahead as it picked up speed. Ours didn't have brakes. I didn't think any of them did. I wished I'd asked Danna to wear a bike helmet.

"I'll run right next to the back handle," Turner added, as if he'd read my mind. "I can grab it and slow the thing down if I need to."

"If I'm about to face-plant, you mean?" Danna asked.

"Something like that."

I took a deep breath. "All right. I think it's our turn."

"I'll help push," Danna said. "I don't need to get in until we're lined up."

She and Turner got behind the outhouse and pushed to get it moving.

"Was it this heavy yesterday?" Turner asked.

"I don't think so," Danna said. "Doesn't matter. It's going to get a lot heavier once I get in."

I finished my cracker and directed them. Jim Shermer and a woman with salt-and-pepper hair were pushing his entry ahead of us. I peered at her back. Yep, that was Detective Octavia Slade in the flesh. Jim's wife but in casual Saturday attire, clothes I'd never seen her wear.

I glanced at where our outhouse was headed and swore silently.

"Angle left, guys," I directed. "Quick. You're about to hit the—"

I was too late. The wheels on the right bumped into the lip of the curb at the entrance to the lot. The outhouse tilted left and then forward. Turner yanked back on the bar as the doors on the front flew open.

A person fell out. A dead person.

CHAPTER 4

My breath rushed in. Evermina Martin lay crumpled on the pavement. Her body had stiffened in a sitting position, with her neck stretched sideways and her chin on her chest. A cast-iron skillet had tumbled out after her. A bloody lump stained her blond hair.

"OMG." Danna stared.

Turner joined us. "No wonder it was so heavy," he whispered, the color draining from his face. He brought his hand to his mouth.

I knelt. Evermina looked dead, but I had to be sure. I laid two fingers on her neck. She didn't have a pulse. Nobody with skin that cold and a body that stiff could be alive. She couldn't have cracked her own head with the skillet. This was homicide. And a law enforcement officer was right in front of me.

"Octavia," I called.

She turned. I beckoned. Her eyes widened. She hurried back. Ahead of us somewhere Zeke kept blowing his whistle. Behind us people were asking what the holdup was. All I could see was Evermina and that lump on her head. My eyes blurred with tears at a life cut short, at her violent end.

I sniffed and pushed up to standing. My emotions were way out of whack these days, and I cried at the least provocation, not that murder was the least of anything.

Octavia and the photographer arrived at the same moment. He whistled and aimed his camera.

"Keep your distance, sir," she told him in a stern voice. She pulled a slim ID wallet out of her pants pocket and flashed it at him. "State police."

"Yes, ma'am."

"Robbie?" she asked.

"Our outhouse hit a bump. She fell out, and the skillet with her. Her name is Evermina . . ." My stomach roiled. "Excuse me," I mumbled as I dashed for a row of bushes and lost my breakfast of crackers. I stayed there until I was sure the bout of upchucking was over. I rinsed my mouth, glad I'd tucked a small bottle of water into my bag. Now I really wished Abe were here.

By the time I returned, Jim had approached. A crowd was gathering at the periphery. Octavia spoke into her cell as she gazed at Evermina. Don pushed through the crowd and gasped.

His cheeks paled. "Robbie, this is terrible."

"I'll say." I swallowed.

"You okay, Rob?" Danna asked.

"Sort of. Can you and Turner help keep people back until the police get here? I'm pretty sure our outhouse is now a crime scene." I'd unfortunately been around more crime scenes than I wanted to count.

"You got it." She conferred in a quiet voice with Turner. He nodded.

"Don, you stay back, too," I said.

"I . . . of course." He melted back into the sea of staring faces.

Danna and Turner each took a side and extended their arms straight out, facing the people massing. With Danna's height, she had an impressive wingspan. She inched forward, urging those in front of her to move back. She ignored their questions. Turner also widened the circle and kept his mouth shut.

The photographer squatted and shot more pictures of the body. He turned his camera on our poor outhouse, which made me cringe.

"Do you know the lady's name?" he asked me.

Over my shoulder, Octavia caught my eye and shook her head hard.

"You'll have to get that from the authorities," I said.

Octavia slid her phone into her pocket. "Sir, I'm going to have to ask you to leave and to hold off filing your story."

"But—" he objected.

Zeke hurried up. "What's holding things up? Why aren't you . . . ?" His voice trailed off. He stared at his ex-wife's corpse. "That's Evie." He looked up. "She's my ex. What happened?"

The photographer perked up and murmured, "Got it. Evermina Martin of the Miss South Lick Diner." He got off a couple of shots of Zeke staring at the body.

"Everybody take two steps back." Octavia's loud voice oozed authority. "Now."

CHAPTER 5

We stepped. A police officer in a black uniform strode up, one hand on her heavy duty belt. Blond hair to her shoulders, she wasn't much taller than my five foot three, and she didn't appear a lot older than me, either. I'd turned thirty-one two weeks ago.

"Chief Harris." Octavia nodded at her.

She was the police chief? She must've been older than she looked.

"Ma'am. What do we got?" The chief, who seemed to know Octavia, frowned down at Evermina.

"I'm off duty, obviously." Octavia gestured at her t-shirt and Capris. "This is Robbie Jordan of South Lick. The victim, Evermina Martin, was in Robbie's business's outhouse and fell out. So did the frying pan. I happened to be helping my husband with his entry. Robbie called me over."

The chief squinted at our outhouse. "Pans 'N Pancakes. That your pan?" She pointed her chin at the skillet.

"Not unless someone stole it out of my store and brought it here." I flashed on Camilla's outhouse. "The Cammie's Kitchen entry had one hanging on the outside yesterday when we all delivered our entries."

"Did you know a person was inside this one?" Harris asked.

"No!" I couldn't believe she'd asked that. "How could we? We delivered it empty, but it sat here in the lot all night."

"Who's 'we'?" Harris didn't look convinced.

"Danna Beedle and Turner Rao, two of my employees." I pointed to them. "Yesterday I asked Zeke Martin if he'd arranged overnight security. He said he hadn't." I fixed my gaze on Zeke.

Harris cocked her head at Zeke. "Is that correct, Mr. Martin?"

He swallowed. "Yes."

Two more Nashville officers, both male, hurried up, one holding a roll of yellow plastic tape. A siren whooped its way ever closer. Wendy Corbett, whose outhouse had been one of the first to leave the lot, slipped in next to Zeke and tucked her hand through his arm. She squeezed and murmured in his ear.

It looked like Zeke had moved on, post-divorce.

"All right." The diminutive chief set her fists on her hips. "Mr. Martin, the race is canceled. Ms. Jordan, you and your employees will please adjourn to the police station and wait to be interviewed. You, too, Mr. Martin. Detective Sergeant Slade, thank you for your help."

"Yes, ma'am," Octavia said. "I'm available if you need me."

"We'll see whether they assign us state or the county sheriff. Or both." Harris rubbed her neck.

"You'll call for the MSCU, of course," Octavia added.

The *miscue*? What was that?

"Of course." Harris sounded peeved.

As Octavia turned to go, she murmured to me, "Mobile crime scene unit."

"Ah. Thanks." My confusion must have been obvious.

The chief faced her officers. "Protect the crime scene. Use the lampposts and find a couple of stanchions to complete the circuit."

One of the guys trotted off. The other tied one end of the tape to the nearest post. An ambulance with lights and siren alive crept down the road from the far end of town, people parting in front of it. It went silent, and two EMTs jogged up carrying their red bags.

Wendy nudged Zeke.

"Chief," Zeke began. "Can't the outhouses already lined up be allowed to race? It'll get them out of here, and they've already arranged to transport their entries from the finish line at the bottom of the hill after the run is over."

Harris gave that a moment of thought. "Good idea. Go ahead. Be sure you come by the station after it's over to be interviewed."

"I promise." He didn't look enthusiastic about it, though.

"And I'll need a list of all the entrants' names. These last few outhouses in the lot can exit through the far egress, but tell them they're not going to be able to get to your starting line. This road is closed for the duration."

CHAPTER 6

By nine thirty my crew and I still sat in the waiting room of the building the police shared with the town hall offices. Danna had texted her mom to say our return to South Lick was on hold, and why. I'd used the facilities and had now resumed nibbling on saltines.

At nine we'd heard the roar of the crowd lining the race route from in here, even though we were several blocks away. The competition was over pretty fast.

A dispatcher in a black polo shirt was the only staff member I'd seen, and she sat behind darkened glass.

"I'm sorry you guys had to see the body," I said to Danna and Turner. "Neither of you has witnessed a murder victim before, right?"

"I did." Danna raised her hand. "Remember that woman who was killed and her body dumped behind the pickle barrel in the store?"

"Erica Berry. How could I forget?" I asked. "You came in to work right after I'd found her."

"We'd only been open, like, barely two months," Danna added.

"I'm lucky you didn't quit on the spot." I smiled at her.

"I wouldn't do that to you."

"I'd be happy never to see another scene like that one," Turner said. "It's horrible to think of a murderer attacking Ms. Martin in the middle of the night and stuffing her in our race entry. Who would have done it, Robbie? Do you have any ideas?"

"No." I took a sip of water. I'd grabbed another bottle at the Quick Pick on our walk down here, while Danna and Turner bought coffees. "I mean, she was divorced from Zeke, and they seemed to be arguing yesterday during the drop-off. But I don't know either of them."

"I hope the police don't suspect you," Danna said. "She mounted quite the nasty campaign against Pans 'N Pancakes after she opened her diner."

"Did she actually badmouth our much-loved restaurant?" Turner asked. "Who would think that would ever work?"

I let out a breath. "She seemed to be heading in that direction. I tried to convince her South Lick had room for two breakfast-and-lunch places. She apparently thought hers wouldn't make it as long as mine was still in business."

"She plastered an ad all over the internet only last week," Danna said. "About how you could get a real Hoosier breakfast solely at the Miss South Lick Diner, and how it had the only decent food in the county. I mean, seriously?"

"Now I know why the diner was dark this morning when I drove past," I said. "Evermina was dead." I wondered if the skillet had been the murder weapon. I supposed if she was whacked with enough force in the right spot it could have killed her. Skulls were pretty hard, though.

I glanced at the outer door as it opened.

Wanda Bird pushed through it. A former South Lick police officer—and the cousin of our current chief, Buck Bird—she was now a detective with the Brown County Sheriff's department. Her tan uniform polo shirt strained over her belly. She'd lost a lot of weight before her wedding last year, but now she was over halfway through her own pregnancy and was looking more than full of figure again.

"Hey, Robbie. I heared about the, ah, incident, and thought I'd see what the sitchieation is down here."

"The situation, Wanda, is that we're waiting for someone to interview us," I said. "I don't know if it'll be Chief Harris, you, Detective Slade, or who." What I did know was that I wanted to get out of here. The benches were hard, I was getting hungry for real food, and I had a volunteer doing half the work at the business I owned.

"Haley's good people," Wanda said. "She'll be along soon enough."

"Haley is the chief's first name?" I asked.

"Yeperoo."

Wanda spoke in the same folksy way Buck did. While it didn't sound professional, I'd learned over the years it didn't reflect their intelligence and had no bearing on their competence as law enforcement officers.

"You know what, Robbie?" Wanda asked. "I picked me up a little intel at the victim's diner a couple few days ago."

"You ate at the competition?" Danna pretended to be outraged.

"Hey, after them ads came out, I had to see what was what. And it was Monday, when y'all are closed."

"It's fine, Wanda," I said. "What did you learn?"

"Well, it seems your own brother-in-law was having him a couple few words with old Evermina."

"Don?" I scrunched my nose. "Do you mean they were arguing?"

"I sure as shooting do. He said she owed him a cow-patty load of money. He up and demanded she pay it."

"Money for what?" Turner asked.

"Why, for the renovations on her diner, 'course. She bought all manner of supplies at Shamrock Hardware, but she put it on account. He wasn't a bit happy about her still being in the red with him. Might could be motive for murder."

"What?" I asked. "Don O'Neill is one of the gentlest men I know."

"And if he killed her, she'd never be able to pay him," Danna pointed out.

"I'm sure Chief Haley'll get to the bottom of it all, possibly with our help," Wanda said. "And there she is now."

Sure enough, the chief hurried in. Zeke followed her at a slower pace. If anybody had ever looked reluctant to be in a police station, it was him. His feet dragged and his lips pressed together.

"Sergeant Bird," Harris began. "Are you in possession of information I'm not aware of?"

"Nope. Just thought I'd drop by, hon, and make myself useful."

"Thank you. But until I receive official word, we have this under control." The skin was tight around the petite chief's blue eyes, and her fists-on-hips stance appeared challenging, not under control.

"Okey dokey, then. Be seeing ya, Robbie, folks." Wanda bustled out the door.

"What's she so happy about?" Danna muttered.

"I don't know, but she's a lot more cheerful than she used to be," I murmured in return. Maybe being secure in job, love, and impending motherhood contributed to replacing her former swagger with a sunny disposition. Or it could be hormones.

"Sorry to keep you all waiting," Harris said to my crew and me. "Did you three drive over together?"

"I drove separately," I said. "If you wouldn't mind interviewing me first, ma'am, I really need to be getting back to my restaurant, which is being run by a skeleton crew."

"Very well."

"You two okay with that?" I asked Danna and Turner.

"Sure," Turner said.

"Totally," Danna agreed. "Mom said she doesn't mind staying on. We'll be back as soon as we can."

"What about me?" Zeke's tone was plaintive.

"Have a seat, Mr. Martin," Harris said. "Please come with me, Ms. Jordan."

She might as well have told him to take a number. He sat. I followed her into the back.

CHAPTER 7

The vaulted, exposed-beam ceiling and the wood-paneled cabinets gave the Nashville PD station a country-lodge kind of feeling. Except most country lodges didn't include a uniformed woman with a gun and a tasing device hanging off her belt. I'd been inside the South Lick police station more than once, and had visited the Brown County Sheriff's facility, but I'd never been in here until now.

Harris led me to a stark interview room. After the preliminaries of asking for my name and address, stating the date and time, and acknowledging that she was recording, she folded her hands on the table.

"Please lead me through the sequence of events leading up to the victim's remains falling out of your race entry, beginning with yesterday."

I told her we'd loaded the outhouse onto Turner's father's truck in South Lick after we closed my restaurant.

"You built it there at your store?" she asked.

"Yes, in the barn behind it."

"Go on."

"We drove it here," I said. "We unloaded it in the staging lot. We left. That's pretty much it."

"Who did you speak to yesterday?"

"I said hello to Camilla Kalb. She told me Zeke Martin was organizing the race. And I greeted Jim Shermer, who now owns the art gallery."

"Do you collect art?" Harris asked.

"No. But he was my real estate agent when I bought my country store property a few years ago." And he'd been my boyfriend for a little while, but she didn't need to know that.

Except it might be five years ago already, or maybe four. I'd already been in Brown County for three years, working as a chef right here in Nashville, when my mom died without warning of a burst brain aneurysm at our home in Santa Barbara. She'd taught me carpentry as I grew up, and the sale of the house and her cabinetry business left me a nice chunk of change. I didn't have siblings to split it with, and I was able to buy the South Lick property and use my skills to do most of the reno work myself. Working with my hands to make my dream of owning a restaurant come true had also helped with my grief.

"You probably know Jim Shermer is married to Octavia Slade," I continued.

She nodded. "Who else did you talk to?"

"I found Zeke, told him we'd arrived, and asked him where to leave our outhouse. He didn't have a system in place at all, except to show up at eight this morning and move our entries to the starting line."

"Did you speak to the victim?"

Why did these people never use the dead person's name? "I briefly said hello to Evermina. Before that, I saw Zeke and her having a disagreement. I have no idea what it was about."

"Had you had any prior dealings with her?"

Was she asking because she already knew? It didn't matter. All I could speak was the truth.

"After she opened the Miss South Lick Diner, Evermina mounted a campaign apparently aimed at putting my restaurant out of business." I explained about the social media ads and that I'd attempted to convince her—once—that we could peacefully co-exist. "She didn't seem to agree."

The chief had fired up a tablet and now fast-typed into it. "And where were you between eight p.m. and, say, five thirty this morning?"

Uh-oh. "I was home." With nobody to vouch for me. "This morning I was at my restaurant before six to do breakfast prep. We open at seven. And then I drove here."

"Do you live alone?"

"No."

"Who do you live with?" She gazed at the wedding band on my left hand, the band I'd worn for a year tomorrow.

"My husband, Abe O'Neill, and my stepson, Sean."

"Can they vouch for your whereabouts?"

"No. They left yesterday afternoon on a camping trip."

"Did you come back to Nashville after dark and hit Evermina Martin on the head with a cast-iron skillet?"

I looked into her eyes. "No."

"Did you stuff her dead body into your out-house and close the doors?"

"No." I shut my mouth and stood so I didn't yell at her. "Is that all?"

She pushed up to standing. "I'll be in touch."

Haley Harris might look young and sweet. But this police chief had a will of iron. Which was a good thing—as long as she didn't aim it at me.

CHAPTER 8

I made a high-speed stop at home on the way to the restaurant. My stomach had settled by now, so I wolfed down a cheese sandwich. I suspected things at Pans 'N Pancakes would be too busy for me to be able to eat after I arrived.

I was right. A line of holiday-weekend customers waited to be seated. Len poured and flipped orders at the grill as fast as he could. He looked like he could really use a break.

So did Corrine, bless her mayoral heart. I'd never seen her frazzled before. She'd worked as a waitperson in her past, and she loved schmoozing. But hours of serving and busing and pouring coffee without a break was a lot to ask of anyone, let alone a volunteer. She'd jammed a store ball cap on her big hair. Under her apron she wore a Pans 'N Pancakes shirt over pressed jeans and red sneakers that matched Danna's. Right now the shirt bore a smear of syrup and the big hair hung limp.

I hurried to scrub my hands and tie on a store apron. "Take a break, Corrine." I relieved her of the now-empty coffeepot. To Len I added, "I'll spell you when she's back. Plus, Danna and Turner won't be long."

Corrine slipped out of the blue apron and tossed it in the soiled-linens box under the counter. "We have to talk. About what happened." She arched her well-plucked eyebrows as she patted her phone-carrying back pocket. She made a beeline for the restroom at the back.

I set two more pots of caf and one of decaf to brew.

"What happened, anyway?" Len slid two finished plates under the warmer. "Corrine got a text, and it was like the world stood still."

"I'm sorry, dude, I can't tell you right now. Soon."

"Okay." He pointed. "Those are for Adele and her friend."

My aunt Adele was here? I already felt better. I loaded up the plates and scanned the tables until I saw them.

"Robbie, hon." Adele Jordan, my late mom's older sister, greeted me with a big smile. "You remember Vera?"

"It's lovely to see you again, Vera." I set down the plates and gave each woman's cheek a kiss.

Both had the soft skin of a person in her mid-seventies, with Vera's a darker shade than Adele's. Vera Skinner, a childhood friend of Adele's, lived in Indianapolis, but she visited Adele on her South

Lick sheep farm several times a year. A quilter, Vera also had a passion for antique cookware and loved browsing my retail shelves.

"Did your outhouse win the race?" Adele asked.

My smile crept away. "We didn't even begin. You're going to want to check your scanner when you get home."

"Is that so?" Adele cocked her head.

"Yes."

"You're looking a mite peaked, Robbie, dear," Vera murmured. "I hope you're taking care of yourself."

"I'm trying, Vera. Thank you." All around me people wanted things that involved my time. More coffee. Their food. Their check. "Sorry, but I can't talk until Danna and Turner get back. Enjoy your meal." Off I went to do my job and keep the place running the way it was supposed to.

After Corrine re-emerged, I sent Len on break and took over at the grill. It was almost eleven o'clock, and already diners were asking for burgers and fries. We clearly posted, on the wall and on the menu, that we didn't serve from the lunch menu until eleven thirty, although breakfast was available all day.

Meanwhile, I poured disks of pancake batter, turned sausage links, flipped hash browns, dished up fruit, and folded omelets like they were going out of style.

But my mind was on Evermina's poor, dead corpse, crashing out of our outhouse without a shred of dignity. Who had had such a strong grievance against her they would have committed murder? And violently, with force. This death hadn't been from a carefully planned poisoning. Her killer was a person with enough strength and rage to grab the closest heavy weapon—a cast-iron skillet—and beat Evermina to death with it. I forced my thoughts away. That path might lead to a repeat of my performance into the bushes this morning.

After Len rejoined us, having three sets of hands and feet instead of two made everybody's jobs easier. He took over the front of the house, as it were, even though we were all in the same big space, while Corrine bused and loaded the dishwasher. When the machine was full, Corrine set it to run and sidled over to me.

"I hear Evermina has been, shall we say, dispatched."

"Yes." I folded a Kitchen Sink omelet in half. "And her remains were deposited in the Pans 'N Pancakes outhouse. It was awful."

"I should say. Do you think the killer left her there to set the blame on your shoulders?"

"Why would anyone want to do that?"

"Listen to me, hon," Corrine said. "It was common knowledge she was out to get you. An evil person might could have wanted to make it look like you did the deed."

"I obviously didn't." I checked an order and poured out three disks of pancake batter. I pushed around a pile of sliced mushrooms and peppers for an omelet and laid four rashers of bacon down at the other end.

We didn't have a separate grill for meat. I'd included a disclaimer on the menu to that effect, but we did try to keep the sausages, bacon, and burger

patties to a particular area of the grill. Strict vegetarians had the option of oatmeal, a non-grilled
sandwich, baked goods, and more. I did stock a
gluten-free bread for those who couldn't tolerate
gluten, and we often offered a rice or potato-based
casserole to accommodate them.

"I only hope the Nashville police chief believed
me," I added.

"You met Haley?"

"Yes. How do you know her?"

"Town stuff." When Corrine's phone dinged, she
pulled it out of her pocket. "Danna and Turner are
on their way."

"Good. Take off whenever you want, Corrine.
And thank you so, so much for helping out."

"Heck, it was fun."

Len arrived with three order slips and two
empty coffee carafes.

"Wasn't it, Len?" Corrine asked.

"Wasn't it what?"

"Fun, me and you making this place run smooth
as a well-tuned classic Harley."

"Sure, ma'am. It was a regular party." He barely
kept the smile off his face.

"Well, I appreciate it," I said. "Apologies again
for stranding you both. Len, can you take over the
grill again? Danna will be here shortly to relieve
Corrine, but Turner was supposed to be off this
morning, and he has to get the truck back to his
father."

"Not a problem."

I slipped into a fresh apron, plated up four orders, and delivered them before heading to Adele
and Vera.

"Hey, now, Roberta," Adele began. "That handsome husband of yours going to be in soon?"

"No. He took Sean camping."

Adele's jaw dropped. "But tomorrow's your—"

"First anniversary? Yes, I know. It's fine, Adele. They haven't had a father-son getaway in a long time. They'll be back Monday, and we'll celebrate later in the week."

"I hope they return before the afternoon on Monday," my aunt said. "I wanted to invite you all to a Memorial Day cookout at my place. Four o'clock."

"That should be fine," I said. "Will you still be around, Vera?"

"Indeed I shall."

"It's a deal, then." I spied Danna coming through the door. "Please excuse me."

"Love you, darling," Adele called after me.

I was lucky to have her, my only blood relative in the whole country. At least, the only one living outside the protection of my body.

CHAPTER 9

By one o'clock, all the tables were still full but we no longer had hungry diners milling around as they waited to be seated. I grabbed a quick facilities break and a dish of sweet, local strawberries, the first of the season. Danna and I had agreed to postpone talking about her interview with Chief Harris until after closing time.

That didn't stop patrons from asking about the murder. A woman at a table of two middle-aged couples stopped me.

"We heard there was a murder in Nashville this morning." Her eyes were wide.

"Why, yes," the other woman said. "We were watching the Nashcar race and overheard a fellow say a body fell out of your country store outhouse. Is it true?"

"I'm not at liberty to talk about anything related to the race." I'd been expecting the rumor mill. "I recommend you check the local news channels. Can I top up those coffees for you?"

"No, thank you," one of the men said, giving his wife a stern look. "Just the check, please."

I laid their ticket face down and got out of there as fast as I could. The last thing I wanted was to engage in gossip. Besides, Harris had warned me not to talk about what had happened. Which was fine with me.

Danna was working the grill and I'd delivered two order slips to her when the door opened, and Buck Bird ambled in. He wasn't alone, and, for the first time since I'd met him, he didn't wear the dark blue South Lick PD uniform. A tall woman stood next to him.

Danna glanced over. "Cool. It's Dr. Bird."

"Dr. Bird?" I asked. "Did Buck get a PhD when I wasn't looking?"

"No, silly. That's his wife. She was my pediatrician."

I gave my head a little shake. I'd never met Buck's wife and didn't even know her name. I certainly hadn't realized she was a medical doctor. There was no time like the present to meet her. I pointed myself in their direction.

"Welcome to Pans 'N Pancakes." I smiled at them and extended my hand to her. "Hi, I'm Robbie Jordan."

"Robbie, this is my sainted wife, Melia." Buck rested his hand lightly on her back.

"I've heard so much about you, Robbie." Melia appeared about Buck's age of fifty. Her long auburn braid was shot through with silver. She wore a purple t-shirt, khaki Bermudas, and sturdy sandals that went with her trim build. She gave Buck a fond look. "I finally convinced this galoot to bring me in so I could taste your food myself."

"I'm glad he did. My employee says you're a pediatrician."

"I am." She gazed at Danna. "Is that Danna Beedle? She's gone and grown herself up, hasn't she? I haven't seen her since she graduated to a gynecologist."

"Danna's great. Buck, you're actually off duty?" I asked him.

"Welp, when you're the top dog, you can actually delegate." He gave a sheepish smile. "And it's our thirtieth anniversary this weekend. Melia here wanted to go for a walk in the state park and then go out to lunch, so that's what we took and did." He gestured at his jeans and hiking shoes.

"Wow, congratulations," I said.

"I understand it's your anniversary weekend, too, Robbie," Melia said. "I'm sorry I couldn't accompany Buckham to the festivities last year. I was on call that weekend and had a critically ill baby in the hospital."

"Was the baby okay?" My shoulders tensed and my palms went on autopilot to my belly, as if I could shield my own baby from harm.

"I'm afraid she didn't make it." Her gaze went to my hands. "Don't worry. It was a rare illness. You're going to be fine," she murmured.

I wanted to counter that she couldn't possibly know that, but I didn't. I'd never had so many fearful thoughts about the future before I became pregnant. But dwelling on them only made them worse.

"Thank you." I made myself relax my shoulders as I surveyed the room. A party of four made its way toward the door, and Len was wiping down the table. "You can have that four-top in a minute."

"Thanks," Melia said. "I'll go say hello to little Danna."

I smiled at the description. Not anymore, she wasn't. "Buck, where have you been hiding this fabulous wife of yours?" I asked him after she left.

"Welp, you know." He gave his aw-shucks shrug. "She's busy, and I'm always in here when I'm working, like. We prefer to take and keep our work lives separate from home. But she's been pestering me no end to bring her in to meet you."

"I'm so happy you did."

"I heared about the, uh, problem over to Nashville," Buck said.

"I thought you might have. Did Wanda tell you?"

"I found out here and there."

"It was pretty bad." The tension returned to my shoulders.

"Hey now, Robbie." He leaned down and peered into my face. "It's going to be fine. I'll up and help Nashville if I can."

"Thanks, Buck. I'm worried Chief Harris thinks I did it."

"Because of that business with the victim's diner and all?"

"Right," I said. "This morning Wanda told me something else. Apparently, Abe's brother had gotten angry with Evermina in public."

"Don O'Neill?"

"The same."

The cowbell on the door jangled. I stared at Don standing in the entrance. Had I conjured him out of, well, not thin air, but conversation?

CHAPTER 10

"Robbie, I have to tell . . ." Don's voice trailed off as he took in who stood next to me.

"Morning, O'Neill," Buck drawled.

"Come in, Don," I said. "You have to what?"

Don glanced back the way he'd come, then at us. His posture slumped as he moved closer.

"Did you get to race the Shamrock outhouse?" I asked. "Or were you in line after ours?"

"After. What happened was pretty shocking." He swallowed. "Are you okay, Robbie? I mean, given your condition?"

"I'm fine." I smiled to myself at Don's term for my pregnancy. He was so old-fashioned, even though he was only five years older than Abe, which put him in his early forties. "It was certainly shocking, and tragic, to find Evermina like that."

"The poor, poor woman," Don murmured. "She didn't deserve that."

"Not a single person deserves a violent death." Buck shoved his hands into his pockets. "Seems you had your own share of conflict with the deceased, O'Neill."

Did Buck know more than what I'd just told him?

Don opened his mouth. He shut it. He narrowed his eyes, as if thinking.

"You weren't the only one," I said gently. Maybe that would encourage him to speak.

"Thing is, I let her open an account at the store," Don began "She bought supplies out the wazoo while she fixed up her diner. That thing was a wreck."

"Kind of like this place was when I bought it?" I asked.

Don perked up. "You got it. Except you paid your bills. She didn't. Who can run a business like that? I sure can't. I have to pay my own suppliers."

"What did you say to try to get her to pay up?" Buck asked. He kept his tone mild.

"I told her that her account was due. And that she had to pay for what she'd bought. She kept giving me cockamamie excuses about this and that and all whatnot."

"And then?" I asked.

"Well, and then I went over there and gave her what for."

"Did you threaten her with harm?" Buck cocked his head.

"No! I mean, I threatened to have her business closed down. I never threatened to hurt her."

Buck only nodded.

"Robbie, you know me." Don craned his neck at me. "Come on. I don't even squash mosquitoes."

True. On the other hand, I didn't know Don all

that well. In all the time I'd known him, he'd kept his thoughts and feelings close to the chest. He often didn't come to family gatherings at the elder O'Neills' home, and Abe had said his only brother rarely opened up even to him.

"So you didn't kill her and stuff her pitiful corpse in Robbie's outhouse," Buck said.

"What? Of course not." Don's voice caught. "I can't believe you'd even think that for a second, Bird. How would that help me recoup my costs, anyway?"

He had a point. The same one Danna had made earlier today.

"Calm down, now," Buck said. "It ain't even my case, but I had to ask. Listen, you want to up and join me and the missus for lunch?"

Don pressed his lips together. Melia already sat at the table Len had cleared. Danna gestured at me and hit the bell signaling plates were ready.

"I need to get back to work," I said. "Why don't you eat with them, Don?"

"I don't want to impose," Don mumbled.

"No imposition at all," Buck said. "Come on. We'd love to have you."

"Well, if you're sure. I'm sorry to intrude, Buck."

Buck bobbed his head and made his way to the table.

Don blew out a noisy breath. "When's Abe back, Robbie?"

"Middle of the day on Monday, I think."

"He's out of range, but I'm thinking I might need the name of a lawyer."

"I might, too."

"You?" His voice rose. "Why?"

"Did you miss Evermina's ad campaign against Pans 'N Pancakes? It was pretty blatant."

"I must have."

"I told her there was room for both of us in town," I said. "She apparently didn't agree. The police probably think I had as much motive as you for wanting her to go away."

"You wouldn't have killed her any more than I would have," Don insisted.

"You and I know that. Seems we're going to have to convince a few law enforcement officers."

Don nodded and shuffled over to Buck's table. I straightened my spine. I had even more to think about now. For one thing, was Don so squeaky clean he'd never needed to talk to a lawyer? He'd lived in South Lick his entire life. You'd think he'd at least know somebody to call.

CHAPTER 11

Luckily, no fireworks ensued between Don and Buck. Diners ate, paid, and left. I was able to close and lock the door promptly at two thirty, and my crew and I began cleaning up. Danna scrubbed the grill. Len wiped down the tables and chairs and swept. I stashed most of the perishables in the walk-in cooler, leaving out the ingredients I needed for breakfast prep, and started the dishwasher.

By three o'clock, we sat at a four-top while the mopped floor dried. They sipped the beers I'd offered them. I would keep them company with a non-alcoholic beer, except the thought of a drink tasting even like fake beer roiled my stomach. I stuck with iced herbal tea. Danna replenished the table-top caddies with packets of sweeteners, tiny jars of jam, and little pouches of ketchup, mustard, and honey. Len rolled silverware into our blue cloth store napkins.

My fingers hovered over my tablet. "What would be good seasonal specials for tomorrow?"

"You mean that we already have supplies for?" Danna asked.

"Yeah. It's too late to put in an order for tomorrow." We were always closed on Mondays, so that wasn't an issue.

"We still have plenty of strawberries, I think," Len said. "A coffee cake would be easy."

"I like that idea," I said. "Sliced berries on top of the batter and a crumble topping."

"Perfect." Len nodded. "And it'll be easy to make several big pans of it."

"We need a savory offering for lunch." Danna cut open another box of sugar packets.

"Monday's Memorial Day," Len said. "Hot dogs and potato salad would work."

"Hot dogs *in* the salad?" I asked.

Danna snickered. "I can think of more than a few customers who would like that. Instead, how about we do up a bunch of kielbasas? That butcher in Nashville brings them down from Chicago. They're super tasty, especially on the grill."

"Sounds perfect." I supposed I could drive back to the county seat this afternoon.

"Isaac and I are meeting friends for drinks in Nashville at five," Danna said. "We'll pick up a few dozen and I'll drop them off, since I won't be here tomorrow."

"That'd be great, Danna, thanks." I sipped my tea. "I'll get you cash before you leave. Be sure you leave me the receipt. You'll drop the kielbasa in the walk-in?"

"You bet."

"Speaking of Nashville, how did your interview with the police go?" Earlier I'd given Len the thumbnail sketch of our aborted Outhouse Race.

"As you might expect," Danna said. "I told them probably the same things you had. We showed up Friday with the outhouse, which was empty. On Saturday, when we began pushing it into place, it was heavy. We hit a bump. She fell out. What more is there?"

"Chief Harris must have asked if you had any ideas about how Evermina got there and who might have been responsible," I said.

"Sure." She glanced up at me and cringed to herself. "I, like, had to tell her about that nasty ad campaign. I'm sorry, Robbie."

"It's okay. You had to. I did, as well."

"On the way back, Turner said he'd answered the same way." Danna drained her beer bottle.

Len had been following the conversation. "The Miss South Lick Diner, right?" He thumbed his phone and whistled. "That was nasty, all right. Did this lady think nobody wants more than one option for breakfast and lunch? Check out this ad on Insta." He held out the display.

I didn't want to look. I'd already seen them all.

"Wow." Danna now worked her own phone. "She even made a couple of TikTok videos. Radical."

"Too old, much?" Len said. "Dude. She basically had no idea what the app is even for."

I wasn't more than a decade older than college-student Len, and Danna was closer to his age than mine. Being a business owner, a wife, and a mother-to-be made me feel as if I were of a different generation and out of range for things like TikTok. I did post food photos to our store's Instagram and Facebook accounts regularly, but I didn't share my personal life in either place. That was private, and I intended to keep it that way.

"I didn't kill Evermina, obviously," I said. "And I'd like to know who did."

Len scrunched up his nose. "Is there anyone holding a grudge against you, Robbie? A person who would want you to look guilty?"

"I have no idea."

"To change the subject," Danna began. "I saw Jim Shermer around there this morning. What's he doing in the area?"

"Who's he?" Len asked.

"Long story," I said. "Old story. He doesn't matter. But to answer you, Danna, he apparently now owns the Hickory art gallery in Nashville."

"Seriously?" she asked. "Isaac has a couple of pieces for sale there."

Her boyfriend produced gorgeous metal and wood sculptures. The ones I'd seen would be too big for a storefront shop.

"He's making smaller works these days, and Jim was happy to display them." Danna finished resupplying the last caddy. "But here's an idea. What if Octavia wigged out and was jealous of seeing you, Robbie? Maybe she killed Evermina to make it look like you did."

"No," I said. "Just . . . no. She has no reason to

do that. She's the one who stole Jim from me, sort of. Anyway, she's a state police detective, and I happen to know she loves her job. That's pure fantasy, Danna."

"You're the one who has wigged out," Len told her. He finished his last roll and stashed the box under the counter.

"Hey, simply brainstorming, here." Danna stood. "Okay if I push off?"

"Of course. Get out of here, both of you. I'll get the coffee cake dough mixed up along with the rest of the prep before I leave."

"See you next weekend," Len said. "Did I tell you I'm flying out to see Lou tomorrow?"

"No. Give her my love. Is she still coming in August?" His big sister was my good friend and biking buddy Lou—Louise—who'd finished her doctorate at Indiana University and landed a tenure-track teaching position in Albuquerque. I missed her.

"She is."

"Good. I hope I'll still be able to bike with her by then." Having never been pregnant before, I didn't have a good sense of when I was going to have to stop doing my favorite—and primary—form of exercise. Any ride around here was a hard workout because of Brown County's signature hills.

They let themselves out. I sat quietly sipping my iced tea and thinking. I flashed on Wendy Corbett's arm through Zeke's. What if she and Evermina had had conflicts over Zeke? Maybe an affair between Wendy and Zeke had been the cause of the divorce, and the ex had been causing problems. Demanding money. Threatening something. Wendy could have had cause to kill Evermina, with or without Zeke's help.

It wouldn't be dark tonight until nearly eight. I didn't have anyone to cook dinner for this weekend, or even to eat with. I needed a good, long bike ride after I was done here. And now I had a destination in mind.

CHAPTER 12

I pedaled hard up the last hill before Nashville. A
stiff wind smelling like rain blew in from the
west, the direction we usually got our weather
from. I hoped it was a light, quick storm. A down-
pour could ruin Abe and Sean's camping trip. On
the other hand, the two were of sturdy O'Neill
stock, and they'd gone prepared for any weather.
They'd be fine.

After I crested the hill, I coasted down into
town, braking when I reached the lot where the
race staging had been. The entire area was now
cordoned off by yellow police tape, with our poor
Pans 'N Pancakes outhouse sitting forlornly in the
entrance, albeit *sans* corpse. A single officer re-
clined in a folding chair next to it, thumbing his
phone. He didn't glance up.

The lot might have been closed, but the former
race route was now open. I pedaled slowly the rest
of the way into town. The sidewalks were full of
what looked like tourists on this long holiday week-

end. They shopped, bought ice cream cones, ate at Cammie's Kitchen, and popped into the Stonehead Tavern, named after the much-vandalized iconic stone mile marker a bit south of here. Flags advertising the Abe Martin Festival hung from lampposts. A talent show and concert was taking place elsewhere in town tonight.

I found a bike rack not far from City Hall and locked my steel steed. I might have popped into the Stonehead for a beer, myself, if not for my condition, as Don so quaintly put it. Instead I drank from my bike's water bottle and clomped along on the cleats of the stiff-soled bike shoes, carrying my helmet.

Nashville Treasures was only a block off the main drag. A dog dish full of water sat out front, and the gift shop's door was propped open to the balmy air. I was gambling on owner Wendy Corbett working this afternoon, but maybe she had employees running the place.

When I walked in, I was struck by how much the store resembled another gift shop in town, the Covered Bridge Bazaar. This one featured the same shelves of country-themed gifts. Carved wooden signs with cute sayings, a bin of rainbow-hued saltwater taffy, silk scarves painted with scenes of covered bridges, flour sack dishtowels stenciled with whimsical grinning vegetables, and crocks of handmade wooden utensils.

Shoppers browsed, including two who'd eaten lunch at my restaurant earlier in the day. I selected a nylon rainbow flag and brought it to the checkout counter at the back. June was Pride Month, and even if Wendy wasn't here, it wouldn't hurt to own a rainbow flag.

My gamble paid off. Wendy, wearing a sleeveless silk top in a brilliant royal blue, stood behind the cash register. I waited until she finished waiting on a customer. I smiled and greeted the shop owner.

"Robbie Jordan." She frowned. "Are you okay?"

"I'm fine." Didn't I look okay? *Oh.* She probably meant about finding the body. "Although, what happened this morning was quite a shock. It must have been to you, too."

"It was. No, I meant . . ." She gave her head a shake. "Never mind." She reached to her right to straighten a display holding Nashville postcards, her sleeveless top showing off a muscled arm.

"What did you mean?" I asked.

She leaned closer, lowering her voice. "I heard you'd been arrested."

"What?"

"For the you-know-what." She drew her finger across her neck.

The gesture was what people used to indicate murder, even though Evermina hadn't had her throat cut.

"Why would I be detained for that?" I pressed.

"It's well known Evermina wanted to put you out of business."

"She apparently did, but I wasn't arrested, and I never would have hurt her." I really wanted to pivot this conversation away from me. "Was she giving you a hard time, too?"

Her gaze shifted away from mine. "Me? Why do you say that?"

"This morning it looked like you're dating her ex. Those relationships can get complicated."

"I am seeing Zeke. But it's not. Complicated, that is."

"Were they legally divorced?"

"I don't think that's any of your business." She bit off the words.

Maybe, maybe not. I had other ways of finding out.

A young couple approached. Time for talking about a motive for homicide was over.

"Can I ring that up for you?" Wendy asked me in a bright voice.

"Yes, please." I tapped my card on the reader and accepted the paper bag she handed me. "Thanks. Take care."

She didn't respond, instead turning to the customers behind me.

All righty, then. Out on the sidewalk, I stared at the bag. What had I been thinking? I hadn't brought a backpack, and I still had to ride home. I hadn't ridden my around-town bike, the one with the basket on the front and another place to carry things on the back.

On the other hand, bike shirts came with a row of pockets on the back the cyclist could access with one hand while riding. The pockets were usually used to stash an energy bar, a phone, keys, and other necessities. If I took the flag out of both the bag and its cellophane wrapper, maybe I could roll it up and stick it in a pocket. But the bag was essentially new. Should I go back in and return it to Wendy? I doubted she wanted to see me again.

I stood paralyzed by decisions, which was not like me at all. Another consequence of pregnancy? Maybe.

"Robbie, are you okay?"

I glanced up to see Octavia Slade. I must not look okay. She was the second person to ask me that.

"I'm fine, Octavia. Thanks." I held up the flag. "Trying to decide how to transport this home."

She cleared her throat. "I might be heading your way before too long. I could bring it to your store if you want."

I took another look at her. She'd changed her clothes. Her blazer, tailored shirt, and dark slacks made her look a lot more like a detective than she had this morning.

"Have you been assigned the case?" I asked.

"I've been asked to help out."

"No surprise, since you're local now."

"Were you speaking with Wendy Corbett in there?" Octavia asked.

"She sold me a flag, so, yeah. I spoke with her."

"But you're not getting involved in the investigation, correct?" Her tone indicated I'd better not be.

"Who, me?"

She glanced away. And back. "I'm serious, Robbie. Nobody wants you to get hurt in the pursuit of justice. You aren't trained, and actual professionals are on the job. Please."

"I have to be getting home now," I said.

She let out a breath. "Do you want me to deliver your purchase?"

"No, thanks. I can manage."

"Ride carefully."

"Always."

She headed into the gift shop. I tossed the bag and packaging in the nearest trash can and made my way back to my bike, stuffing the flag in one of my back pockets when I got there.

No way was I committing to not looking into this case. Not when my own innocence was in question.

CHAPTER 13

After my ride and shower, it was already six thirty, and I was starving. I'd heard of pregnant women whose morning sickness hit them around the clock. For me it really was only the morning, for which I was grateful. The exception was my aversion to the thought of alcohol or coffee, which was present twenty-four seven. To that I said, "Smart body." I wasn't supposed to have those drinks, anyway.

I zapped a plate of leftover lasagna and ate it out on the brick patio. The menfolk had taken Cocoa, Sean's black Lab, on the trip with them, but our cats Birdy and Maceo joined me in the fenced-in yard. Sean had adopted Maceo, his second all-black pet, only in March, and I'd been relieved my tuxedo longhair decided to play nice with the interloper.

A male cardinal lit on the lilac tree near the back fence. The beautiful red birds and their more modestly dressed mates were ubiquitous around here. A patch of daisies brightened a corner, and my seedlings of basil and lettuce thrived in the raised bed Abe had built. A lawnmower droned in the neighborhood. The air smelled of cut grass and fragrant honeysuckle, although clouds still loomed, and the air was humid.

My thoughts were on Evermina's death, though, not this lovely and peaceful garden. I ate. I sipped my seltzer. I mused.

First off was the way she'd been murdered, if in fact the skillet had been the cause of the contusion on her head. How much force was needed to whack a woman's head hard enough to cause death? Whoever had done it must have had considerable muscle as well as a height advantage. But why would Evermina have stood still and let a cast-iron pan come down on her head. Maybe she and the killer had been arguing, and Evermina had turned away to leave. That scenario would work, just.

No matter the method, the most important question was who killed her. I knew I didn't. Zeke might have, if he owed her money or she been demanding too much of him. He was plenty taller than Evermina, and looked reasonably fit, so he had the muscle. And the only time I'd seen them interact was from a distance, and it hadn't looked friendly.

Or Wendy could have done the deed, if she thought Evermina wanted Zeke back, or was keeping him from starting anew, romantically. Was Wendy strong enough? She had the height, for sure. One piece of information I needed was to find out if Zeke and Evermina were officially divorced.

I hoped Don was innocent. At five ten he was an inch taller than Abe. While not in the best shape of his life, he was still a reasonably fit male and could easily have wielded a heavy object. It would be horrible for Abe's whole family if he was guilty, and for Don's wife, Georgia. They'd met later in life, when her husband was quite ill with dementia. After he'd died, Don and Georgia happily tied the knot.

That was a pretty small pool of suspects. Other people in Nashville might have had issues with Evermina. Anyone from her past could have surfaced. She'd certainly been flirting hard with Jim on Friday. She might have also pulled that behavior with a man whose wife wouldn't stand for it. I planned to ignore Danna's suggestion of Octavia as killer for now.

It was time for me to do a bit of internetting. I carried my plate inside and brought my tablet out to the teak table. I could poke around out here at least until the rain hit. But where to begin?

Evermina herself seemed like a good choice. Hers was a unique name, for sure. My search on her name plus divorce decree didn't get me anywhere. Maybe they weren't divorced, or maybe I didn't know how to find the appropriate record. But to dig into her past, I was going to need her unmarried last name.

She certainly would have filed legal papers to buy her diner, get a building permit, and so on, and legal filings usually included full names. I headed, virtually, to Brown County's web site and the Recorder's Office.

But I found the deeds area hard to navigate and

gave up. *Okay.* How about news stories? I plugged in "Evermina Martin" and "Miss South Lick Diner" and found several articles, one in the *Brown County Democrat,* which was published in Nashville, both online and as a weekly actual paper. None included Evermina's name before she'd married Zeke.

Her obituary would include her maiden name, but nobody would have written it this soon. The evening of the day she was found murdered was also too early to read a news piece about her homicide. Wasn't it?

I snapped my fingers. Birdy perked up from where he snoozed on the bricks at my feet. It was too early to read about the murder, yes, but not too early to watch coverage on a television news channel.

After I changed my search to "Nashville murder," several newsclips popped up. I clicked on the Indianapolis station. I tapped *Play* and sat back to watch. The clip was short in duration and information and long on drama. I hit *Stop.* They didn't even mention Evermina's name. So much for that avenue.

My yawn was wide and long. The day had been even longer, and fraught with tension. Was seven thirty too early to go to bed? Probably. On the other hand, I needed to get in the habit of taking care of myself. I was more of a go, go, go type of gal instead of a put-your-feet-up-and-relax person.

Still, there was no time like the present. I maneuvered my feet onto the chair next to mine and set the tablet on the table. Maceo jumped onto my lap and relaxed as I stroked his smooth, short black coat. Birdy hopped onto the chair next to my feet, his purr a vibration on my tired bare feet.

The rain was still distant. Twilight was imminent, but it was too early in the season for mosquitoes to be too bad.

I didn't need to be an amateur investigator right now. Or ever again.

CHAPTER 14

A bell startled me. *What?* My feet were wet. It was dark. Rain pattered on the wide umbrella overhead. On the table, my phone was lit up and vibrating. The cats were gone. My exhausted, pregnant self must have fallen asleep in my chair.

Another bell sounded, this one more distant. The phone rang again. I grabbed it and connected the call.

"Robbie? It's Wanda Bird. I'm at your door."

"Okay." I gave my head a shake to clear it. "Be right there."

I grabbed the tablet and hurried in, only to be greeted by two dry cats who'd had the sense to come in through the cat door after the rain began. I checked the peephole in the front door to make sure it was, in fact, Wanda, who stood on the porch. A murderer roamed free out there. One couldn't be too careful.

But it was Wanda. Water dripped onto her nose from the hood of an open rain jacket.

I unlocked the door and stepped back. "Come in."

"Thanks, Robbie." She stepped inside. "It's a real frog-strangler out there." She still wore her sheriff deputy's uniform, duty belt and all.

"You can hang your jacket here." I gestured to the coat tree in the entryway. I waited until she'd shed the garment and wiped her feet on the mat. "What's going on?"

"You mean to bring me to your front door on a Saturday night?"

"Yes."

"I been tasked with asking you a couple few more questions. See as how you're in the family way like me, I thought I'd make what you might call a courtesy call at home."

My previously relaxed shoulders tensed. "Okay. Come on back."

"How come your hems are wet?" She pointed at the bottoms of my pale-gray yoga pants.

I glanced down. "I was sitting outside and fell asleep, but my feet weren't under the umbrella when the rain started."

I gestured for her to sit at the counter separating our dining table from the kitchen area.

"Can I get you a glass of water?" I offered. "Herbal tea?"

"What I'd like is a beer, but you and me both know that's verboten for the duration." She hoisted herself onto a stool. "Anyhoo, no thanks."

I remained standing across the counter from her. I didn't want her to get too comfortable. I waited. She fiddled and adjusted and didn't meet my gaze.

"So?" I tilted my head. "You wanted to talk with me?"

"Yes." She straightened her spine. "I read your statement to Chief Harris. About what you saw. What you know. I'd like you to go through it again, please." She pulled a tablet out of her bag and tapped it to life.

Wanda dropped her folksy way of speaking. She could be all business without a trace of dialect when she wanted to be. I'd heard a linguist on a show refer to it as code-switching. That was what Wanda was doing right now, changing her speech to fit the situation.

I repeated what I'd told the chief.

"Did you see anything suspicious that evening?" she asked. "Anyone acting oddly?"

"I told Chief Harris that Evermina and Zeke seemed to be arguing, but I couldn't hear them." I thought back. "There was a woman checking out the diner outhouse."

"The Miss South Lick Diner?"

"Yes. I don't think I've ever seen her before, so I don't know if she's a local or not." Not that I knew everyone in Nashville, but the county seat wasn't that far from South Lick, and my restaurant was popular with the city's residents and visitors to it, as well.

"What did this woman look like?"

"About my age, but taller and slimmer. Strong arms. Dark hair above her shoulders." I shrugged. "I didn't talk with her, and I didn't see her interact with Evermina. She was probably interested in how to build a race outhouse and that was the closest one."

"All right. And this morning, what happened?"

"We were moving the outhouse to the starting line. Danna and Turner were pushing, and I was ineptly directing. They hit a curb. The Dutch doors popped open. The body and a skillet fell out. That's all."

She glanced up with a kind look. "Tough stuff when you're pregnant."

I gave a nod. Seeing a murdered corpse was tough no matter what one's condition was.

"I seriously don't know anything else, Wanda."

"Did you have digital communications with Ms. Martin about her ad campaign against you?"

Uh-oh. "Yes." Birdy sauntered up and arched his back against my calf. I reached down to stroke him. "I contacted her a couple of times."

"And?"

"Her replies were minimal."

Wanda smiled and put a hand on her belly. "She's kicking."

"You know the gender."

"We sure as heck do. With the strength of these kicks, this little one's bound to up and win a gold medal in one sport or other, I can plum guarantee it." She cleared her throat and got back to both business and standard speech. "What was the content of your messages? And were they texts or emails?"

I blinked at her reversal. "Texts. I wrote that I thought South Lick had plenty of room for two breakfast establishments and that her campaign seemed a little unfair."

"No answer?" she asked.

"She said she had a business to run, then she

launched another wave of sponsored social media posts and flyers in public." Wanda had better not try to confiscate my phone. She'd need a search warrant for that. Anyway, if they had Evermina's cell, they could see my side of the communications.

"Did you confront Evermina in person?"

I let out a breath. "I stopped over there one afternoon. She was painting inside. I told her I liked what she was doing with the place. That I thought we could be friends."

"Did you threaten her?"

"No! Really, Wanda? How long have you known me?" I needed to pee, urgently, and I was so done with these questions. "I did not threaten Evermina Martin, and you can quote me on that."

"Okey dokes." Wanda switched off the device. "Thanks for your time. Please let me know anything you might learn or overhear."

I barely nodded.

"Mind if I use the little girls' room?"

I showed her to the powder room off the hall. What grown woman, and a sheriff's detective, no less, uses the term "little girls' room?" *Sheesh.*

After she emerged, I showed her to the door.

As she shrugged into her wet jacket, she said, "You're all done with private snooping, I hope."

"Good night, Wanda." I shut the door after her and double-locked it.

What I was done with was her, plus talking to the police without a lawyer.

CHAPTER 15

The rain had blown through overnight, leaving the world washed clean and sparkling in the sunlight. I hoped my mind would stay washed clean of thoughts of murder, too. I'd slept well and gotten to work on time at six thirty, an hour later than usual, because we opened an hour later on Sundays.

We'd been slammed with customers ever since I unlocked the door of Pans 'N Pancakes at eight. We had the pre-hiking crowd along with the birders, who had already been out for a couple of hours. The attire of the before-church folks stood in contrast to that of the outdoorsy diners, tasteful slacks and shined shoes as opposed to shorts, many-pocketed vests, and sturdy footwear.

My team and I fed them all. The strawberry coffeecake was predictably popular, but our regular menu also was. We served up eggs in many forms, sausages and bacon, cheesy grits, pancakes—naturally—and biscuits with or without gravy. It was business as usual, and I tried not to dwell on yesterday's homicide.

I also attempted not to dwell on the state of my stomach, although I felt the smell of coffee didn't turn it as much this morning as it had. Was I moving beyond the morning sickness phase? Please, let it be so. I still needed to nibble saltines, but my insides weren't roiling as badly as before. *Good.*

By ten o'clock the rush of diners ebbed a bit. It was too early for post-church, and the lazy-morning Sunday brunchers wouldn't be in for another hour or two. Turner set to scrubbing and cubing potatoes for the lunch salad. Len worked the grill, as Danna had the day off. And I poured coffee and water, took and delivered orders, bused and collected money.

I glanced up when the bell on the door jangled. Every time it had sounded this morning, I'd feared seeing Octavia, Wanda, or Chief Harris stride through and aim for me, handcuffs at the ready. Instead of a law enforcement officer, a man walked in, his arms full with an enormous array of flowers. I headed his way.

"Robbie Jordan?" he asked.

"Yes, that's me."

"Congratulations." He smiled and extended the vase.

"They're for me?"

"The person you married a year ago ordered them. Happy anniversary."

My eyes filled. I tried to blink away the happy tears. I should give him money. "Um, let me get you a tip."

"Please don't. It's enough to see the love in your

eyes. Believe me, ma'am, it's a lot better than delivering sympathy bouquets." He turned and slid out the door.

I set the vase on the desk. It was filled with dozens of mini carnations in pink, white, and red, plus the usual sprays of baby's breath and greens. I swiped at my eyes and picked out the note in the little plastic holder. I hadn't opened it yet when Turner's voice rang out.

"Happy first anniversary to Robbie and Abe!"

The restaurant broke out in applause. I turned and smiled through the tears that now fell freely. I waved.

"Thank you."

The noise died down. People returned to their breakfasts. I read Abe's note.

Happy first anniversary to my favorite wife, chef, and mother-to-be. I'm sorry to be apart today, but I hope you know how much I love you.

Aww. I slid the card in my pants pocket to savor later. The bell jangled again. Once again it was blessedly not anyone in uniform but my aunt and Vera who came through.

"Hey, hon," Adele said. "Somebody up and send you a big honking bouquet?"

"Abe did." I sniffed again as I greeted them.

"They're awful pretty," Vera said.

Len hit the ready bell and signaled to me that diners needed my attention.

"Grab any open table, ladies," I said. "I'll bring coffee as soon as I can."

"You're looking a touch better today, Roberta," Adele murmured.

"I'm feeling a bit more settled." And I hadn't been arrested. Yet.

They headed for a table. I gave the flowers a wistful pat and returned to my work.

"We're almost out of coffee cake," Len said. "Want us to make more?"

"Strawberries, too?" I asked.

"They're running low."

"No. Let's call it on the morning special. It's ten thirty. I'll go erase it from the specials board. Plate up two servings for Adele and Vera, though, please, before it runs out. I'm sure they'll want to try the coffee cake."

I grabbed the coffee carafe. After I erased the special, I poured for Vera and Adele at the four-top where they'd settled in. "Don't tell anyone," I whispered, "but we saved you each a strawberry coffee cake serving."

"Bless you, Robbie," Vera said. "I was hungering for a taste of that."

"She's a good girl." Adele beamed.

I rolled my eyes a little.

"Listen, hon," Vera said. "My late friend Rosemary Carter gave me the tastiest recipe for apple dumplings. I brought you a copy. They might be a popular item here in the restaurant."

"Thanks, Vera." I scanned the sheet of paper she gave me. As with many passed-down recipes, it was a little scant on details. We chefs knew how to fix that. Maybe I'd bake a pan as a trial and bring it to Adele's cookout tomorrow.

"She was a Quaker lady from up Russiaville way," Vera went on. "Real nice, lived on a farm with her passel of young ones. One of her sons even became a professor."

"Cool." I spied customers wanting my attention all over the place. "I need to get back to work. What can I get you to eat beyond the coffee cake?" I jotted down their orders. I folded the recipe and slid it into my pocket along with Abe's note and turned to wade into the fray. At a hand on my arm, I turned back.

"I mighta heared a snatch of interest about, you know, yesterday," Adele murmured. "I'll tell you when you get a little minute."

I nodded. Except thinking about a killer instead of carnations roiled my stomach all over again. Seeing a state police detective standing at the door didn't help one bit.

CHAPTER 16

If Octavia was here to see me, I was in trouble. Or not. I had a restaurant to run, which didn't include time to be grilled by the police.

"Sit wherever you'd like, ma'am," I called. That seemed better than addressing her as "Detective" at volume in front of a roomful of diners.

"I got ya covered, hon," Adele said to me. She half stood and waved at Octavia. "Yoo-hoo. Come join us here."

I made a beeline for the grill. Octavia joining Adele could be good or bad. Good if Adele finagled news out of her. Bad if the officer wanted to extract information from her about me.

"Hey, Turner," I said after I stuck Vera and my aunt's order up on the carousel. "I can take over with the potato salad."

"I could use a quick break," Len said. "Grill, my man?"

"Sure." Turner pointed to the big pot already on a lit burner. "The potatoes are taking a while to boil, but the cubes are small enough they'll cook quickly once they do."

"I'm on it," I said. "I'll get going prepping the rest."

Len stripped off his apron and pointed himself at the restroom. Turner shifted over to the grill, checking the orders and going to work with one of the heavy spatulas. I made my way into the walk-in cooler. The heavy door clicked shut behind me, and I leaned against its solid core, cool and smooth.

I hated that I was involved in another murder. Now, while I was carrying Abe's and my child. The homicide of a woman who'd had a beef with me, even though I hadn't returned the sentiment.

At least the killing hadn't happened on my own property, like what had gone down in March directly upstairs from where I stood. When I let myself think logically, I knew I was good at ferreting out the facts of a crime and putting them together. My puzzle brain liked solving this kind of conundrum. Maybe tonight I'd haul out the graph paper, ruler, and pencil, and create a crossword, as I often had in the past. I usually didn't finish it, but doing the exercise helped me organize my thoughts.

Now, though? I had ingredients to gather and a job to do. I loaded up my arms with celery, fresh dill, a gallon plastic jar of mayo, and one of the white paper-wrapped bundles of kielbasa Danna had dropped off last evening.

I smacked my forehead, or would have if I'd had a free hand. Desserts. Did we still have cookies and brownies for lunch? When was the last time our baker—my friend Phil MacDonald—had delivered? Not yesterday, for sure. Customers generally liked a bit of sweet after their midday meal. Glancing around the shelves, I didn't see any plastic-wrapped pans of deliciousness. I'd have to come back in and search for the trays he delivered the baked goods on.

A four-inch metal disk on a thick rod extended from the door, a device designed to let one exit the cooler with full hands. I faced away from it and pressed the disk with my back to open the door. Nothing happened. I leaned forward and back again. Often you had to hit it at the correct angle. The door didn't budge. What was going on here? I peered at where the rod went into the door. It was straight and looked fine. A mechanism inside must have jammed.

I swore out loud. Nobody could hear me. And that was part of the problem.

No need to panic, I told myself sternly, even as my throat thickened. The cooler had come with a red emergency button inside next to the door. My phone was in my pocket, and the store was full of people, several of them the most trusted members of my immediate circle.

Still, I shivered, and not from the cold. A person could have messed with the mechanism. Someone like a murderer, for example? I wasn't unknown in the county for my prior successes with homicide cases. But I hadn't been snooping around in public. Not much, anyway. Not yet. I swallowed. My hands would have pressed protectively over my belly if they hadn't been holding food.

I'd never had to test the red button and couldn't remember if it set off an alarm or only released the latch. I didn't want to test it. An alarm whooping would be like yelling "Fire!" in the proverbial crowded theater. But I needed to get out of here before my nerves turned into a panic attack.

Once more I stepped away. I carefully made contact with the opener, crunching my abs as I pressed my back into the disk. I nearly fell backward into the restaurant as it swung open. *Whew.*

Len, re-aproned and with his arms full of ready breakfast plates, gave me a raised eyebrow. I regained my balance, both in my body and my psyche, and shrugged. Let him think I was a klutz. I didn't mind.

I unloaded my burdens. "Turner, did I forget to ask Phil for more desserts? I didn't see any in the walk-in."

"You mean him?" He gestured over his shoulder with his thumb.

I whirled. Phil sauntered toward us with his arms full of covered trays.

"You are so just in time, my friend." I smiled as I made room on the counter for the desserts.

"You called Friday, Rob," he said. "Remember? You asked for a small order, since you didn't think you'd have enough for today, but you're closed tomorrow. I'll bring a full order on Tuesday." The smile slid off his handsome dark face. "But when I do, we need to talk."

Uh-oh. What did that mean? "Sure."

"Listen, I gotta run. My sweetie and I have tickets to the opera in Indy." Phil, who had the most gorgeous, resonant speaking voice I'd ever heard, was also an aspiring opera star.

"Have fun. And thanks." I stashed the trays under the counter. They didn't need to be chilled for the hour until we began serving lunch. Phil would tell me his news, whatever it was, when he was ready.

I tested the potatoes—done—and dumped the pot into our biggest colander in the sink. I rinsed and diced celery. I shifted the potatoes into a giant bowl and drizzled vinaigrette over them to absorb while they were still warm. I did not make eye contact with Octavia Slade.

CHAPTER 17

I added the last dollop of mayo to the cooled potato salad. So far, I'd successfully avoided going near Octavia.

The next time I glanced up, Buck sat at the table with the ladies. His wife wasn't with him, and today he wore his South Lick PD uniform.

Len brought an order slip. "Buck wants to talk with you," he told me.

"About police business?" I asked.

"He didn't say."

"I guess I'll go see." I gave a final stir to the salad and checked the wall clock. "Eleven thirty. Feel free to dish up any time it's ordered."

Len fished a clean spoon out of the drawer and tasted it. "Excellent, Robbie. I like the dill. Nice touch."

"Thanks. I can take over orders if you want."

"You got it," he said. "I'll go add the kielbasa and salad to the specials board."

I grabbed the carafe and moved as slowly as I could toward the four-top, pouring as I went.

"Hey, there, Robbie," Buck said.

"Morning Buck, Octavia."

Octavia's bowls formerly holding oatmeal and fruit were mostly empty, as were Adele and Vera's plates.

"Did you want to order, Buck?" I poured coffee for him.

"Nah. Young Len there up and wrote down what I want."

I held up the carafe. "Anybody else for coffee?"

"No, thanks, hon," Adele said.

Vera shook her head.

"I'd like more hot water for my tea, please," Octavia said.

"Sure. Be right back." I returned with a second metal pot of hot water and another tea bag. I turned away.

"Now, hang on a chicken picking minute," Buck said. "Me and the detective want to have a word with you."

"Sorry." I set my fists on my hips. "That's not going to happen until after we close and I leave for the day."

"But . . ." His voice trailed off. "Well, shoot, guess you got yourself a point there."

I left their table without saying anything else. The next time I heard the bell on the door jangle, it was Octavia leaving the restaurant. *Good.* I guess she didn't want more tea, after all.

It was funny. I'd known Buck for the entire time my store had been open for business. I trusted him and wouldn't mind speaking to him about the

murder if I got a minute. I felt a lot less warm and
fuzzy toward Octavia. I was glad I'd asserted myself
about not doing police business during my business hours.

When Buck's enormous order was ready, I
loaded my arms with his lunch. He'd ordered a
double cheeseburger with the works, a heaping
bowl of potato salad, a grilled kielbasa, a side
order of cheesy grits, and two brownies. I carried it
all over to him. How he stayed so skinny was an un-
solved mystery for the ages.

"Thank you, ma'am." He groaned at the sight of
the full plates. "Died and gone to heaven. You
know, my stomach was emptier than the Grand
Canyon during a hundred-year drought."

I smiled. "Enjoy."

Adele stood. "Sorry to desert, you, Chief, but
me and Vera gotta run. Robbie, want to hit a big
estate sale with us in the morning? It's down
French Lick way, and it's supposed to have a heck
of a lot of cookware."

"She means old stuff, like you sell," Vera added.

"I'd love to. My shelves are getting a little bare."
Antique and vintage cookware was the "Pans" part
of my store's name, and it was a big draw with certain customers. That was how I'd first met Vera, in
fact. She'd come in with a tour group perusing various antique stores and flea markets. She'd run
into Adele and they'd reconnected after decades
of being out of touch. Now they visited each other
frequently and were as tight of friends as they'd
been when they were girls.

"Thought so," Adele said. "We'll pick you up at
eight thirty."

Vera laid down cash for their meals. "Detective Slade left this, too." She pointed to a twenty-dollar bill.

"Thank you." I leaned toward my aunt to kiss her and murmured, "What did you want to tell me? You know, about yesterday."

"I'll call you tonight." Adele made the thumb-and-pinky phone gesture. "See ya, Buck." She and Vera headed for the door.

"I'll see if I can get back for a minute after you've eaten," I said to Buck.

Mouth full, he only nodded.

I cleared a few tables, took a few orders, delivered a few plates. Three women came in outfitted in their Sunday best of heels, handbags, and hair spray. I sat them at the only available four-top.

"You're Miz Jordan, aren't you?" a dark-haired one asked.

"I am." I smiled. "This is my store and restaurant." I was pretty sure I hadn't seen any of them before.

Her platinum-locked friend spoke up. "We understand you were the person to find our poor deceased Sister Martin."

Uh-oh. The news must be out. I'd forgotten to check.

"Unfortunately, I was the one, in a way." I blinked. "She wasn't a nun, though, was she?"

The third woman laughed. "We all go to the same church. At Covenant Hope, that's how we refer to a sister in faith."

"I'm very sorry for your loss," I said.

"We heard she was murdered," Platinum whispered. "May she rest in peace."

"I heard the same." I cleared my throat. "Which station did you get the news from?"

"Not a TV station," the third one said. "Sister Cooper told us this morning. We came here directly from services."

It was time to for me to cut off this conversation before it went any further into speculation and the gossip they'd picked up from whoever this Sister Cooper was.

"Coffee?"

"Surely, ma'am," Dark-hair said. "And thank you."

As I turned away, it hit me. If a news station hadn't mentioned my name, how did these ladies' fellow churchgoer know it?

Sister Cooper could have been at the parking lot. Dozens of people must have witnessed our outhouse stopping the lineup process after the doors burst open. They would have seen the police tape and the EMTs. Word spread fast. Anyone could have made an educated guess that the owner of Pans 'N Pancakes had been on the scene when Evermina's lifeless corpse hit the pavement.

CHAPTER 18

All our tables were full when several very tall women sauntered in. They were followed by more until ten or eleven had assembled. In matching red shirts, black sports pants with a white stripe down the sides, and red sneakers, the young women moved easily and stood glancing around and looking hungry. An older woman, not as tall but looking fit, brought up the rear.

This had to be a basketball team and its coach. IU's? Possibly, considering the red shirts and shoes. They might be hungry, but unfortunately, they were going to have to wait. I made my way toward them and gazed up at the closest athlete. Way up.

"Welcome, ladies. I'm Robbie Jordan, proprietor."

"Hi." She extended a dark hand with long fingers that must make it easy to control a basketball. "I'm Janae."

"Sorry, I work with food. I never shake hands at work."

She stuck her hand in her pocket. "No worries."

"It looks pretty busy in here." The pale-skinned blond woman next to her said, her hazel eyes searching the room. "Any idea how long the wait might be? We came from practice."

"Let's see. I have a table that seats eight." I pointed with my chin. "I think those folks are about done, and you can have the next four-top that opens. You don't have more than twelve?"

"No," Janae said. "Thanks."

"It shouldn't be too long," I said. "Can I guess that you're the IU basketball team?"

"Easiest guess you've had all year, right? We're the Indiana Hoosiers," the blond woman said.

"Redundant much?" Her teammate grinned. "Anyway, we're only part of the team. IU's out for the summer, but those of us who are in the area practice and have friendly games with other schools."

"Feel free to browse the retail shelves while you wait," I said. "Or, if you want to hang out on the porch, I'll come and find you." I spied Buck waving at me. "Excuse me." His was the four-top most likely to open up before any others.

"Looks like you're busier than a mosquito in a nudist colony." He stood and pulled out money.

I snickered at the saying. "We are at least that busy, but it's all good." As long as my feet lasted.

"That was a tasty meal, hon," Buck said.

"Thanks. Did you have anything in particular you wanted to ask me about the, you know, case?" I began stacking his dishes.

"Welp, I know Don O'Neill is your brother-in-law and such, but have you seen him acting odd, like, recently?"

"No." My heart sank. Don's name again. "I haven't seen him at all lately except Saturday morning after the . . ."

"Right. If you do happen to speak with him, I'd be much obliged if you'd take and pass along to me any interesting bits you might learn."

"Um, sure."

"I'd best get back to it, then." He glanced toward to the door. "Say, if that ain't the lady Hoosiers. And little Ellie Seaton."

"You know one of the players?"

"I do, indeedy. That tall blond drink of water with the braids? The one looks like she should oughta be in Sweden? She's my wife's cousin's girl, or some such. Haven't seen her in a month of Sundays."

Little Ellie, indeed. She might have been little before her growth spurt. Not anymore.

"See you, Buck."

He stopped by to speak to the braids on his way out. I carried his dishes to the kitchen. Len was loading the dishwasher. He paused.

"OMG, Robbie, that's the IU team, or part of it." Len's eye shone. "They came this close to winning the championship at the start of last month." He held his thumb and index finger a quarter inch apart.

"That's them. They're waiting for Buck's table and the eight-top."

Len tilted his head. "Buck just hugged Seaton."

"She's some kind of relative of his." I wasn't surprised Len knew the players by name. He was nearly as tall as they were and had played the sport in high school, before he'd transitioned, when his name was still Leah.

Turner hit the ready bell twice. "Team? Food's ready and it's stacking up."

"My bad," Len said.

"I mean, I'm as excited as you are by the team, but we're a restaurant." Turner raised his unexcited eyebrows. He was totally not a follower of basketball, women's or men's. "A full and busy restaurant."

"My bad, too," I said. "Sorry, Turner. Len, why don't you swap jobs with him?"

I grabbed the rag and spray bottle and cleaned Buck's table as the party of six was preparing to leave. When both tables were ready for the group of tall, hungry athletes, I motioned them over. Janae and Ellie and two others took the four-top.

"We have two specials on the board," I told them. "Otherwise, you can order anything on the regular menu, breakfast or lunch."

Janae said she was a vegetarian and ordered the potato salad with a grilled cheddar-tomato-avocado melt on dark rye, while Ellie chose a Western omelet with home fries and bacon. I took the other women's orders.

"So, one of my co-chefs is a big fan of your team," I said. "The tall one. Okay if I send him over to say hello?"

Ellie checked out the grill. "Looks like he should be playing basketball instead of cooking."

I laughed. "You'd have to ask Len about that. I'll be back with your drinks."

Before I could leave, the bell on the door jangled once more. Janae narrowed her eyes and muttered under her breath to Ellie.

"It's okay, Jannie," Ellie said. "You don't work for her anymore."

I followed their gaze. At the door stood Wendy Corbett and Zeke Martin. I didn't think either of them had been in before, either. Why now? Morbid curiosity about Zeke's ex's body? An involuntary shudder ran through me.

"You worked at Wendy's gift shop?" I asked Janae.

"For too long." She stared down at her hands.

I was dying to linger and find out what had happened. Except I didn't have time for that.

"I'll make sure to seat Wendy and Zeke on the other side of the room," I told Janae.

"You will?" Her expression turned to surprise. "Hey, Robbie, thanks."

"Not a problem." I jotted down what the women at the big table wanted and stuck the slips on the carousel for Turner.

"Those three settled up." Len gestured toward the church ladies.

"Thanks." I headed for the newcomers. My eyes widened as I approached.

The dark-haired churchgoer stood face-to-face with Zeke, her arms folded on her chest, her eyes flashing.

"If I wasn't a good Christian woman, Zeke Martin, I'd give you a piece of my mind, you two-timing, no-good, mendacious sewer snake."

"Ma'am, I don't even know who you are." He

sounded like he was trying to stay calm, but his voice quavered.

"You ought to be ashamed of yourself, deserting poor Evie like you up and did." Her ire shifted to Wendy. "I'd watch this man with a high-powered telescope, hon. He'll treat you exactly like he did our sister in faith. And now look at her. Dead and alone on a coroner's cold slab. But heck, you were probably the slut who stole Mr. Martin away from his lawfully wedded wife."

Wendy gasped and stepped back.

"Serves you right," the woman went on. "You got the piece of gutter trash you deserve."

Applause sounded from the basketball players. Janae stood, beaming, and clapped for the churchgoer. Ellie rose to join her. The other teammates joined in. Their coach looked worried and motioned for them to sit.

The two other ladies pulled the irate speaker away from Zeke and Wendy and hurried her through the door.

CHAPTER 19

I turned the sign to Closed after the last customers left at about three fifteen. We kept later hours on Sundays. I stayed leaning against the open doorway for a moment, gazing at the beautiful spring day out there. Leaves were in full green leaf. Pansies bloomed in the window boxes atop the porch railing, and the creamy white flowers on the pagoda dogwood tree across the road strutted against a cerulean sky. The breeze was mild and not too hot.

If this weather held, it would be perfect for parades, cemetery visits, and cookouts tomorrow. Too bad it was marred by questions about Evermina's murder, including whether the at-large killer would strike again.

Earlier, after the church lady had accosted Zeke and Wendy and the basketball team supported the tirade, Zeke had conferred in a whisper with Wendy. He glanced over at me.

"You have quite the clientele here, Robbie." Zeke

folded his arms over his chest. "We've changed our minds about lunch."

"Are you sure?" I asked, ignoring the jab at my outspoken customers. "It won't be a long wait."

"Quite sure." Wendy grabbed his arm and nearly dragged him out.

Whatever. I'd hoped to finagle a chat about Evermina with them, but I couldn't hold the couple prisoner. A law enforcement officer I was not, and I was glad of it.

I turned back to the job at hand. It took several trips to carry baskets of food into the walk-in. On the last one, I also snagged my tablet and surveyed our supplies, tapping in the start of an order for next week.

Back in the restaurant, Turner scrubbed the grill as Len slid the last plates into the dishwasher.

"Uh-oh." He shook the dishwasher pods box. "We're out."

"Oops," I said. "I think I loaded it last. I'll get another box." I made my way to our small utility area by the back door and pulled open the supplies cabinet. Search as I might, I couldn't find a single box of pods. I returned, shaking my head. "It looks like I forgot to order more."

"Want me to run over to Shamrock and pick up some?" Len asked.

"No, but thanks," I said. "I'll head over and grab a few supplies after we're done and come back to turn on the machine."

Turner cocked his head. "You always say never to leave it running when nobody is in here."

Right, in case it sprang a leak. Where had my brain disappeared to? Forgetting that, plus not ordering more pods. If I ran the machine after we were done, I'd have to stay and monitor it. But there was no prep to do for tomorrow, because we'd be closed. "I'll stay and babysit it. But take a look around and see if there are other supplies we're low on, both of you, or any hardware we need, okay?"

When we finally sat to fill caddies and roll napkins, I couldn't believe how happy my feet were to be resting, and I wasn't even carrying weight yet. That would come later.

"That little show was really something, wasn't it?" Len asked.

"You mean when the church lady told off that dude?" Turner asked. "That was the murder victim's ex-husband. And his new girlfriend."

"Zeke Martin and Wendy Corbett," I murmured.

"Wow," Len said.

"Robbie, do you know anything about the Martins' divorce?" Turner asked. "I mean, was he cheating on her while he was married like the lady claimed?"

"I know nothing. Seriously." That could be useful information, though.

"It's a dirty thing to do, if he did," Turner added. "Those netters weren't shy about supporting the church lady, either."

"When you're that tall and fit, you don't have to be," I chimed in. "Who's going to push them around?"

Len laughed.

"Are they as good as the men's team, Len?" Turner asked.

"Are you kidding?" Len asked. "They're way better. The Larry Knight days are long gone."

"What was that like?" I asked. "Who was he, anyway?"

"Robbie took the words out of my mouth," Turner said.

"You guys are hopeless," Len said. "Back a few decades, like forty years ago, maybe, Knight was an amazing men's basketball coach at IU. Rude, loud, and completely effective at coaching winning teams year after year. But he's gone, and now the girls are so much better than the guys. At least this year they were. Man, they almost beat the Gamecocks." He glanced at my blank expression. "The South Carolina team, which was, like, the best."

"To change the subject," Turner said. "Do you know when you're getting the outhouse back, Robbie?"

I couldn't help but shudder. "I'm not even sure I want it back. But no, nobody has mentioned returning it. They probably have it sequestered at the county sheriff's facility to go over it for evidence. Listen, let's finish up, guys." I tapped the tablet on the table. "Thoughts about specials for next week?"

"When's the deep fryer coming?" Len asked.

I groaned. We always had so many customers asking for French fries, fritters, and fried chicken, not to mention onion rings, donuts, and deep-fried catfish, I'd finally broken down and found a refurbished model. It was supposed to be delivered in two days, but a deep fryer was the last thing I wanted to deal with. Hot oil could splash up and burn the cook. We'd have to set aside a place for

draining the fried food after it came out of the baskets. I'd need to learn how often to change the oil
and figure out where to dispose of it.

Plus . . . pregnant. For the moment, the mere
thought of smelling deep-fried food all day turned
my stomach. But I'd already paid for the thing.
This trusty crew would help me figure it out. And
the morning sickness would pass, according to
those in the know.

"They told me the fryer would be delivered on
Tuesday." I said. "I wouldn't count on us being up
and running with it for a few days, though."

"I have a great cheese fritter recipe from my
grandmother," Len said.

Turner's face lit up. "Ooh, and we can offer
samosas from time to time, too."

"Let's plan on starting there. I'm sorry, gang. I
should have prepped for this better. I don't even
know if we can keep up with hand-cut fries or
where to buy good frozen ones."

"It'll be fine, Robbie." Len smiled. "It always is.
You run a good show here."

"I guess," I said. "I think Cammie's over in
Nashville has a deep fryer. I can pick Camilla's
brain a little." She might have information about
people like Wendy and Zeke, too.

I knew finding Evermina's killer wasn't my job,
and I had to be even more careful now I was responsible for two lives, not one. But it would be
such a relief not to have to think about murder
right now, on top of everything else.

CHAPTER 20

I wove my way through the narrow aisles of Shamrock Hardware half an hour later. It was a delightful Alice's Restaurant type of old-fashioned hardware store. You could get pretty much anything you wanted. Not Alice, of course. Not fancy designer towel rods or lamp shades, and not lumber other than dowels.

But Don had you covered for high-quality tools, bolts and hooks and light bulbs, paint and industrial cleaning supplies—including non-chemical "green" versions—garden supplies and equipment in season, and so much more. It really was one-stop shopping, and I loved it.

My red plastic basket already held a bag of dishwasher pods, enough to tide us over until I could order a more economical size. I'd also thrown in a few packages of yellow dishwashing gloves, and two spray bottles of the unscented, vinegar-based cleaner we used on the tables between diners. We usually refilled the ones we had from a gallon jug, but that was nearly empty. I had not been keeping up with ordering, which worried me.

I poked my nose into the open door of Don's office as I passed. His brow furrowed, he peered at a laptop screen, a pen in his hand poised to scribble on a pad next to the computer. He sat perpendicular to the doorway, and I could see a spreadsheet open on the screen.

"Hey, Don."

"Wha?" He started and the pen in his hand flew up and behind him. He stared at me, then slapped the laptop shut, swiveling his wheeled office chair to face me.

"Sorry, I didn't mean to startle you," I said.

"Good," he blurted. "Fine. I mean, hi."

Nervous much? But about what? I held up the basket. "I was doing a little shopping and thought I'd say hello."

"No problem." He mustered a smile. "Are you finding everything you need?"

"Always." Without being asked, I perched on the edge of the other chair. I had to perch. A box of toner cartridge filled the back half of the seat. The rest of the office wasn't any tidier, with papers and boxes piled around. I suppressed a sneeze. The room could benefit from a good dusting and the application of the cleaning supplies for sale only steps away. "Got a minute?"

"I'm pretty busy. But for you, Robbie, sure." Except he didn't look happy about it, proved by the low groan that slipped out. "I suppose you're wearing your private investigator hat."

"Not really." I gestured toward his laptop. "Were

you working on your books there? It looked like you had a spreadsheet open."

"Well, I . . ." He glanced at the smudged cover of the large, clunky laptop. "I have a lot to keep track of in this business."

"Every small business owner does, me included." I folded my hands on my lap. "Yesterday you talked about Evermina owing you money and you threatening to shut down her business. Has a detective interviewed you?"

"She called me." He swallowed. "I, uh, haven't had time to call back."

Time or inclination? I suspected the latter. "She as in Octavia Slade? Or did you mean Wanda?"

"Wanda. I guess they're working together on this, the state and the county."

Wanda loomed in the doorway. "Did I hear my name?"

Don's face faded to an even paler shade than it usually was.

"Hi, Wanda," I said. "We were just talking about you."

"Hope it was good." She beamed.

Don stared at the desk.

"We hadn't gotten that far," I said.

"Got time now for a quick chat, O'Neill? Seems you had time for old Robbie here." She shifted from foot to foot as if they were bothering her.

They probably were. She was normally heavier than I was and now she was further along in her pregnancy weight gain, too. I picked up my shopping basket and stood.

"Here, take my seat," I said. "I have to get back to a dishwasher full of food-encrusted plates."

"Thanks so much." Wanda heaved the items from the seat onto the floor and sank into the chair with a satisfied sigh. "I was going to have to ask you to go, at any rate. Interviews have to be confidential. Shut the door on the way out, would you, please?"

Don cast a desperate look my way. I couldn't save him. I closed the door.

I hadn't learned much from my little visit except that he was nervous about whatever was on his laptop. And that he really hadn't wanted to be interviewed by the police.

CHAPTER 21

I'd slid my key into the lock of my restaurant's front door when a car pulled up behind me. Having been attacked on this porch more than once, I whirled, glad it was still daylight out.

Octavia stepped out of a dark SUV. She presented a different kind of threat than a murderer with a weapon, but I was innocent. I could handle her questions.

I greeted her and unlocked the door. "Come in." I didn't wait, carrying my Shamrock Hardware bag over to the kitchen area. I loaded in a pod and pushed the dishwasher's *Start* button. Finally, I turned to face her.

She stood near the door. "I'd like a few minutes of your time."

"Fine." I sat at a four-top and pointed at the chair opposite mine. I didn't want to be too close to her. "You're lucky to catch me here at this hour."

"I've called you several times today with no response." She sat and laid a tablet on the table.

"I always put my phone on 'do not disturb' when I'm working." I had exceptions set for Abe, Sean, and Adele, but Octavia didn't need to know that. "I haven't had a chance to change it back yet." Actually, I'd forgotten. She didn't need to know that, either.

She tapped a button and went through the routine of date and time, plus my identification and permission to record, a routine I was unfortunately too familiar with by now.

"Let's begin with Friday night," Octavia began. "Where were you, and who were you with?"

"I told Chief Harris all that on Saturday morning at the Nashville station. She didn't share her interview report with you?"

"Please answer the question."

I supposed I had to. "After my employees and I delivered the store's outhouse to the Nashville parking lot at about four thirty, we came back here. I did breakfast prep, locked up, and went home at about six." I thought of the possible irony of Wanda interviewing Don at the same time and wondered how he was faring.

"Who else was in the house?"

"No one but two cats."

"Where was your family?"

"Camping." I didn't offer any information she didn't ask for. A lawyer had recommended that to me once.

"Are they back?"

"No."

"Very well. Were you at home all night?"

"Yes."

"What time did you leave your house?"

"Before six. I came here to set up for breakfast," I added. I knew that would be her next question. Might as well get the answer out of the way.

"Were you here until you left for the race in Nashville?"

"Yes."

"How did Ms. Martin's body come to be inside your race entry?" she asked.

"I have no idea. The lot wasn't locked or guarded overnight. Our outhouse had nothing to steal from inside, so its doors weren't locked, either."

"How well do you know Zeke Martin?"

"I don't know him at all. I only met him for the first time when we dropped off our entry."

"How is that?" She tilted her head, as if she didn't believe me. "He was the race organizer."

"I filled out a race application form online, and it didn't list him as the organizer. I repeat, I'd never met Zeke or even talked with him until Friday end of day."

"Are you aware of anyone who might have wanted the victim out of commission permanently?"

"Not really. I assume you're looking at Evermina's husband. She and Zeke weren't together anymore, and I don't know if they were officially divorced or not. He's apparently now seeing Wendy Corbett. But I don't have any information on how they all got along or anything."

"Your brother-in-law had a problem with Ms. Martin."

"I understand it was a matter of her owing him a lot of money," I said. "Not an issue most people commit murder over, and certainly not Don."

"How about Camilla Kalb?"

"What about her?" Why was she asking about Camilla?

"Do you know her, did you have dealings with her, did you witness conflict between her and the victim?" She ticked off the questions on her fingers.

"Let me think. I've met Camilla a few times, since we are both in the small-restaurant business. She's always been cordial, but I haven't had dealings with her other than on a superficial level. The only time I ever saw her in the same place as Evermina was Friday at the outhouse staging lot. I don't think I saw them interact."

"Thank you. Do you know an Isabelle Cooper?"

"No." Although I'd heard that last name earlier from the church ladies.

She scrolled a bit more. "I understand you and Evermina Martin had a, shall we say, difference of opinion about your respective restaurants. Please explain."

"I didn't have a difference of opinion with her, other than that I didn't like that she was trying to malign my business. I told her there were enough hungry diners to go around. Pans 'N Pancakes is popular for a reason, and I was confident that, between locals and visitors, we'd get enough customers to stay afloat, indeed, to thrive. She probably would have, too, depending on how she ran her diner and who was cooking."

"You're saying you didn't have a reason to kill her."

"Of course not!" My voice rose like an escaped

helium balloon. "She was conducting a fairly malicious social media ad campaign against my restaurant and by extension, against me. But one hires a
lawyer and brings a charge of libel for that, not
kills the libeler. I asked her to stop. She didn't. She
was murdered by someone else, Detective Slade,
and you're wasting your precious time suspecting
me." I rose and folded my arms.

She regarded me with a gaze I couldn't interpret. Had I doomed myself by protesting too
much? Except everything I'd said was true.

"If you'll excuse me, I'm still not done with my
work for the day." I returned her gaze with my un-
smiling one even as I turned my chair upside down
on the table. My cleaning service came in on Mondays to deep clean the floors, counters, restrooms,
baseboards, and everything else. The last task for
the day was to clear the floor of chairs, boxes, and
anything else that could get in their way.

Octavia stood. "You realize I don't enjoy being
your adversary, Robbie." Her voice was gentle.
"Homicide is the most serious crime there is. I
have questions I have to ask in order to exact justice, no matter how much you don't like them."

I nodded, not quite trusting myself not to blow
up at her again.

"I'll let myself out." She headed for the door.

You do that, honey, I muttered silently. I finished with the chairs. I might have used a teensy
bit too much force with several of them.

Seeing the restaurant like this always made me
think of elementary school, when each student
had to set their chair upside down on the desk be-

fore heading for the bus or the bike rack. It made me smile and forget my anger for a bit. So did the big vase of flowers.

Yes, the world needs justice. It also needs beauty, and these pretty blooms were going to look lovely on my dining table at home.

CHAPTER 22

Before I headed home, though, I had a B&B room to get ready for new guests arriving on Tuesday. The last round of visitors, a family of six, had left on Friday, but I hadn't had a free minute to go upstairs to the three color-themed rooms, each with its own bath.

I'd decorated the spaces in shades of pink, blue, and green, and for my own purposes named them the Rose, Sapphire, and Green rooms. The family had used all three, but the incoming guests were only a couple. I stripped all the beds and towels and stuffed the linens into three bags, each labeled according to the room.

The cleaning people who scrubbed down the restaurant every Monday also cleaned up here after guests left, including doing the laundry. My financials were sound enough to let me outsource more and more of that kind of work.

But I liked to make up the beds myself to make sure the sheets were drawn taut and the covers

were smooth. I drew a fresh set of white linens—
because . . . bleachable—out of the hall closet and
headed into the Rose room. It was the nicest of my
B&B offerings, with windows facing the big trees at
the back of the building, and it offered a bit more
space.

Except a woman had been murdered in here on
Saint Patrick's Day only two months ago. Not so
nice. In mid-April, I'd made the emotional and
business decision to reopen the Rose room and
not inform guests of its history. I'd helped the police resolve that case, and it was time to move forward. No lodgers in any of the rooms had reported
hearing ghostly sounds or screams, so I was pretty
sure the victim wasn't haunting my building.

The towels I left on the desk. The cleaners
would array them nicely in the bathroom before
they left. In here, I smoothed out the fitted sheet
and shook the top sheet over it. Two hospital corners, two pillowcases, and one dusty-rose flowered
comforter later, I stood back to check my work.
Perfect.

I picked up my keys but lingered. Western sun
slanted in the window on that side. I sank into the
rocking chair in the corner, musing for a moment.
How had I, owner of a modest business, no more
than a middling cook and carpenter, become involved in solving murders? What had it been by
now, a dozen or more? I had not a lick of professional law enforcement training.

A couple of times, the murder had been associ-
ated with my store, including the body discarded
behind my pickle barrel. I'd had to lock up and
turn away customers more than once. Keeping my

livelihood's bottom line intact was great motivation for digging into a crime.

Abe's father had been investigated one Christmas season, and Abe himself had been a person of interest in what I now called the Rose Room Murder. Who wouldn't want to clear the name of a person they loved?

I'd also gotten involved when Danna's half brother was a person of interest during a different holiday season, and after Turner's father had been suspected of the homicide of a tree scientist. The police had even suspected Adele once or twice.

And now Don was acting funny. He'd argued with Evermina. Was he about to be arrested? Thinking of him made me think of my own neglected bookkeeping.

I pushed up to standing. It was time for this girl to head home. After I had a bite to eat, I could pay attention to my financial in and out boxes. Or work on a puzzle to help me think through the current case. Or both.

CHAPTER 23

After cooking all day, plus making up beds, the last thing a chef wants to do is make herself dinner. I fed Birdy and Maceo their small portions of canned dinner, washed my hands, and changed into cozy sweats.

I found a couple of chicken tamales in the freezer and stuck them in to be nuked. I treated myself to one of the excellent non-alcoholic microbrews that had been appearing in stores lately, popping it open and decanting it into a pint glass. A glass of milk to accompany Mexican food was simply unacceptable. Lucky for me, the taste and smell of the NA beer didn't repel me tonight.

The flowers did, indeed, look lovely in the middle of the dining table. I sat facing them instead of on a stool at the counter. I'd never gotten around to reading the weekly *Brown County Democrat*, the actual paper newspaper Abe insisted we should subscribe to. It was nice to spread it out and read as I ate. This was a small-town rag, and I loved the quirky public interest stories. This edition included a piece about a ninety-year-old woman who volunteered in a kindergarten class, and the police log mentioned a carcass in the road as well as a suspicious person whistling. The authorities determined the whistler did not present a threat.

The smell of the newsprint and the crackle of the paper reminded me of reading the Sunday *Los Angeles Times* with my mom when I was growing up in Santa Barbara, and the *Santa Barbara News-Press*, too. Certain Sunday mornings we'd take breakfast to the beach, just the two of us. We'd eat and stroll and swim and make elaborate sandcastles. When we stayed home, we'd sit quietly at the kitchen table and read. I'd read the comics, and then would do a jigsaw puzzle or play while she perused the paper's sections. By the time I was in middle school, a tidbit one or both of us read would spark real discussions about politics, science, or culture.

I stroked my belly. Being pregnant made me miss Mommy more than ever. I didn't ache for her every day as I had in the first year after her sudden and unpredictable death. How I would have loved for my child to know her, to explore the beach with her, to learn from a loving and talented grandmother who had created beautiful pieces of fine wooden furniture. My mom had raised me to think for myself, be independent, follow my dream. And I had. She'd also been fun and lively and inquisitive.

I couldn't reverse what had happened. I could talk about Grandma Jeanine to my child as she or he grew, as well as model my mother's best traits. I would try to be as lively and fun a mom as she had been, and as encouraging of the child's intellect.

Abe would help with that. He almost always had a twinkle in his eye, and I knew he would be a devoted father to our little one. I'd admired the way he fathered Sean ever since I'd met both of them. Even when Sean's mom was alive and the boy spent less time with his dad, Abe was always there for him, teaching him, supporting his dreams, playing games, and also providing gentle discipline when needed.

I didn't have my mom, but I knew what a lucky woman I was in all other respects.

A story about the Covenant Hope church on the back page of the paper caught my attention. Was that the place of worship the ladies this morning had mentioned? I read the article and sat back. It described a major donor to the church. The source had asked to remain anonymous but had raised red flags about the financial stability and management of the organization. It would be a shame if tithes and donations from the members weren't being used for the charitable works they'd been promised to.

I closed the paper and savored my last bite of tamale, a food I'd grown up with. Its soft cornmeal covering wrapped around a savory meat filling and then steamed always tasted like comfort. I'd planned to work on creating a crossword puzzle this evening to organize my thoughts about Evermina's murder. I hated being even remotely suspected of the homicide. The sooner the case was solved, the better.

First, though, something was bugging me. I hadn't checked the recent news. Just because those church ladies had said they'd heard the news about Evermina from this Sister Cooper didn't mean the murder wasn't being discussed publicly. I thumbed my phone, searching.

A couple of places mentioned a death at the beginning of the Nashcar race and that authorities regarded it as suspicious. I couldn't find Evermina identified anywhere. Instead, I read the usual verbiage about the name being withheld pending notification of family. Who was her family? I hadn't heard anyone mention her pre-married last name. Octavia and her team were surely working on that.

Before I started creating a crossword, I had one more thing to do. Seeing Don work on his business accounts, if that was what the spreadsheet had been, had reminded me to take a look at mine first. I hadn't done it in a while.

I brought my laptop to the table and opened the application I used to manage the store's finances. Money in, money out. Payroll. Capital expenses, like that deep fryer. Maintenance expenses like adding a motion-activated front porch light or fixing a tread on the stairs. Retail income. Balancing the checkbook, so to speak, and paying taxes of all kinds.

It was a lot. I'd always excelled at math, but I was going to have an important new priority in my life come Thanksgiving. I might as well establish a relationship with a good accountant now, while I could. How to find one, though, especially a professional who understood the food business? I wasn't sure they needed that specific expertise, but it couldn't hurt.

Camilla ran a successful restaurant in Nashville.

She might have a reputable accountant on speed dial. I could take another ride out there tomorrow and ask her.

Or not. I was going to the estate sale in the morning. Putting in an order for the week and doing breakfast prep. Making a dish to bring to Adele's. And welcoming my family home in the afternoon. Such a full day might not have enough hours in it for a ride. On the other hand, Cammie's owner could also be in possession of information about Zeke. Or Wendy. Or Evermina.

Did I have her cell number? I might. Last year there had been a mixer in Nashville with all the restaurant owners in the county, which was where I'd renewed my acquaintance with her. Before I bought my store, I'd worked as a chef at the Nashville Inn and had met her casually.

I'd spoken the truth about that to Octavia, not that I'd lied in any of my answers. I rarely ate at restaurants in the county seat, especially ones that didn't serve dinner, so I hadn't run into Camilla recently before Friday. I again wondered why Octavia had asked about Camilla. If she was a person of interest, I had no idea why.

I found Camilla's number and gave her a call, but she didn't pick up. Well, it was Sunday evening. I left a text identifying myself and asking her to call, saying I wanted to pick her brain about a few things.

A yawn overtook me. Today had been a super-full day, too. I settled in on the couch and tucked my feet up, wishing Abe were next to me. Tomorrow. He'd be home tomorrow.

CHAPTER 24

A ringing phone startled me for the second
evening in a row. I sat up. Birdy leapt off the
couch. I must have fallen asleep. Was this Camilla
calling back, or had Abe found himself with cell
service?

I grabbed the phone, which read Cammie's
Kitchen.

"Hi, Camilla." My voice had sandpaper in it.

"Robbie, you wanted to talk?"

I cleared my throat. "Yes. Thanks for calling." I
described my interest in an accountant. "Do you
have someone good you use?"

"I do, Ann O'Sullivan. She's in business with her
husband. She really gets my business model and
handles all my stuff. My taxes, too."

"That sounds good. Can you text me her contact info after we're done talking?" Now I had to
figure out how to steer the conversation around to
murder.

"Sure. Hey, how are you doing? It must have

been a huge shock to have Evermina's body fall out of your race entry."

"You bet it was." I smiled to myself. She'd done the steering for me. "The detective has been after me, asking all kinds of questions."

"What, she thinks you killed Ev?"

Ev? She and Evermina must have been friends. "It kind of seems like that. Which, obviously, I didn't. How about you?" I wrinkled my nose. That had come out sounding like I was asking if she was the murderer.

She didn't speak for a couple of seconds. "What about me?"

"I mean, has Detective Slade been to see you?"

"Why would she?"

"You know a cast-iron skillet fell out after Evermina." Birdy jumped up next to me again with the little chirping sound that gave him his name. I stroked his long, smooth coat.

"It did?"

I didn't believe her feigned ignorance. Even if she hadn't seen the skillet herself, she must have heard about it, but I couldn't remember if she'd been close by on Saturday morning or not.

"Yes," I said. "And on Friday at the drop-off I saw one like it hanging from your outhouse. Saturday it wasn't there. I thought maybe the killer used it as the weapon."

"Oh." She drew out the syllable. "I wouldn't have a clue about that, Robbie. But, yes, Slade came to see me. She wants me to go to the station tomorrow to be interviewed."

"Did you know Evermina very well?" I grimaced. I should pull back from sounding like I was interrogating her. I didn't want her to be suspicious of me.

"I'd met her a few times. Talked business. That kind of thing."

I'd leave their interactions there. "I wonder if Zeke is grieving her loss. I mean, I know they were divorced. But sometimes . . ." I let that thought go. I had nothing more to say. I did find it interesting that she referred to Evermina by a nickname, despite claiming she didn't know her well. Ev was a shortening I hadn't heard anyone else use.

"I doubt he's sad at all," she said. "Zeke Martin got rid of her like a hot coal, or maybe like a millstone around his neck. Once Wendy got her claws into him, he didn't even have the decency to wait until he was free of his wife, may she rest in peace." She made a *tsking* sound. "My husband was no saint, but he and I stayed faithful until the day he died."

"I'm sorry. I didn't know you were a widow, Camilla."

"It's been a couple few years, Robbie. I miss the old coot, but missing won't bring him back. That's the thing about death. There's no fixing it."

No, one couldn't fix death. I knew that as well as I knew my own face. "Is Wendy divorced, too?"

"She is, for years now. She probably figured she'd better snag another man before she got too old."

"You might have heard that Evermina had been trash-talking my restaurant all over South Lick," I said.

"I did."

"I'm sure she was trying to drum up business for

her diner, but she took a malicious approach to it. Did she mount a campaign against your restaurant, too?" I hadn't seen ads or flyers to that effect, but I didn't spend much time in Nashville. I easily might have missed them.

Again she didn't speak for a moment or two. "As a matter of fact, she did. Or tried. It was downright ridiculous, Robbie. I opened Cammie's Kitchen, what, twenty years ago? Nearly. We weren't even in the same town, and she definitely wasn't in my league. I couldn't believe it."

"Did you ask her to back off?"

"Well, sure. Didn't you?"

"Yes." I suppressed a yawn. "And did she?"

"Did she what?"

"Stop. Cease and desist."

Camilla snorted. "Not for a minute. The girl was relentless. Hey, I gotta run. A show I like is coming on."

"Gotcha. Thanks for the name. You'll send me your CPA's number?"

"Yep. See you around."

She disconnected, putting an abrupt end to our chat. It was fine. I'd learned a few things, and I might have snagged an accountant, too.

Still, I felt like I needed to know more about Evermina. Maybe I hadn't searched as deeply as I might. I put Mr. Google to work again. This time I scored, big time. Typing in "Evermina Indiana" got me to a news story from the *Indianapolis Star* about Mrs. Smith's Diner in Martinsville, a city on the road between Indy and Bloomington. It apparently was a family-run restaurant, in which all the

Smith children worked. Including daughter Evermina.

I checked the date. The article had been published over twenty years ago, apparently preceding
her marriage to Zeke. Maybe the diner named
after her mother had inspired her to open her
own.

My plan for the evening had been to create a
sleuthing puzzle. I decided a new and more attractive plan was to work somebody else's puzzle. In
bed.

CHAPTER 25

Tour bus travelers who stopped at my restaurant to eat also loved shopping for cookware. It was a great lure, but the "pans" section of Pans 'N Pancakes was running low on items for sale, and I needed to restock. I stared at tables and shelves groaning with vintage cookware the next morning at nine and gave a happy sigh. Adele hadn't been kidding when she'd described the sale as big.

The owner of the sprawling home set on a knoll down a quiet country lane had been a chef who'd apparently outfitted his home kitchen with more implements than most restaurants are stocked with. He'd retired in the mid-1950s, so everything was vintage if not officially antique. Now a decade after he'd died, his children had put the property on the market rather than keep it in the family.

This sale wasn't a live or online auction. Things were priced to move. The cookware cost more than it would have at a flea market but items were still inexpensive enough I could clear a profit on resale. And the selection was amazing.

Vera said the man's wife had been a quilter, and everything in her sewing room was also up for grabs. In fact, the contents of the entire house were.

I foresaw two problems. One was going to be identifying what I wanted and piling it all in one place. The second would be transporting it to the cashier and from there to Adele's car. Pans could get heavy and unwieldy, but Adele and Vera had wandered off. I'd text my aunt when I was ready for help.

After I sorted through dozens of cake and muffin tins and picked out fifteen in decent shape with interesting stamping in the metal, I came to a high table of sharp objects. Ice picks and nut choppers, cleavers and corers, plus a wooden block with knives, each in its own slot. Good thing the surface was at bar-table height. I'd hate for a child to grab for one of these implements.

An antique sugar auger made me shudder. A few years ago, a murderer had come after me in my store with one of those. Sixteen inches long with a wooden handle and lethally sharp edges and points, it had been used in days of yore to loosen up usable chunks from big cakes of sugar. Ever since that attack, my store's cookware display had included a locked, glass-fronted cabinet for anything with a blade.

"That thing looks pretty nasty," a woman said.

"You bet." I turned to see Melia Bird smiling at me from a few feet away. "Melia, what a nice surprise."

"Good morning, Robbie. Are you here to stock up for your store?" Instead of hiking clothes, today she wore blue Capris and a blue-and-white striped top, a comfortable outfit that was stylish at the same time.

"Exactly." I glanced around. "Is Buck here?"

"No, he had to work. I drove down with a few girlfriends. We're making a day of it. Lunch, shopping. You know."

"That sounds fun."

"I'm a quilter when I'm not minding children's health. One friend collects antique books." She gestured toward a woman picking through a collection of cast-iron pots and pans. "That one is a neurosurgeon, but also an amazing amateur chef."

A neurosurgeon who loved to cook. Who knew?

"Robbie," Melia lowered her voice, "I heard something interesting."

"About?"

"About what happened in Nashville." She shot me a pointed look.

Ooh. I tried to hide my surprise.

"Well," she continued, "about one of the people who might be involved."

"Okay. I'd love to hear it."

"It's this way. I met Zeke Martin last year when he designed a series of information sheets for our pediatrics practice. We like to hand out short pieces on things like asthma, immunizations, nutrition, and so on to our parents, and we create our own so we vet the facts and don't rely on anyone else's presentation."

"Sounds like a good idea," I said.

"The handouts have to be attractive and read-able so they don't scare folks off. Zeke gave us a reasonable quote, and we liked the look of his portfolio. We hired him. But . . ."

"But?"

"As he did the work, he kept finding reasons to tack on additional costs. And when I met with him in person, he badmouthed his wife, whom I didn't even know. It was in very poor taste."

"That's too bad." But why was she volunteering this information?

"I told Buck, and he said he'd pass it along." As if she'd read my mind, she went on. "I know you like to do your own investigations, and you've been very helpful to my husband in the past, un-covering details he wasn't able to."

"Thank you. So, you're thinking Zeke might have been the one who . . . did it." I didn't want to say the word *murder* aloud in here.

She shrugged. "It was a thought. He might have been paying alimony to his ex. If he's prone to fi-nancial mismanagement, which it seemed to me he was, he could have wanted to get out from under that burden."

"Using extreme measures."

"Indeed." She gave a little laugh. "Nobody I know does what someone did to Evermina to get out of a debt owed."

"Same here."

"Listen, I'm glad I caught you, but I need to get over to the sewing room before everything's gone."

"Go," I said. "It was good to see you again, Melia. And thank you."

By telling me about Zeke, it seemed she wanted to pay me back a little for helping Buck in the past. I welcomed the gesture. And the information. Zeke's financial situation definitely bore looking into—if I could figure out how.

CHAPTER 26

Adele drove Vera and me back to South Lick. A tarp covered my pile of cookware purchases in the bed of the battered red truck.

"Did you find much, Vera?" I asked.

"I picked up a few sewing notions and a pile of fat quarters in gorgeous shades of purple and turquoise. The sewing room got emptied fast, though."

"What's a fat quarter?" I twisted to face her where she sat in the window seat. I'd volunteered to cram in the middle again. Adele's ride was not a new fancy truck with a back seat in the cab, but an old workhorse she used on her sheep farm. At least it had a sizeable bench seat.

"They're twenty-two by eighteen-inch pieces of the same type and weight of cloth, usually cotton, in colors that might look pretty together in a quilt," Vera replied. "They're folded in quarters, and fabric stores bundle them together. It's a convenience the lady of that house apparently enjoyed but never finished using up."

"Our Vera here's a right talented quilter," Adele said.

"Go on, now." Vera blushed. "I do confess that I like stitching pretty things folks can use."

We drove in silence for a few minutes, which brought back thoughts of what Melia had told me about Zeke and his several kinds of bad behavior.

"Adele, what do you know about Zeke Martin?" My aunt definitely knew everyone in South Lick, but I wasn't sure how far her circles reached into Nashville.

"I've had me the odd run-in with him over the years."

"What do you mean by odd?" I asked.

"Let me think a minute, here. It was back when I was mayor. Martin came around saying he could give us a competitive price on the design for a job of signage we had out to bid. The other two artists submitted a package price. Martin's proposal looked to cost less at first, but when I dug into the fine print, he was tacking on a whole slew of extra costs that put his offer way over our budget. When I pressed him on it, he said that was normal in the biz. I thanked him and said goodbye."

"Doesn't sound like it was normal if the others approached the bid differently."

"You got that right, Roberta."

What she'd said sounded similar to Melia's experience with Zeke. Padding costs was distasteful and a bad business practice, but it wasn't illegal. At a soft snore next to me, I glanced at Vera. Her head resting against the window, she seemed to be having a contented late-morning snooze.

"How about Wendy Corbett?" I asked Adele. "Do

you know anything about her? She runs the Nash-ville Treasures gift shop."

"Owns it, too. Wouldn't touch that girl with a ten-foot fishing pole."

"Really? Why?"

"Land sakes alive, hon. Because she's as un-scrupulous as they come. She come up to the farm last year, year before, something like that. Wanted to make a big-old fuss about selling my yarns in her little shop. In fact, she proposed to take and slap a new label on the wrapper. *Treasures Precious Wool.* What a load of he-cow patty."

"With no credit to you?"

"Not a word except for 'Hand-spun in South Lick.' But not by whom, not a word about how the dang wool came from sheep raised in our pretty little town, and certainly not my name."

"I hope you declined the offer," I said.

"You can bet your sweet aardvark I did. She wanted to buy the stuff at half wholesale price, too. Forget it."

I sold skeins of Adele's wool in my store, along with the hats and mittens and socks she knitted with it. But the labels on the skeins were her labels, with full identification and attribution. Same with the knitted products. She also sold directly from her farm and maybe elsewhere. I was pretty sure she didn't need the money, particularly.

"You know, I ran into Melia Bird in the kitchen of the estate sale."

"Yes, I spoke with her, as well. She's a sweet-heart, and smarter than all get-out. Buck's lucky to have her."

"I'd have to agree," I said. "I met her for the first

time on Saturday when he brought her into the restaurant. Anyway, she'd had a similar experience with Zeke and a work proposal as you did."

"Them two, Zeke and Wendy, they're made for each other." She snorted. "In the worst of ways."

Were Zeke and Wendy made for each other to the extent that they might murder together? The thought made me shiver. Still, Evermina had been killed, by whom I didn't know. I didn't feel an inch closer to the truth about the crime.

We passed the sign for Gnaw Bone, home of the legendary breaded pork tenderloin sandwich. The town's name was apparently a local rendering of Narbonne, what the French trappers had dubbed the hamlet centuries ago. Other Hoosier town names had similar origins. I like the current spelling better. A public sign that invariably makes you smile when you see it has to be a good thing.

We skipped the entrance to Nashville and headed toward South Lick. Adele took a back road I rarely used. It was direct but had been in poor repair since I'd moved to the town. The ride today was as smooth as riding in a luxury limousine with great shock absorbers and new, well-padded seats.

To my right loomed a gigantic, sprawling building with a roof that swooped up to a point at one end. The parking lot surrounding the pale-yellow structure was also enormous but stretched out mostly empty.

"What in the world is that?" I asked.

"The Covenant Hope church. You never seen it before?"

"I have not. How many people come to services here, a thousand?"

"Probably ten times that. It's one of them evangelist megachurches. From what I hear tell, there's lots of praising the Lord, folks finding Jesus, rousing hymns, and tithing. They're encouraged to be generous with the collection plate, except via automatic withdrawal from their bank accounts instead of dropping bills or coins into a dish on the Sabbath."

"Do they handle snakes and speak in tongues?"

"No idea. I've never been."

"I wonder if those things really happen," I said. "It doesn't matter, one way or the other. Everyone is entitled to their own way of finding God or whatever spiritual life they want."

Those church women in my store yesterday had seemed genuine and happy with their chosen house of worship. The church might have paid for the road upgrade, but the article I'd read had mentioned financial mismanagement.

I blinked. The women had said it was a Sister Cooper who told them about Evermina's death, which sparked another memory. *Yes.* It had been Octavia who'd asked about Isabelle Cooper, a person I'd never heard of. Was the passer-on of news the same person? I might have to do a little digging on Sister Cooper later.

CHAPTER 27

After Adele and Vera dropped my purchases and me at the store, I priced and set everything up on the shelves. One of the cake pans was heart-shaped with flowers embossed into the bottom. The pan would need serious greasing, but the cake it would produce once baked and up-ended would be pretty, especially with a pink glaze or even frosting.

Should I slide this one onto the "not for sale" display shelf, or maybe add it to my collection in the store's kitchen? I doubted I'd use it often, and it would make another baker very happy. I slapped a price label on it and set it front and center on one of the shelves.

My first job done, I gazed around the restaurant. The floor and counters gleamed from the cleaners' work. Hiring them was worth every penny not to have to scrub down the place myself. I'd grown to trust the couple enough to hand over a key. Letting them in was no longer a Monday morning chore.

It was now eleven o'clock, and I was genuinely hungry. I washed my hands and fixed a sandwich, cheddar cheese and ham on rye, for an early lunch, slicing a dill pickle to accompany it. I'd realized on the drive home from the estate sale that my stomach hadn't threatened to expel its contents all morning. What a relief to feel I was moving beyond the sickness phase of this pregnancy.

As I ate, I ran a search on my phone for Isabelle Cooper. I doubted she was the Vice Provost for Undergraduate Education at Stanford University. Or the artist who featured nature in her sculptures and paintings, who seemed to live in England. Sister Cooper might have been the one who was married in Pennsylvania last year, but probably not. *Aha.* Here was one listed as the surviving wife to a Bernard Cooper who'd died a couple of years ago in Indianapolis at age eighty-two.

At least this Isabelle was a Hoosier. But if she was Sister Cooper, how did an elderly woman find out about the murder victim's name before the news had been made public? Or that it was murder at all? Isabelle must have moved to our area from Indy if she attended Covenant Hope. It was more than an hour's drive here from the state capital. That was a lot for weekly services, especially if you were in your eighties. Churches like that often held midweek worship, too.

I popped in the last bite of pickle. Enough of this futile searching and musing. I had work to do.

I grabbed my tablet and headed into the walk-in to figure out what I needed to order.

Surveying the shelves, I thought fast about possible specials for the week. Once the deep fryer was set up and running, we could do those cheese fritters Danna had mentioned. And samosas, with Turner in charge. I gave myself a little head slap for forgetting to ask Camilla last night about good frozen products for a deep fryer. That could come later.

I ordered several bags of three kinds of pre-grated cheese for the fritters. I checked all the supplies and ordered enough perishables for the week. My team and I could brainstorm specials for the weekend tomorrow. We didn't need to offer a special beyond the usual menu every single day. Our normal fare was plenty popular.

For now, I wanted to make up a test pan of the apple dumplings, so I loaded the carrying basket with butter and apples. When I was alone and my hands were busy with cooking, my brain usually did its best work.

The first step in the dumpling recipe was making a pie crust. I always used a no-fail dough from a Julia Child cookbook. The recipe called for a food processor, and I loved that the iconic chef wasn't above revealing that she loved a time-saving appliance as much as the rest of us.

As I smeared the crumbly mix, bit by bit, onto the counter to bring it into a coherent dough, I again thought about Don's behavior yesterday. He'd wanted to hide whatever was on his laptop from me. But what had it been? Maybe Abe would have insights about his brother and what he was up to.

I returned to the thought I'd had in Adele's truck after she said Zeke and Wendy were made for each other. What if they had collaborated on the murder? It could have been one's idea and the other aided and abetted, in cop show lingo. Had Evermina been an emotional thorn in Zeke's side or maybe a financial albatross?

I wrapped the disk of dough in plastic wrap and stuck it in the fridge. As I kept thinking, I buttered a rectangular baking dish and washed and dried six apples.

Camilla had feigned ignorance on the phone last night when I'd asked her about the skillet. She had to know the skillet from her outhouse was missing. How could she not? But she'd pretended she wasn't aware. Why? And she'd paused before answering my inquiry about whether Evermina—Ev—had campaigned against her restaurant in the same way she had against mine. It was a simple question. I didn't know why she had to think about it.

I cored and cut the apples into quarters, then tossed them in a big bowl with cinnamon and nutmeg. I mixed sugar and water until the sugar dissolved and put it on to boil. I also set the oven to preheat. These dumplings baked in a sugar syrup, which seemed like a neat trick.

I wanted to dig into Wendy's past. And Evermina's. It was always possible that an entirely different person had murdered Evermina, but all I could do was follow the information I had.

After I set aside the hot syrup, I readied the counter for rolling out the dough. When it was an even eighth-inch thick, I used a sharp knife to cut it into squares. An apple quarter went into the middle of the first square. I stretched up the sides and pinched the edges together, laying it in the prepared pan. Rinse and repeat.

Was there any merit to including Jim Shermer in the mix? Evermina had come on strong to him that evening. Everything I knew about Jim pointed to a gentle man. But I hadn't been acquainted with him long before he'd moved on from our romance. He might have a hidden streak of violence and had gotten fed up with Evermina's advances. But, no. Octavia was a good judge of character. A detective had to be. She wouldn't have married Jim if he were prone to violence. At least, I hoped not.

By now the pan was full of two dozen little packets. I poured the warm syrup over the pan and popped it in the oven. As I cleaned up and washed my hands, I wished I could wash my hands of this case, too. But I knew my mind wouldn't rest until it was solved.

CHAPTER 28

I stepped through the open door of Hickory Fine Art at a little past one o'clock. With the dumplings cooling and my breakfast prep for tomorrow completed, I'd driven to Nashville to see what I could learn. Abe was back in cell range and had texted that they'd be home around three, and we weren't invited to Adele's until four thirty. I had time to squeeze in a little sleuthing.

The gallery walls were white, perfect to showcase framed art. Most of the visual art was paintings or drawings of nature or people, but I spied a few artistic photographs, too, and a couple of abstract pieces. On blocks here and there sat various kinds of sculptures, with a display in one area of fanciful metal figures not even a foot tall. A grinning dragon faced a sassy catfish standing with hands on hips, and a raccoon held a half-eaten apple. Maybe those were Isaac's new creations.

Jim was helping a customer. He glanced over at

me and frowned. I smiled, giving a little wave, before turning away. The wall nearest me was hung with an assortment of lovely watercolors of shops, ponds, and birds. One captured the glint of sun on water. Another showed the happy expression of a child gazing up at a white-haired man smiling down. I peered at the signature, which I thought read E. Smith.

I wandered along the next wall, which featured black-and-white photographs of people, most appearing unaware their image was being captured.

Pausing at one, I leaned closer. It depicted rows of people in chairs, all facing front. The focus of the photograph was of a woman whose hands were folded in her lap, but her face tilted upward with unmistakable rapture in her gaze. A shaft of soft, unearthly light lit her visage. It was the church lady from my restaurant yesterday, the one who had so roundly chewed out Zeke.

Just beyond her in the composition another woman looked straight into the camera lens. Nostrils flared and lips pressed together, she was about my age, with dark hair in well-cut layers falling almost to her shoulders. The picture caption read, "Rapture and Judgment."

Who would go into a church and take pictures of worshipers? That pursuit of art struck me as a step too far.

"What do you think?" Jim asked, now next to me.

"I think this photographer shouldn't have been sneaking a camera into a church service." I faced him. "Doesn't that seem like a violation?"

"Maybe. But it could have been a phone, which

everyone has, and maybe the artist attends that church regularly."

The photographer's name wasn't familiar to me, which didn't matter. I still didn't approve.

"Can I help you with anything, Robbie?" he asked.

"I'm not sure. You've set up a nice place here."

"Thank you."

"How long have you had it?"

"We moved back to the area about two years ago. I opened before the holiday shopping season six months later."

"Has business been good?" I asked.

"Not bad. The only other gallery is much more sort of folk art, country design, that kind of thing. I have the market on fine art."

"Good." I pointed to the watercolors. "Those are really nice."

A shadow came over his face. "They are."

I moved over to the metal sculptures. "I bet these are Isaac Rowling's."

"They are. Do you know him?"

"Not well, but he and one of my staff are a couple." I stroked the catfish and examined the tag, which read two hundred and twenty dollars. Pricey, but artists had to make a living, and so did Jim. I decided to splurge. "I love the attitude on this one. I'll take it."

"It's yours." He carried it to the counter.

I handed him my credit card and watched as he wrapped the fish in tissue and bubble wrap. He didn't make eye contact with me.

"Terrible about Evermina, isn't it?" I kept my tone casual.

That made him meet my gaze.

"Yes," he said. "Tragic."

"She looked really cozy with you on Friday. You weren't cheating on Octavia, I hope."

He gaped. "Me? Of course not. How in the world could you think such a thing?"

"Old habits die hard?" I tilted my head.

Jim opened his mouth. He closed it. He gave me my card and a bag holding the sculpture.

"Thank you," I said.

"For the record, Robbie Jordan," he said in a low, hard voice. "I did not cheat on you before we broke up."

"Before you broke up with me, you mean."

"Whatever you say. By the way, Evermina had a lot of talent. She painted those watercolors."

I gaped. Jim turned his face away. A couple stepped inside. The woman began exclaiming about Isaac's "cute" creations.

I stepped toward the door. "Take care," I said. "See you around."

"Do come back, now."

I didn't care that he didn't mean it. I bobbed my head. Aiming for the door, I slid past the newcomers. The bright sunshine nearly blinded me as I left the store, and I collided with a passerby.

"Oof," a man said.

"I'm so sorry." I moved away and, shielding my eyes with my hand, looked up. "Zeke, it's you."

"Might want to watch where you're going, Robbie."

"I apologize. The light hit my eyes."

He cleared his throat. "You certainly have the oddest customers in your restaurant, or should I say rudest?"

I smiled and shrugged. It had sounded like he and Wendy had deserved the tirade. I wasn't going to apologize for my customer.

"Looks like you bought a piece of fine art." Zeke eyed my bag.

"I did, a small sculpture."

"Or maybe you were snooping around, playing at being a real detective." His sneer was obvious.

Whoa. "You have a good day, Zeke." It was time for me to clear out of here.

"Better watch where you step. Bad guys are around every corner."

He strode down the street. Was that a threat? I stood still for a moment. In fact, I was trying to do a bit of investigating. And Zeke Martin didn't scare me.

What Jim had said about Evermina being a painter had stunned me, though. With so much artistic talent, she'd wanted to open a restaurant instead?

I considered my next steps. Maybe I could hit up the courthouse and find out if Zeke and artist-turned-restaurateur Evermina were officially divorced.

I glanced up and down the street, where the lampposts were all hung with red, white, and blue buntings. I wouldn't be requesting any records. Today was Memorial Day, a holiday. The county courthouse would be locked up tight.

My stomach gave a growl. I'd had that sandwich, but maybe my pregnant body was making up for lost time—and calories. Cammie's Kitchen was down the block. I was eating for two, and there was nothing wrong with a second lunch. Maybe I could also find out why she'd hedged while we were on the phone last night.

CHAPTER 29

The police station was on my route to Cammie's Kitchen. I carefully crossed the street and tried not to look at the building. The last thing I wanted today was to be invited back inside for more interrogation. I hurried on toward Camilla's restaurant.

"Hey, there, Robbie," a voice called.

I slowed and groaned when I glanced across the road to see Wanda. In uniform. Coming out of the police station.

"Where's the fire?" She made her way across to me.

"No fire. What's happening?"

"Nothing much of consequence, unfortunately. You got a minute?"

"I guess." I kept my sigh silent.

"Want to grab a bite to eat or a cup of tea with me?" Wanda rubbed her belly. "Seems I'm hungry all the time these days."

Did I want her company at Camilla's place? Not really, but I might as well.

"I was headed to Cammie's Kitchen. You can join me."

"Perfect."

She lumbered along at my side. Three minutes later we perched side-by-side on stools at the long counter. Camilla approached behind it, set down a glass of water for each of us, and laid two straws in paper wrappers next to the waters.

"Afternoon, ladies." She gave me the side eye. "Working with the county sheriff now, Robbie?"

"No," I said. "We just found ourselves heading in the same direction."

"I plum shanghaied her." Wanda sounded way too cheerful about waylaying me. "How's it shaking, Camilla?"

I'd been about to introduce them to each other. If I'd thought about it, I might have realized Wanda would be a regular in here.

"Fine. What can I get you both?" Camilla, who was pushing sixty, still had mostly dark waves, but a dramatic white stripe split the hair near her temple. She was broad-shouldered in a black V-necked shirt, her white half apron snug around a waist that looked sturdy, not fat.

"I'll have me a cheeseburger with the works," Wanda said, "and a glass of chocolate milk, if you please."

I scanned the paper menu on the counter. I was headed to Adele's in a few hours. I didn't want to stuff myself here. "I'd like a cup of the catfish chowder, please."

"You got it. Anything to drink for you?" Camilla poised her pen above the order pad.

"Just the water will be fine, thanks, and I don't

need a straw." Too much plastic got tossed in a place like this. I didn't drink water with a straw at home. Why would I want one in a restaurant?

Camilla turned to the pass-through window and stuck the order slip on a carousel exactly like the one we used in Pans 'N Pancakes.

"You're working on a holiday?" I asked Wanda.

"Sure am. Duty calls and all that." She cleared her throat. "And speaking of that, can I assume you're doing your own investigating on this, uh, current business?"

Camilla was clearing the place next to me. Her hands slowed, and if human ears could actually perk up, I'd swear hers did.

"Why would you think that, Wanda?" I shifted my eyes toward Camilla, trying to signal to Wanda that the proprietor was listening.

"Merely thinking about what you done in the past. You gotta promise to share any juicy tidbits, hear?"

"Um, okay." Except thinking of murder in terms of *juicy tidbits* made me wince. "But I'm not investigating anything."

"Right." Wanda snorted.

I waited until Camilla carried the dishes into the kitchen. "Wanda, don't talk about the case while she's nearby," I murmured.

"You think she was listening?"

I nodded. "I'll tell you later."

In a couple of minutes, Camilla set Wanda's plate in front of her. It was fully loaded with a fat burger, a pickle spear, and a mound of crispy fries. In front of me she placed my cup of soup, plus a packet of oyster crackers.

"Thanks. Those fries look great," I said. "Camilla, I'm finally getting a deep fryer for my place. Do you hand cut the potatoes?"

"Seriously?" She cocked a hip and an eyebrow. "We don't have time for that. No, I buy big bags of frozen. They come out good, though."

"Can you share the brand?"

"Sure. You want I should write it down?"

"Actually, could you please text it to me?" I asked. "You have my number from last night."

"Will do. You girls all set now?" Camilla asked.

Wanda, already deep into her burger, gave a nod.

"Yes, thanks," I said.

I dipped my spoon into the chowder, making sure I included one of the pieces of bacon crumbled on top, and tasted it. As chefs do when eating someone else's cooking, I rolled the flavors on my tongue. The thick, creamy chowder was delicious.

I'd guess heavy cream was on the ingredients list. Diced potatoes added to the creaminess. Corn kernels that weren't overcooked added tiny nuggets of crunchiness. I loved catfish, and in a landlocked place like Indiana, the tasty river fish was a perfect substitution for clams or saltwater fish. I detected a subtle hint of hot pepper, but the Californian in me wanted more. Luckily Camilla had brought a bottle of habanero hot sauce with the chowder. A couple of drops added exactly the right touch.

A fish chowder would make a great special in my own restaurant. I might add minced parsley, or maybe minced scallions. A squeeze of lime juice could brighten the flavors.

"That must be good," Wanda said. "You've been lost in thought for a while there."

I laughed. "I was trying to deconstruct the soup and figure out how I could make my own version for Pans 'N Pancakes."

"I'd eat that."

Right now, it seemed Wanda would eat anything. I continued to savor the chowder until it was nearly gone.

Camilla returned. "How is everything?"

Wanda, now with another mouthful and a nearly decimated plate, gave a thumbs-up.

"This chowder is delicious, Camilla."

"Thanks, hon." Camilla beamed at me. "It's one of our most popular items. Who doesn't love catfish?"

"I could name more than one person, but they aren't locals." Wanda held her hand in front of her mouth as she finished chewing.

I happened to love the sweet flavor of farmed catfish, and the flesh rarely cooked up too dry.

"Say, Camilla," Wand said. "I seem to recall seeing a couple few ads around town comparing this joint to Evermina's diner, and they sure as shooting weren't all that complimentary to your cooking. Were you aware of that?"

I turned to look at Wanda. It was as if she'd read my mind, asking that question, which was fine with me. It was her job. This way I wouldn't get on Camilla's bad side.

"Aware?" Camilla's voice rose. "Are you kidding? Of course I was. And I told her in no uncertain terms to stop what she was doing. Heck, we weren't even serving the same customer base."

"When was that, when you told her to cease and desist?" Wanda asked.

"Last week."

"Was it late Friday night?" Wanda lowered her voice. "Did you kill Evermina Martin to make her stop?"

Camilla slapped our check on the counter and folded her arms on her chest. "No." She whirled and strode away. She turned back, opening her mouth, glaring at Wanda. She seemed to think the better of adding any further response and pushed through the swinging door into the kitchen.

"You didn't sugarcoat that at all, Wanda," I murmured.

"Nah. What's the point? You all done?" She popped the last bite of pickle into her mouth and stood.

I slid the cracker packet into my bag. I still wasn't sure I was over morning sickness. I rose.

"Lunch is on me."

"Thanks."

She grabbed the check and laid a twenty and a ten on the counter. "You're a cheap date, Robbie Jordan." She headed for the door.

Before I followed Wanda, I glanced into the pass-through window. Camilla's gaze bore into me. I gave a shrug and turned away. I couldn't help what Wanda had asked her, although doing it here in front of customers seemed inappropriate. Still, had Camilla's response been a bit too heated for that of an innocent person? Maybe.

CHAPTER 30

Nashville Treasures wasn't far from Cammie's Kitchen. I could stop by to talk with Wendy at her shop and poke my nose into another hornet's nest.

Except at this point in my day, I wanted to get home and be relaxed to greet Abe and Sean—and energetic pup Cocoa—when they arrived. Plus, using my own bathroom would be a bonus.

I climbed into my car and began my drive home. I swerved at the last moment onto the road Adele had taken this morning, the one that led by the gigantic church. I glanced in the rearview mirror. *Huh.* A big silver SUV had turned immediately after I had. Probably another driver taking the same shortcut on this much-improved pavement.

The route was mostly wooded and was sparsely populated by humans, with only the occasional house set back along a long drive. Nobody else was out driving right now, either, other than the SUV and me. I lowered my windows to enjoy the country air.

I loved the salt-scented breezes of my native Santa Barbara, but nature smelled pretty darn good here in the southern Midwest, too. A few evergreens mixed in with the deciduous trees wafted a piney scent, and a fragrant honeysuckle in blossom added a floral touch.

Thoughts of Camilla's reaction to Wanda's questions detracted from this being a pleasant drive. And she'd glared at me after Wanda headed for the door. Camilla must have thought I was in fact working with Wanda, even though I'd said I wasn't, instead of semi-casually grabbing a bite to eat with her. But what did Camilla have to hide?

At least Wanda hadn't strong-armed me for more questioning inside the police station or asked me to come into the sheriff's office building, which was also in Nashville but on the outskirts of town. Was I off the Persons-of-Interest list? I hoped so.

A flash of light in my rearview mirror made me gasp. *Yikes.* Sunlight reflected off the SUV's windshield. It was following way too close. True, this two-lane road was too curvy to safely pass. But what was the driver's hurry? I couldn't speed up much, and I didn't want to in any case.

This was ridiculous. And dangerous. If an animal ran in front of my car and I needed to brake suddenly, I'd be rear-ended. The shoulder looked soft and dropped off into a ditch. I had no room to pull over.

I swallowed, hard. What if one of other persons

of interest—that is, Evermina's killer—thought I was getting too close to identifying them? I wasn't. But I was guilty of doing what I always did, trying to find the truth.

Ahead loomed Covenant Hope, along with its mega parking lot. I wrenched the steering wheel to make a quick turn into the entrance. If the silver vehicle was merely being driven with a lead foot, my getting out of its way was a good plan. If the driver was an ill-intentioned person out to get me, this was a very bad plan. Not a single other car was parked here on this holiday afternoon.

The SUV turned in too. I grabbed my phone, but my sweaty fingers kept slipping. Should I make a dash for it? My throat thickened. I had to protect my baby, but if I sped out of here, the much bigger and more powerful car might keep tailing me. Its driver could run me off the road in a more dangerous spot than this flat expanse of pavement.

The SUV pulled up on my left at enough of an angle that its right front corner blocked my driving straight. *Great.* The passenger window lowered. I ignored my jackhammering heart and turned to face whoever it was.

The driver leaned toward me. She looked about my age. Her glossy dark hair fell in waves. A sleeveless blue top showed off toned upper arms. This was too weird. I stared into the face of the woman from the church photograph. And the one from the outhouse staging area.

"Hey, there," she called. "Do you need help finding someplace? You were driving slow, like you were looking for an address."

"No, I'm fine." My voice creaked. I cleared my throat. "You seemed to be in a hurry. I thought I'd get out of your way."

"This beast has a mind of its own. Likes to go fast." She stroked the dashboard as if she approved.

Seriously? As far as I knew, self-driving cars weren't legal in Indiana.

"Well, if you're in need of a church, you came to the right place," she went on. "You can find God here like so many others have."

"Thank you, but I'm all set in that department." I gestured toward the road. "You can go on ahead of me. I don't want to keep you."

"That's okay. I have business here. You won't have to worry about me tailgating you. I'm Isabelle, by the way."

Isabelle Cooper, perhaps? I swore silently. I didn't want to be alone with anyone Octavia had expressed interest in with regard to Evermina's murder.

"You sure I can't give you a tour of the inside?" she asked. "It's pretty impressive."

"Nice to meet you, Isabelle. Thanks for the offer, but I really need to get home. I'm Robbie, by the way."

Her smile slid away. "Do you live in South Lick?" I nodded.

"You must be Robbie Jordan who owns the country store."

"I am."

"Then we're related, in a roundabout kind of way. Don O'Neill is my stepfather."

My jaw must have dropped, because she barked out a harsh laugh. "And you haven't heard of me.

That's okay. He and I never did get along. Haven't seen him in years. You take care, now." She rolled up the window and drove to a parking space close to a side door in the building.

Just . . . wow. Don had a stepdaughter he was estranged from, which meant he'd been married before. Nobody had ever breathed a word about either Isabelle or an ex-wife. Not Don, not Abe, not their parents. At least not to me.

Now that I was out of danger, at least from this mysterious Isabelle, I put my little car in gear and pointed it toward home. Toward safety, kitties, and a list of questions for Abe.

CHAPTER 31

I waited until Abe and I were in the car on the way to Adele's before I raised the subject of Don's stepdaughter.

We'd had a lovely but quick reunion, since the guys had been delayed by traffic. Abe and Sean had unloaded the car and admired the flowers. Sean, after begging off going to the cookout, had taken Cocoa for a walk, saying he'd put away the camping gear when he returned. I figured he was probably also heading to his girlfriend's house, but that was fine. Abe had grabbed a quick shower while I zipped over to my store to get the dumplings and pick up a carton of vanilla ice cream at the market.

Now at four thirty, I drove us out Beanblossom Road toward my aunt's Ovinia Farm.

"You totally surprised me with those flowers yesterday, Abe," I said. "They're so pretty."

"Hey, one year of happy marriage is something to celebrate." He squeezed my knee.

"Absolutely. I have a surprise planned for you later in the week, too." It was as yet an ill-formed idea, but I'd thought of making him a special dinner and a decadent chocolate dessert on Sunday night when neither of us had to work in the morning.

"I like the sound of that." He turned to me and winked.

"Sean seems to be doing well with us as a family, doesn't he?" I asked.

"He adores you, Robbie, and he's excited about the baby—at least when he's not embarrassed that his father is, you know, doing the thing that makes babies." He grinned.

"He's a teenager. I would expect no less."

"Anyway, it's all good. So, tell me. How was your weekend? Did you guys win the Outhouse Race?"

I glanced over at him as the car bumped over a stretch of bad pavement. It hit me that he knew zero about the murder. Did I want to get into the whole story now? I did not. I'd have to later, but I wanted to savor this warm, cozy moment of being with him again.

"We didn't. Adele took me to an estate sale this morning, though, and I picked up quite a few great vintage cookware items to restock the store."

"Perfect. You were needing more pans, right?"

"I was. Abe, I met an interesting woman on my way home from Nashville today."

"Oh?"

"Yes. She told me her name is Isabelle." I glanced at him.

Abe stared straight ahead. His shoulders rose and fell with a deep breath.

"I had no idea Don had a stepdaughter," I added. "I didn't even realize he'd been married before he found Georgia."

"I know."

The sign for Adele's farm came into view at the bottom of the gently sloping hill with its fenced-in pasture. Her cottage and barn sat at the top. Sheep dotted the green field on our left.

"Pull over here for a minute." Abe pointed to a wide spot in the road to the right. "I don't want to talk about this among company."

I pulled over and shut off the engine.

"We've known each other, what, four years?" he asked.

"About that."

"Well, the story about Don's family is a long and unhappy one, and it was basically over before you and I met. Yes, he was married. His wife had a daughter from a short-lived previous marriage."

"Isabelle."

"Yes. Don did his best, but the girl never accepted him, and her mother turned out to be mentally ill."

"How sad. Did Don have children with his wife?" I asked.

"No. He wanted a family, but it's probably for the best no babies came along. The wife ended up so ill she took her own life when Isabelle was in high school."

"That must have been so painful for her and for Don."

"Completely." Abe's voice was low and full of sorrow. "But Isabelle decided her mother's death had been Don's fault. The minute she got her high school degree, she moved out and cut ties with him."

"Had he adopted her?"

"No. His wife wouldn't let him." Abe rubbed his forehead. "Sweetheart, I'll talk more about Isabelle later, I promise, about the whole mess. I should have told you long ago. But right now I'd like us to go on to Adele's and just enjoy ourselves for the rest of today. Can we do that, please?"

I reached for his head and gently brought our foreheads together. "Yes. Absolutely."

"I missed you so much while we were away," he murmured.

"Same here, favorite husband." I kissed him, restarted the car, and drove the rest of the way up the hill.

I hoped I could slip Adele and Vera a word not to talk about homicide for the rest of the day, either.

CHAPTER 32

Adele's border collie, Sloopy, greeted us at the car after I parked on the grass next to a few other cars. As soon as I opened the door and stuck my feet out, he yipped, raced around to Abe's side, then back to me.

Abe laughed. "He's trying to herd us toward the others in our flock."

"As always. Hey, Sloops." I stroked his head before lifting the pan of dumplings from the back seat. "Can you bring that insulated bag, please? It has the ice cream."

"Sure." He grabbed it along with the six-pack of beer he'd brought.

We rounded the corner of the house to a patio behind it, where a scattering of people sat or stood. My heart sank a little to see Buck and Melia among them. Not because I disliked their company, but that was two more people I hoped wouldn't bring up homicide. I probably should have told

Abe on the way over. It was too late now. That train
had left the station.

I put the ice cream in Adele's freezer in the
kitchen and rubbed her kitty below the ears, a
massage Chloe loved. Outside, Abe already had a
beer in his hand and was talking with Adele's eighty-
something boyfriend, Samuel, who was Phil's grandfather. I waved a general greeting to the group.
Adele sat with Buck and Melia. If I went over there
right now, I might be able to slip the three of them
a word about keeping mum regarding the weekend's news.

Instead I took a chair next to Phil and his girlfriend, Noreen Connolly. If the news of Evermina's death, and my involvement with it, came
out while we were here, I could deal. I'd tell Abe in
a few hours, anyway.

"Isn't this nice, Robbie?" Noreen gestured around
at the group. She held a purplish drink with blueberries floating on top and a stir stick topped with
mini marshmallows.

"The company is perfect, and so is the weather
and the setting." It was as lovely a vista as it had
been a year ago during our wedding and the following festivities. Clouds scudding, meadow greener
than Ireland, sheep grazing, gardens weed free and
flourishing in the full flush of late spring. "What's
that?" I pointed to her drink.

"My red, white, and blue Memorial Day cocktail
invention." Phil laughed. "Except the blueberry
syrup and cranberry juice combined to make it
purple."

"And the marshmallows are the white?" I asked.

"Yes, plus white rum."

I zoomed in on the diamond sparkling on Noreen's ring finger. "Do you guys have news to share?" I pointed to the ring.

Phil laid his arm around Noreen's shoulders as she blushed and held out her left hand.

"I asked this sweet, brilliant, beautiful woman if she'd marry me," Phil said. "And she said yes."

"I am so happy for both of you." I beamed. Noreen had lost her father to murder a few years ago. I was delighted she'd found love with Phil, especially since it had been during the aftermath of the homicide when the two had met. "Have you set a date?"

Phil pulled a face that was both wry and amused. It was an expression that, combined with his sticking-out ears and dark skin, always reminded me of former President Obama.

"I'm trying to pin down my peripatetic parents," he said. "They travel almost more than Peepaw and Adele."

"We wanted to have the ceremony this fall, but it might have to be spring." Noreen gave Phil a quizzical look.

In return, he gave a little shake of his head. Adele approached holding two champagne flutes filled with an amber-colored bubbly. Her other hand gripped Abe's, who held a similar glass. She extended one of the glasses to me.

"Can I have everybody's attention, please?" she called out. "If you don't have a drink, grab one."

"Adele," I whispered. "I can't drink."

"It's sparkling cider, you silly goose," was her retort.

Abe pulled me up to stand next to him. The group quieted.

"I want to wish Robbie and Abe a very happy first anniversary," Adele announced. "May your marriage be long and joyful."

"That's the plan." Abe smiled at me.

"Here's to Robbie and Abe." Buck lifted his glass of beer.

Everyone else echoed the toast. Not to my surprise, my eyes filled. Abe squeezed my hand.

"Thank you, from both of us." I was glad I'd worn my favorite long dress. In a black-and-white geometric design, it was casual and comfy while being a step above the Capris or jeans I might have donned. Plus, anything tight around my waist was growing increasingly uncomfortable.

"Don't go draining those glasses yet," Adele announced. "We have one more thing to celebrate. These two fine young people have decided it's their turn to tie the old knot." She gestured for Phil and Noreen to stand. "Here's to Phil and Noreen."

"To Phil and Noreen." I echoed the others.

Noreen, her pale Irish skin still blushing, lifted her glass. Those two were going to have darling biracial babies, with Phil's big smile and startling blue eyes, and her quintessentially Celtic coloring and curly auburn hair. Whose complexion would our baby have? The olive skin I inherited from my Italian father or Abe's lighter, northern European look? Either way, the little one was almost guaranteed to have brown eyes, since we both did.

Adele enlisted Abe to help her with the grill. Phil and Noreen went to talk with Samuel. I drifted over to Buck and Melia and sat in the next chair.

"You staying out of trouble, Robbie?" Buck asked.

"I'm trying to." I wrinkled my nose. "I thought somebody was following me today." I told them about the silver SUV and meeting Isabelle Cooper.

Melia frowned. "I don't like the sound of that."

"She tried to make it sound innocent," I said. "As if her car had a mind of its own about speed, and claiming she had business inside the church. But I kind of didn't believe her."

"I'm sure you know this Robbie," Melia said. "But in light of that SUV, you need to, well—"

"I know," I said. "I need to stay well clear of danger. Believe me, that's the last time I take a short-cut alone."

"Wanda was telling me about this Cooper lady," Buck said. "She's related, sort of, to Abe's brother, isn't that right?"

Ugh. Isabelle was on Wanda's radar? I didn't like the sound of that.

"Yes. She's Don's stepdaughter. I only learned about that today." I tilted my head, gazing at Buck. "There's nothing illegal about that."

"Indeed there isn't." He tapped the side of his beer bottle and lowered his voice. "Homicide, though? It's about as illegal as they come."

CHAPTER 33

The picked-clean bones of several barbecued ribs plus two cubes of the best potato salad I'd ever eaten were all that remained on my plate an hour later. It was even better than what we'd prepared in the store yesterday. Adele had served grilled asparagus spears, too, of which not a trace could be seen. My helping was right where it belonged, in my stomach.

Adele and Vera sat across from Abe and me. "Adele, those ribs were fabulous," I said. "What's your secret?"

She chortled. "Bought 'em sauce and all from Janko's Little Zagreb, that's what. Not much of a secret, when you come right down to it. All's we did was warm those babies on the grill."

"Really?" Abe asked.

"Yeperoo." She grinned. "Why do the work when that cute little restaurant does it better? They've been in business for decades now."

"They have," Abe said. "I remember going there as a boy."

"I just call me in an order and drive over to Bloomington to pick it up," Adele said. "Didn't I do exactly that yesterday, Vera?"

Vera, who was still working on extracting every shred of meat from her last rib, nodded.

"I've never eaten at Janko's," I said. "Based on this dinner, I'd like to remedy that situation."

"They're in an old-style restaurant on the other side of the train tracks, hon." Adele took a swig of her wine. "On the west side of town. Easy to find."

"I'll take you to eat there whenever you want," Abe said. "By the way, my darling, maybe I should go away more often." His expression turned mischievous.

"Why's that?"

"Look at that empty plate." He pointed. "My being absent seems to have cured your morning sickness."

"Maybe." I smiled. "Except I think the passage of time is what did it. But you can go away whenever you want."

Vera snickered.

Abe stretched out his legs. "So, dear wife of mine, Adele tells me you had a little excitement this weekend." His tone was casual.

Uh-oh. He'd heard about the murder from Adele, probably while they were grilling dinner, and I knew him well enough to hear the hurt because I hadn't told him myself.

"It's true," I said. "Being there when a body falls out of your race entry isn't the kind of excitement I was seeking out, believe me." I added in a mur-

mur, "I was going to tell you later, my love, but I didn't want to get into all of the sordid details on our way here."

"It must have been an awful experience for you." He now frowned.

"It wasn't much fun," I agreed. "Nor for Danna and Turner, who were right there. It was awful and shocking and so very sad."

"I'd guess our Roberta's already been nosing around about who was responsible, haven't you, sugar?" Adele asked.

"Guilty as charged, but I've been investigating only carefully, peripherally," I said. "Besides, Octavia Slade and Wanda seem to be assigned to the case, which is as it should be, plus the Nashville police chief."

"A relatively young woman is the new department head, I heard." Abe took a sip from the bottle of beer he held.

That was his second drink, I thought, or maybe third. I didn't mind. I was our designated driver for the duration of this pregnancy, a job I gladly accepted. And I'd never known Abe to drink more alcohol than he could handle.

"Yes," I said. "The chief's name is Haley Harris. Her entire team is made up of men. I wonder how they feel about that."

"If they want to keep their jobs, they'd better feel fine about it," Vera said. "But we all know how subtle remarks and actions can sabotage what looks like a bold move of equal hiring."

As a Black woman in her seventies, she'd had a lifetime of becoming way too familiar with that kind of sabotage.

"Did you pick up any new intel this afternoon?" Adele asked me.

"Not really," I said. "Can we change the subject?"

"You don't want to upset that little bun in the oven," Adele said.

That wasn't why I wanted to move the conversation along. Talking about murder among loved ones on a beautiful evening was too dark to bear and would spoil the happy mood, if it hadn't already. But I didn't contradict her about the reason.

"I get it," Adele went on. "I'll tell you one thing, I sure can't wait to have little imps running around this place."

Vera smiled, too. "That will be so fine."

I smiled. It would be fine, even though the imps would come one at a time, and the baby I was carrying wouldn't be running for a couple of years. I did love the image of Abe's and my child kneading bread with Adele and learning to help with the sheep, being close to my side of the family as well as to Abe's. We could also take the little one to Italy to meet my father. He'd already said he wanted to have regular video chats with his new grandchild.

"Adele," I began. "Did you ever want children of your own?" It was a highly personal question, but I'd known my aunt since before I could remember, and I realized I'd never asked her.

When a stricken look passed over her face, I wished I hadn't asked. The look slid away as fast as it had appeared.

"Sure, hon," she said. "Thing is, it didn't turn out that way. We take what life gives us, don't we?"

Samuel strolled up and laid a brown, age-spotted hand on Adele's shoulder. She covered it with her own lighter, weathered one.

"Addie could have had any boy she wanted back in the day," Vera said. "She was one hot ticket."

"She still is," Samuel said.

Adele's cheeks pinkened. "You go on, now."

We all sat quietly with our thoughts for a few moments. After I set my plate on the ground, Abe laid a hand on my knee. A sheep in the field baaed, inciting an ovine chorus. A man laughed in one of the other circles of guests, and a truck bumped over a pothole out on the road.

The reality of Evermina's murder felt distant, hazy, instead of being a terrible thing we'd witnessed the aftermath of only the day before yesterday. Right now? Distant was fine with me.

"Who's ready for dessert?" I asked.

CHAPTER 34

By eight thirty Abe and I were snuggled on the couch at home, me with a mug of chamomile tea and a novel, not that I'd opened it yet, him with his still-dark tablet. Sean, the dog, and both cats were in Sean's room as he finished homework for tomorrow.

Abe had final exams later this week for his certificate in wildlife education and had said he needed to study. He already had a job lined up at Brown County State Park, but he'd told me acing the course would mean more pay and possibly better opportunities elsewhere, should he need them.

I covered my mouth as I yawned. Both Abe and I had had a full day in different ways. On our drive home, he'd said he understood why I hadn't wanted to talk of homicide on our way to Adele's. But he'd urged me to share the experience and what I knew about a suspect pool after we got home, which was now.

I first filled him in on the horror of a dead Evermina crashing out of our outhouse and what had happened directly after.

"You're sure the shock didn't affect the baby?" he asked gently. "You're feeling okay?"

"I'm fine, Abe, truly. This little one is still very little, and he's well-cushioned in there."

"Or she." He winked. "I keep imagining a mini-Robbie emerging next fall."

"And I find myself thinking we'll have a son." We had agreed to do it the old-fashioned way and not learn the gender before the birth.

"Can we go back to the death for a minute?" Abe asked.

"Sure." I didn't particularly want to, but I'd said I'd share.

"Who do you think they're looking at for the homicide?" he asked.

"You mean, besides me?'

"What?" He twisted to look at me. "No way."

"Yes way, but I hope not seriously."

"Wait. Is this because of that ridiculous ad campaign, where Evermina tried to smear your restaurant's reputation?"

"Apparently. But since I didn't kill her, here's who else seems to be in the pool. Zeke Martin, her ex-husband. Wendy Corbett, his new girlfriend." I ticked the names off on my fingers. "Maybe Camilla Kalb, who runs Cammie's Kitchen."

"Interesting. Is that all?"

"Unfortunately, it isn't." I cleared my throat. "Don apparently had more than one public argument with Evermina about a lot of money she owed him."

"My Don?" His voice rose again.

"Your older brother, Don. Also impossible. But the thing is, I've also heard Isabelle Cooper's name several times coming out of the mouth of a detective."

Abe let out a low groan. "If she's a murderer, that would destroy my brother. But . . . why Isabelle? What was her connection with the victim?"

"I have no idea. I hope to find out, maybe from Wanda or Buck. Do you know any of those first three names? Any connection with them, now or in the past?"

"Let me think."

I took a sip of tea. The next time I glanced over at Abe, his eyes were as closed as my book. *Good.* He needed the rest. I was tempted to shut my own eyes and join him, but I knew that would make it harder for me to fall back asleep once I was in bed.

My store wasn't going to open itself tomorrow morning at five thirty as the sun peeked over the horizon. And I doubted I could still this busy brain. Abe had a gift for relaxing completely, on the spot, when he needed to. He could take an evening snooze on the couch and still fall right to sleep when he went to bed. Me, not so much, my last two evening's naps notwithstanding.

Sipping my tea, I left my book unopened. How could I find out what Isabelle's connection with Evermina might have been? Don wouldn't know, not if he'd been estranged from his stepdaughter. Octavia wouldn't tell me if I asked, and I doubted Wanda would, either.

I picked up my phone and paired the two names in a search. Which yielded exactly nada. Okay. What about Isabelle herself? I removed Evermina's name and added the name Covenant Hope church. Now we were getting somewhere. Sister Cooper was a deacon, whatever that meant, and head of the development committee. Didn't that mean fundraising?

Why would a big church like that need to raise funds? The building had looked fairly new. Maybe they had debt to pay off.

The melody from the Sister Sledge song, "We are Family," played from Abe's phone, which vibrated at the same time. It was the ringtone he'd set up for calls from Don.

Abe's eyes flew open. He sat up, looked around, blinked, and grabbed his phone from the coffee table.

He poked at the cell. "Don?" Abe's voice was gravelly. He listened, frowning.

It was after nine o'clock. This couldn't be a casual call.

"What? Why?" He turned to stare at me. He listened for another few moments.

What had happened to Don? I had a terrible suspicion that it might be connected to the homicide.

"Calm down, now. Yes, I'll call her, and I'll be over there as soon as I can. Don't say a word to them."

Don's raised voice came through the phone, although I couldn't make out the words.

"No, not a single word," Abe repeated. "Keep your mouth shut and shake your head. Promise?" He listened. "Okay. Sit tight. I'm on my way." He disconnected.

"Has he been arrested?" I asked.

"No, but they insist on keeping him for more questioning. Or detained, or whatever. I have to call my dad's lawyer and get over to Nashville."

"I thought you meant call Georgia."

"She's out of town. Possibly because of marital problems." Abe gazed at me. "And you know Don. He can make a disaster out of the smallest thing."

"But this is already a kind of disaster. If they brought him into the police station instead of questioning him at home, that's serious." I held up a palm. "Mind you, I don't believe he killed Ever-mina. But it's naive to think that just because a person is innocent, the system won't work against them."

Abe stood. "Which is why I'm going to my clue-less brother's rescue. He obviously did something we don't know about."

"Who's the lawyer?"

"That woman who helped my dad that Christmas, remember? When he was suspected of murder himself."

"Good. Corrine gave me the name of a criminal lawyer not that long ago, in case your dad's person is away or can't handle it."

"Thanks, sweetheart. You're the best." He leaned down to kiss me. "I don't know how late I'll be."

"Are you okay to drive?"

"I had two beers hours ago, my sweet. I'm fine."

I smiled at him. "Good luck."

I heard him tell Sean he had to go rescue his uncle. Water ran in the bathroom, keys jangled, and the back door clicked shut.

What could Don have done to get himself in

trouble with the cops? It might have to do with his nervous reaction to me coming in when his laptop was open. I wished I'd gotten a better look at it. Wishing would get me nowhere.

But preparing for bed and sliding into a deep sleep would accomplish what I needed. Abe could handle Don's troubles. All I had to do was get my rest and gear up for the work week.

CHAPTER 35

The morning was shaping up both good and bad. The good was severalfold. First, even now at six thirty, the smell of coffee brewing in the restaurant didn't turn my stomach. I thought I might even pour a mug of decaf, dose it with whole milk, and see how it went down.

Second, when Abe had slid into bed at one of the wee hours of the morning, he'd murmured that Don had kept his mouth shut and let the lawyer be his voice. Abe had driven him home, but it had been super late. Before I'd left the house, I'd scribbled a note for Abe to give me a call or stop by the store if he could.

Third, Danna had arrived bright-eyed and on time. We were moving in our well-rehearsed chore-ography of readying the restaurant to open at seven, sharp.

All good. The bads were the massive dark thunderclouds and strong wind gusting in from Illinois to our west. Who wanted to go out to breakfast in the pouring rain, not to mention lightning?

Not that long ago, a thunderstorm had knocked out power to all of South Lick. The Pans 'N Pancakes grill was powered by gas, as were the stove and oven. As long as they were already lit, we could keep cooking. But the coffeepots were electric, and we didn't have a big urn. What we did have were a half dozen insulated carafes.

"Let's make as much coffee as we can now, while we still have power, in case it goes out," I told my co-chef. "I've already filled two of the insulated carafes, and that red one is full of decaf."

"I'm on it." Today, over a red t-shirt, she wore a brown overalls dress that hit her above the knees and a tan sweater, with a green scarf tying back her golden-red dreads. Yellow Converse high-tops completed the outfit. She twirled. "What do you think? Today's National Hamburger Day."

I stared, then burst out laughing. "And you are all of it. Meat, bun, mustard, ketchup, and lettuce."

"Or pickle, depending on your taste." She set to work making more coffee. "Our lunch special can be the hamburgers we always have on the menu. It's also National Brisket Day, but we would have needed a lot more advance planning to serve that."

"How was your Memorial Day?" I slid a pan of biscuits into the oven.

"We relaxed and grilled yesterday, but a buddy of Isaac's scored tickets to the Five Hundred on Sunday. So we went. It was awesome, Robbie."

"I totally forgot about the race." The iconic speedway race was held every year on the day before Memorial Day. But the speeds and the spectacular, occasionally fatal, crashes were not to my liking. I was sure that was why I'd forgotten about the popular event. "Me, I'd rather see the IU bike race."

"The Little Five Hundred? That's more your speed. You could compete in it."

"Yeah, with all the other pregnant thirtysomething bicyclists? I don't think so. Anyway, it's for college students."

"Hey, any news about our outhouse tragedy?" she asked.

I tensed and a noise emerged from my throat as I paused the rolling pin on the next disk of biscuit dough.

"What?" Danna stepped next to me. "What happened, Robbie?"

"Don O'Neill was taken in last night. Abe had to go try to rescue him."

"Taken in by the police?"

I nodded. "Well, by the county sheriff."

"You mean Wanda."

"Yes, and to the police station in Nashville. Abe got hold of a good lawyer for him, thank goodness, but it's concerning all around."

"You don't think Don killed Evermina Martin, do you?"

"No, I do not." I glanced at the wall clock. "Danna, I'd love to pour a cup of decaf, sit down with you, and hash this all through, but it's six fifty. Can you please get the sausages cooking and everything else we usually have on the grill by now?"

"You got it." She hustled back from the walk-in with the basket full of links, rashers, and the containers of peppers and onions I'd cut up yesterday. When she'd gotten meats sizzling, she said, "You know, I think my mom has a line on that gift shop lady."

"Wendy Corbett?" That could be interesting.

"Yes. She's made a few shady moves, according to Mom."

"What kind of shady moves?" I asked.

"I don't know. But she's Mr. Martin's new squeeze, right? She could have wanted to get rid of the ex, like, for good."

"Agree. I've wondered the same. Thanks for that tip, Danna. I'll text Corrine when I get a chance."

Knocking sounded on the front door a few minutes later. The clock read seven.

"Time's up," I said.

"The hungry hordes hovered hellishly at the hatch to—" Danna announced in a deep, dramatic voice.

Until I interrupted her and headed for the door. "Let's feed the hungry hordes while we can."

CHAPTER 36

I unlocked the door and welcomed the dozen diners waiting on the front porch. They didn't constitute a horde, exactly, although the twelve certainly looked eager to eat as they hovered. The last person to enter was Buck, again in uniform.

Yesterday at Adele's he'd spoken about Isabelle in connection with the murder. Don's stepdaughter, Isabelle. Had Buck had a hand in detaining Don last night? I was determined to find out if I got a free minute, which was unlikely to happen until Turner came on shift in an hour.

"Your table should be open, Buck," I said.

"I appreciate it." He leaned over a little to peer into my face. "Everything okay with the family?"

"No, I would not say it's a hundred-percent okay." I set my fists on my hips. "I gather you know about Don."

"Yes, but I didn't have nothing to with him being detained and all. Just so's you know."

Maybe he didn't, or maybe he did. "I'll bring

coffee." I left the tall, skinny chief to find the two-top he preferred at the back, where he could observe the comings and goings as he ate. I had coffee to pour and orders to take, plus a teensy bit of ire to get over.

Within twenty minutes, every chair in the place was full, with a cluster of ten customers waiting to eat. I was moving faster than Lucille Ball in front of a sped-up candy conveyor belt. Or, more accurately, as fast as a short-handed restaurant owner. Luckily, I didn't have to stuff any sausages down my bosom.

It was as if all these people had information I didn't. Was a tornado on the horizon and everybody wanted to make their last breakfast a great one? It didn't matter. Work was work, and we always aimed to please—within limits.

I finally brought Buck his usual gargantuan breakfast order. "Here you go. Pancakes, sausages, biscuits and gravy, and a ham and cheese omelet with home fries."

"Thanks, Robbie. My middle's so empty you could drive one of them double-wide trailers through it and it'd come out clean."

I gave a little snort. How he kept coming out with new and ever-more hyperbolic expressions for being hungry was beyond me.

He tucked his napkin into his collar and picked up his fork.

"Any news about the case?" I kept my voice low, in case any neighboring diners were listening.

Buck shook his head, his mouth full of food.

"You know Melia gave me a tip about somebody yesterday, right?" I asked.

He frowned and gave a single slow nod. *Interesting.* Had he not approved of her speaking about Zeke to me?

"Enjoy your breakfast." I flashed a quick smile without much feeling behind it. "I'd love to know more about Isabelle when you learn anything."

I saw him about to try to speak with his mouth full of pancakes. *Just. No.* Danna dinged the ready bell. I headed back to the kitchen area to fetch more plates full of hot, delicious food for diners who blessedly had nothing to do with murder.

It was still before eight when Buck stood, laid cash on the table, and gave me a wave from across the room. I'd learned nothing. But I was too busy to dwell on it. By now I'd swapped with Danna. I was rather frantically flipping pancakes, turning omelets, and sautéing peppers and mushrooms on the grill. I wouldn't have had time to follow Buck to the door for more questioning, anyway.

I wished I would hear the details about Don from Abe.

Five minutes later, Turner pushed through the door, followed by Corrine. Danna had told me, when we'd switched jobs, that she'd texted her mom about my interest in Wendy. Corrine wore her full mayoral attire of red power blazer, black pencil skirt, four-inch heels with the red sole indicating an expensive designer brand, and her usual big hair. She must be making time for me on her way to work. Or maybe she simply wanted breakfast.

Turner came straight to the kitchen, but Corrine stopped to greet a diner she knew.

I greeted Turner. "How was your holiday?"

Danna approached and held up her palm to him for a high five.

"Great, actually." He slapped her palm, washed his hands, and slid into an apron, but his neck turned red as he tried to wipe away a smile.

"Dude, what's her name?" Danna elbowed him.

"What?" He pretended innocence.

It didn't work. "Come on, Turner, dish," I said. "But quickly."

"It's too soon to get my hopes up," he began. "But she's brilliant, and gorgeous, and she's a cook."

"What's brilliant and gorgeous doing slumming with you?" Danna teased even as she loaded her arms with ready plates and turned away to deliver them.

"I have no idea what Laila sees in this geek, but she was the one who asked *me* out," Turner murmured.

"I want to meet your goddess, this Laila." I smiled. He hadn't had a steady girlfriend since I'd known him. I hoped the relationship worked out. He deserved to be happy in love.

He gave himself a little shake. "Where do you want me, boss?"

"Let's see. I started on the grill a minute ago, so you can bus and deliver and pour coffee and all the rest, beginning with those, maybe." I pointed to the sink.

"Will do." He dug into the waiting pile of dirty plates and silverware, rinsing and loading them into the dishwasher. He headed out into the room.

A moment later Corrine strutted up. Maybe she didn't mean to strut—or maybe she did—but how else could she move in heels that high?

"How's it shaking, Robbie?" she asked. "My girl says you wanted to talk with me about a certain gift shop owner."

"I do. Thanks for stopping by." A sausage popped and bacon sizzled. "You don't want to get too close to the grill, Corrine, or your mayoral outfit is going to acquire a set of grease stains."

She took a step back and to the side. I took another glance. Her hair and clothes were dry.

"It's not raining yet?" I asked.

"No, but it's sure fixing to, and soon."

"So, Danna mentioned shady moves," I said in a low voice.

"And that's a little bit of an understatement." Corrine raised her eyebrows. "That Wendy Corbett is a lady to keep your eye on."

"Why? What were her shady moves?"

"For starters, I think she was already bonking old Zeke while he was still married to poor Evermina, may the good Lord bless and keep her departed soul."

"Adultery is never good." I flipped three pancakes and turned a half dozen sausages. "Except they wouldn't be the first couple, and I'm sure they won't be the last."

"Ain't that the truth? But there's more. Did you know Wendy lives in South Lick?"

"I didn't." I plated up pancakes and bacon, two over easy with links, and a serving of biscuits with gravy. "Even though her shop is in Nashville?"

"Yep. She wanted to open another one right here in town, but the lady lied ten ways to Sunday on her permit application."

"Why would she do that?" I set the plates under the warming light and hit the ready bell.

"Search me. It's not like we wouldn't find out she hadn't gotten either a loan approval or a building permit for the renovations she'd already up and started. Appears she lost money on the deal after it all got canceled."

Which gave Wendy even more motive for getting Evermina out of the way, but only if Zeke had been, in fact, paying his ex since the divorce. I needed to look into that, and soon.

CHAPTER 37

Ten thirty seemed to cause everything bad to happen at once. Was it an ill-fated half hour? I had no idea. What I knew was that lots blew up all at the same time.

First, our deep fryer was delivered. Nothing wrong with that. I'd ordered the appliance, and it was paid for. But the delivery guy parked out front, taking up two customer spaces. I hurried out and asked him to drive around the side, where our service entrance was. I went back inside to unlock the door.

A terrific crunching noise permeated the side wall. A shelf of antique jars shuddered. What in heck?

I pushed open the service door to see the large panel truck scraping forward along the brick chimney that stuck out from the side wall, a chimney that now housed our furnace exhaust. The dude must have cut it too close as he backed in. He cut the wheel, extricating the truck.

It took me giving him traffic directions, along with cursing—he under his breath and silently from me—but he got the large box holding the fryer inside and mostly out of the way. I could worry about setting it up later. A lot later. His truck appeared to have suffered far more than my brickwork. I took pictures of both, just in case.

Next, Phil arrived not only with a full complement of desserts for the next few days but also a nervous smile.

"Thanks, Phil," I said. After we got the sweets stashed, he turned to leave. Business was in a bit of a lull, and I had time to talk. I touched his arm. "What's wrong?"

"I need to talk with you." His expression turned stricken.

"Come." Hoping no one in his family had died, I led him to my desk in a far corner. I didn't do much actual work here, but I kept my ordering tablet in the antique Art Deco desk, and the cushioned love seat next to it provided a place to sit and schmooze away from the restaurant tables. I sat in the swivel chair and pointed at the love seat.

He perched on the edge. "I almost told you yesterday." He kneaded his hands in his lap.

"Phil?" I kept my tone gentle. "You can talk to me." Let it not be news that he'd learned he had a fatal illness.

"I got a fabulous new job with an opera company," he said.

Oh! "And that's bad news, how exactly?"

"It's in Madison."

"I'm guessing you don't mean Madison, Indiana." Madison, a town on the Ohio River about an hour and half southeast of here, was too small for an opera company.

"Wisconsin. Noreen's going with me. But I'm leaving you in the lurch for desserts. I'm so sorry, Robbie."

I stared at him and burst out laughing.

"Is that funny?" he asked, now appearing confused.

"Not at all. But I thought you were going to tell me you'd had a death in the family, or you'd gotten a really bad diagnosis. Phil, I'll miss you terribly, and we'll have to find a new baker. But that you found your dream job, and in a cool college town? That's fabulous news. Please don't worry."

"Really?" His shoulders relaxed, and the stricken expression was replaced by hope.

"Of course. I can't wait to see you perform at the Met, or at the Dorothy Chandler Pavilion in Los Angeles." I stood and held out my arms.

As we hugged, though, a much louder noise shook the building than when the delivery truck hit it. The crack was followed by the sound of giants rolling bowling balls—in the dark. We'd lost power.

"I guess the storm's here," I muttered.

Octavia hurried inside. The windows darkened as rain beat against them. The generator outside hummed into life, but it was only strong enough to power the walk-in cooler and the chest freezer.

"When do you leave?" I asked Phil.

"In three weeks. Lots to do."

"I bet." I had a flash of inspiration. "You know what? Sean loves to cook and bake. If you send

him your recipes, maybe that can be his summer
job while I look for someone more permanent."

"Good idea." Phil squeezed my hand. "Thanks
for being such a good friend, Robbie."

I squeezed back. "We'll miss you. I'll miss you."
My phone dinged with a text from our food whole-
saler.

Am at door with your order.

Great. My order for the food for the week that
now might be at risk from inadequate refrigera-
tion if the power didn't come back on ASAP. I
headed for the service door again, but Octavia
waylaid me.

"We need to talk, Robbie," she said.

"I suppose, except not right this exact minute."
And maybe not ever. "Are you here to eat?"

She gazed left and right. "I might as well."

I surveyed the restaurant, which was only half
full by now. "Sit anywhere you want. One of us will
stop by to get your order when we can." I turned
away. At least she hadn't come in to arrest me.

In the kitchen area, Turner was on the grill.

"Danna, our food order is here. Can you help
the driver with that, please? I'll grab the meat for
lunch from the walk-in and anything else we need
for burgers and BLTs." And grilled cheese and
fruit salad and all the other parts of lunch. "After
you put away the order, make sure the door shuts
tight, okay?" If anything went wrong with the generator, I'd be out a lot of inventory.

I turned to the tables full of customers and
clapped my hands twice to get people's attention. I
waited until the room quieted.

"Hey, everybody. Please stay and finish your meals, or go ahead and order if you haven't yet. We'll get to you as soon as we can. I'm afraid there won't be any more coffee until the power comes back on, but the grill and stove are gas-powered, and we'll do our best to stay open."

"We're good, Robbie," a man called.

"Who needs light when the food is this yummy?" a woman said, followed by laughter from the other ladies in her group.

"Good thing it wasn't yesterday," a white-haired customer remarked. "Would have ruined the ceremonies at the cemetery. On a Tuesday? Who cares if we get a deluge?"

His buddies nodded, two of whom wore ball caps indicating they were veterans.

I cared if it lasted too long, but I hadn't seen a recent forecast for the storm's duration. The bell on the door jangled. I glanced over to see what else could go wrong. Instead, I caught sight of a soaked and dripping Abe.

CHAPTER 38

I gave Abe a little wave before picking up an armful of ready plates and carrying them to their waiting diners. When I glanced at Abe again, he'd shed his jacket and was looking at his phone. Good. That meant he was staying, at least for a little while.

I pointed myself in his direction. I didn't care if Octavia was glaring at me. Family came first.

When he saw me, my darling husband opened his arms. His hug was a blessing, but I kept it short.

I stepped back. "Is he—?"

"He's—"

We both laughed at speaking simultaneously.

"Yes, he's okay." Abe stopped smiling and let out a sigh. "But he's a basket case, hon. I have to go take care of him, and possibly the hardware store, too."

"Instead of studying."

"Instead of studying."

I studied him. I was eager, or maybe it was anx-

ious, to hear what Don had said about why the authorities had detained him. What he'd told Abe in
private. Why being questioned for hours at the station had so shaken Don, an adult who owned a
successful small business. Except I didn't have
time at the moment for a leisurely debriefing.

"Taking care of family," Abe said. "That's life,
and speaking of life, I see your power's out. Can I
still get a bite to eat?"

"Always." I checked the wall clock. "It's already
past eleven. Breakfast or lunch?"

"I'd love two over easy with hash browns and
bacon, if you can. And grits?"

"It's yours, all of it. Sit anywhere. I have to get a
few things from the walk-in, then I'll give Turner
your order." I turned to go.

He reached for my hand. "How are you feeling
today, sugar?"

"Pregnancy-wise?"

He nodded.

"I'm doing a lot better. And you're a sweetheart
to ask. Other, uh, shenanigans have been going
on, but not in here." I rubbed my belly. "Now let
me go. I still have customers to feed."

"Can I help?"

I tilted my head and smiled at him. "You're the
best, you know that? A little help would be awesome." I pointed at Danna lugging boxes from the
service entrance toward the walk-in. "Give Danna
a hand?"

"I'm on it."

I headed to the walk-in to grab the lunch stuff,
swapping places with Danna and Abe when they
arrived carrying boxes. Lunch stuff stashed in our

kitchen fridge, Abe's order given to Turner, I grabbed the last two full coffee carafes and made the rounds, pouring and taking orders and money, until I reached Octavia.

"I might be able to heat tea water on the stove for you," I said.

"Don't bother. Cold water is fine. Could I please have a spinach and Swiss omelet with wheat toast and a bowl of fruit?"

The detective was a vegetarian who'd never ordered anything but the healthiest items on our menu.

"You got it." I jotted her request on my order pad.

"Thanks." Her expression was serious, but she kept her tone level and not harsh. "You seem pretty busy. If you get a minute free, I'd like to ask you a few questions."

Polite went a long way to making me want to cooperate. "I'll see what I can do."

"Thank you. I'd appreciate it." She focused on her phone again.

On my way back to the kitchen area, I took an order for three lunches and cleared a table.

I stuck the new slip up on the carousel. "We have Burger Triumvirate at the far four-top. One hamburger, the works. One cheeseburger, no veggies. One turkey burger, with mushrooms and provolone, extra onions."

"Got it." Turner lowered his voice. "I bumped Abe's order to the head of the line. If you dish up the grits, it's ready to go."

"That's great, thanks." I dished and looked around.

Abe had apparently finished helping and now sat alone at a two-top. I brought his food over.

He thanked me. "I guess stress makes me hungry."

"I can understand that."

"And I'm afraid I'm going to wolf this down and head out."

"I was thinking of taking Don a little food after we close. Good?"

"He'd love that," Abe broke his yolks and moved the potatoes into them, which is the same way I prefer to eat that combo.

"Then I'll do it. Was his power out, too?" I asked.

Abe swallowed. "I don't know. I won't find out until I get there. But I saw the guys out." *The guys* being Abe's former electrical lineman coworkers. "Your electricity should be back before too long." He forked in another bite.

"I hope so. Love you."

His smile was all I needed to see.

I turned back toward my livelihood. Danna was coming out of the restroom in the back, which made me aware that I could use a break, too. As I passed her, I indicated where I was going. When I emerged, refreshed if not rested, she and Turner had swapped places. He could probably use a break, too.

The bell on the door jangled and kept jangling. A handful turned to a half dozen and then a crowd of people seeking lunch. They all looked wet, but the patter of rain on windows had lessened, and I thought the skies might be brightening. Abe slipped out after the last few entered.

I told Turner to take a break while he could. He stripped off his apron, and I changed mine for a fresh one.

I jumped when a new and deafening crack sounded. Almost immediately thunder followed, making an impressively loud noise. We were limping along on low light and cooking with gas, but if lightning struck this building or my barn—or heaven forbid, a person—things could change in an instant.

The bell jangled once more. I swore under my breath at what I saw. It wasn't exactly a lightning strike, but the expression on Chief Harris's face was as stormy as they come. And she was staring straight at me.

CHAPTER 39

Was it something I said? The Nashville police chief had seemed friendly at the beginning of this whole mess. Now she was giving me a look as if I were the killer at large. I'd rather have palmed her off on one of my coworkers, but Danna was already hard at work at the grill. Turner was on break. And we had a dozen or more people to seat along with the officer.

I greeted the newcomers as a group and told them my name, ignoring Chief Harris for now.

"We didn't know if you'd be open." A tanned woman rubbed the water out of her short hair.

"Glad you are, though," a man added. "It's a freaking deluge out there. And Lou told us you had the best food round."

"Lou Perlman?" *My* Lou?

"The same," the woman said. "We're high school friends from Lafayette, and she rides with us when she's home visiting her dad."

"I'm glad we're open, too." I took another look.

All these newcomers wore biking shorts and wicking tops in bright colors under their now-wet, neon-green windbreakers. "You've been out cycling in this storm. That's no fun. Feel free to use the restrooms in back to grab paper towels and dry off. I hope the power will be back on soon, although there's no guarantee. In the meantime, we can offer food but no hot drinks."

"It's all good," the man said. "Should we grab open tables?"

"Please. Menus are on your place mats." I wouldn't mention specials, since we didn't have any. As they clomped away in their biking shoes, I turned to Harris and mustered a polite smile. "Would you also like a table, ma'am?"

"What I'd like is to speak with you about a few matters of police business."

"I'm afraid I don't conduct police business while I'm at work, Chief Harris." Unless she had a warrant for my arrest, that is, in which case I would have no choice. "If you'd like to make an appointment to come back at four o'clock, I can accommodate that."

She did a prissy thing with her lips. Opened her mouth. Shut it. Finally, she spoke. "Very well. I suppose I might as well eat while I'm here."

I wanted to say, "Nobody's forcing you to stay." I didn't. The damp cyclists seemed to have occupied nearly all of the available seats. Abe's vacated two-top was free, as was a place at Octavia's table.

I gestured with my chin. "You can have that small table, once I reset it, or you might persuade Octavia to let you join her."

Harris did a little double take, as if she hadn't

seen the detective sitting quietly eating her vegetarian breakfast. "That's good. I'll sit with Slade."

Excellent plan. They could do their police business together without me. On the other hand, if I
had information to offer, even a little, maybe
they'd share in kind. *Nah.* That would happen
when pigs fly.

"You might have heard me say we can't offer
coffee or tea, but we have plenty of cold drinks
and water," I told her. "I'll be by soon to take your
order."

She bobbed her head and turned away. I delivered a check to one table and cleared another,
scooting around Turner, who had his arms full of
hot lunches for hungry diners. I took orders from
the cyclists and delivered their drinks. I could
avoid Harris and Octavia no longer. They sat con-
ferring in low voices wearing serious expressions.

"Excuse me," I said. "What can I get you to eat?"
I asked the chief.

"A double cheeseburger, please, with coleslaw
and a chocolate milk."

"Sounds good. Can I bring you anything else,
Octavia?"

"No, thank you." She glanced up at me. "Haley
says you don't want to speak with us on official
matters during working hours. Is that correct?"

"Yes."

"Seems to me you have at other times in the
past." Octavia sat back and crossed her arms.

"I can't recall." That was the past. This was now.
I wanted to run through the list of how stressful it
was working in dim light while worrying about
food going bad and not being able to make coffee,

all while the danger of a murderer lurked. Instead, I kept it short and sweet. "It's not going to happen today. I'll go put your order in, Chief Harris."

I turned away to ask the folks at the next table if they would like anything else. I was pretty sure I heard Harris mutter something like, "uncooperative." *Huh.* If those two had solved the case, if they'd locked a real suspect behind bars, I wouldn't have anything to be uncooperative about.

CHAPTER 40

It wasn't until one o'clock that I was able to fix myself a grilled cheese and actually sit to eat it. I'd made sure Danna and Turner had had time to eat before I did. After Danna shooed me away, saying she and Turner could handle everything, I carried my sandwich and glass of milk over to my desk and sat with my back to our diners, my store, the door—to everything.

We weren't oversubscribed at the moment. No one was waiting and a few tables sat unoccupied but set and ready. At least I had an appetite, and the act of smelling and tasting food didn't spoil it, unlike in previous weeks. Such a relief.

I was also relieved I'd gotten away with not being grilled by Octavia and by Haley Harris. As she was leaving, I'd told the chief I would call her later when I had time to talk.

I savored my sandwich. The soft, stretchy, tangy Gruyere cheese; the smear of Dijon mustard; the

acidity and sweetness of a slice of tomato, all between two thick slices of crisp grilled sourdough.
Perfection. This kind of grilling was much prefer-
able to accusatory questioning.

Our work conditions at the moment? Not perfect, but I'd been surprised at the steady flow of
customers and how well my team and I had done
at keeping them fed. We'd need to run the dishwasher three times whenever power was returned.
After we'd stuffed it full, we'd resigned ourselves
to rinsing and neatly stacking all the busing. The
rain seemed to have stopped outside, possibly a
good sign for power restoration.

I drained my milk after my last bite of lunch and
stood, refreshed enough to finish out this dismal
workday. The bell on the door jangled yet again.
In came a middle-aged couple pulling wheeled
carry-on suitcases. That must be my B&B guests,
arriving a little early. Check-in wasn't until three.

I left my plate and glass on the desk and went
over to greet them.

"I'm Robbie Jordan. Are you the Blounts?"

"We surely are, Ms. Jordan," the woman said.
"I'm Helen and this here is Fred." She was round
to his angular, blond to his close-shorn dark hair,
and cheery to his stern.

He stuck out his hand.

"Welcome." I smiled but clasped my hands behind my back. "I'd love to shake hands, but I just
ate a messy sandwich. What brings you folks to
South Lick this week?" They'd reserved their room
through Monday.

"We're special guests at the big tent revival over

to Covenant Hope." She smiled up at her husband. "My Fred here has a gift with bringing sinners to God, don't you, honey?"

He cleared his throat. He didn't return her smile and maintained his silence.

"And I am occasionally called to speak in tongues when the Spirit moves me," she said. "You'd be welcome to join us, Ms. Jordan."

"Please, call me Robbie."

"Why that's awful kind of you, Robbie. I'm Sister Helen and this is my husband, Brother Fred."

"Nice to meet you, Helen and Fred." No way was I appending Sister or Brother to their name. "Where did you come from today?"

"We drove up from our litty-bitty town south of Cincinnati," Helen said. "Wouldn't a been too bad of a drive if it wasn't for the rain."

"The guest parking is around the side, but you don't need to move your car right now. I'll show you after you settle into your room. As you can see, we lost power earlier today." I kept battery-powered lanterns in the rooms along with flashlights, and the upstairs hall had emergency exit lights the same as the ones down here. At least guests shouldn't need heat or air conditioning in late May. "I hope it'll be back on soon."

"That's no trouble at all," Helen said. "The good Lord will provide. But listen, hon. My husband and me, we're feeling a mite hungry. We thought maybe we could sample your delicious lunch menu before we settle into our room. Would that be possible?"

"Absolutely." I turned and surveyed the restaurant. "You can have a table for two near the far wall."

"Our sister in Jesus is going to be joining us any little minute now," Helen said.

"That's fine. Why don't you take that open four-top?" I pointed. "You can leave your bags next to my desk over here."

She and Taciturn Fred followed me to my desk.

"I'll come by to get your order after your friend arrives." I picked up my plate and glass.

"Why, would you take a look at that, Fred?" Helen's voice rose. "It's Sister Isabelle, herself."

I turned my face toward the door. There stood Isabelle Cooper in the flesh, with the same perfect hair and the same strong arms. I'd felt vaguely threatened by her yesterday. But I had to welcome her to my store.

Helen beat me to it as she hurried to the new-comer. "Sister Isabelle, thank you for joining us. We can't wait to hear all the details for the week, isn't that right, Fred?"

He strode up next to them. "Glory be to God, Deacon Cooper." He stressed the title, as if in re-buke to his wife. "We are well pleased to be with you."

Now that he'd finally spoken, I heard a voice as low, resonant, and compelling as a charismatic preacher's should be. Why did that make me not want to trust him?

Isabelle shook his hand. Neither smiled at each other.

I joined them. "Welcome to Pans 'N Pancakes, Isabelle."

"Thank you. Robbie, wasn't it?" Isabelle asked. "I couldn't refuse the invitation from my honored brethren."

"I'll let you all get settled." I hoped Don wouldn't come in while she was here. That might lead to fireworks, as least on Isabelle's part. Except, judging from what Abe had said, his brother was unlikely to budge from home. *Good.* The lightning this morning had been enough fireworks to last me until July.

A couple of minutes later, order pad in hand, I headed to the table where Blounts and Isabelle sat.

"I'm afraid we can't offer coffee while we don't have—" I stopped midsentence.

Without warning or fanfare, the overhead lights came on. Refrigerators and drinks coolers and all the other plugged-in things filled the previously much quieter air with a welcome hum.

"The blessed Lord has answered our pleas," Helen pronounced.

"Let us pray." Fred extended his hand to Helen on one side and Isabelle on the other. He bowed his head.

Helen clasped Isabelle's hand and raised her other to me, looking hopeful. I shook my head.

"I'll be back," I murmured.

Fred began to intone his prayer of thanks.

In my decidedly unreligious opinion, they should instead be blessing Abe's hardworking former coworkers. But if paying customers wanted to pray, I wouldn't stand in their way.

CHAPTER 41

With the dishwasher blessedly purring and two pots of coffee perking away like a little percussion band, my mood lifted. It was as if I'd had a gray veil over my face ever since the lightning struck. I could tell my staff felt the same. Turner whistled at the grill, and Danna smiled as she scrubbed a pot.

Turner hit the ready bell. "Lunch for the pious among us," he murmured, casting his gaze over to the Blounts and Isabelle. He'd been raised in his father's Hindu faith, but he'd once told me he practiced more like Christians who went to church only on Christmas Eve and Easter, or Jews who attended high holy holiday services, lit menorah candles, and ate matzo at Passover but otherwise were more secular than religious.

I set the plates on their table. "Soup and grits for Helen, cheeseburger with coleslaw for Fred, and chef salad for Isabelle, dressing on the side. Yes?"

"Absolutely." Helen beamed. "Thank you so much, Robbie. I'm a complete weakling around grits. I cannot resist."

Isabelle's choice of a low-carb, high-protein lunch was probably in service of her regularly worked-out physique. Fred had silver at his temples, but his erect posture and near-military haircut made me wonder if he'd served in the Armed Forces. His trim build certainly didn't show his age, whatever it was.

When he folded his hands and bowed his head again, I expected a prayer of grace would follow, ASAP. I spoke quickly before he could start.

"Enjoy your meals. Would anyone like coffee when it's ready?"

Fred looked up wearing an annoyed frown and shook his head.

"Yes, please, hon, with cream and sugar," Helen said.

"I'd like coffee, too, but black," Isabelle said.

I left them to their prayers. I cleared a table and pocketed a tip, took an order and delivered it to Turner. I checked out who the latest incoming diner was.

Or diners. Cousins Wanda and Buck stood side by side, looking about as different from each other as Helen and Fred did. Wanda's pregnancy only accentuated the contrast between round and skinny, shortish and tall. She beckoned to me.

"Is power back everywhere in town?" I asked Buck.

"Pretty much, thanks to the Brown County REA."

"Glad to hear it." The rural electrical association cooperative was Abe's former employer. "Those line people are the best. Do you both want lunch?"

"That's why we're here," Wanda said. "But now that I see a certain Ms. Cooper, I might could have a word with her, too."

"Why?" I asked.

"Let's just say we have a particular interest." She took a step toward the threesome.

I grabbed her arm. "No police business while people are eating, remember? You can talk to her about church or food or what kind of movies she likes, but I can't have homicide-related interviews in my restaurant. I thought I made my policy clear last time." Not that I could exactly remember when that had been, or if it had been her detective husband whom I'd told. Buck knew my rule, for sure.

"Who are them folks she's with?" Buck asked.

"Fred and Helen Blount. They just arrived. They're staying in one of my B&B rooms through the weekend. Apparently the megachurch is having a revival, and the Blounts are special invited guests."

"Cooper is thick with that church," Buck murmured, almost to himself.

"She's apparently a deacon," I said.

"Deacon or not, the lady's a major donor, from what I've been able to dig up," Wanda said. "And not only to the church, neither."

"She's pretty young to be wealthy," I said. "Did she inherit funds or make a killing in the stock market?"

"You could say that." Wanda snorted. "Married herself a rich old coot. Mr. Cooper was kind enough to take and die a couple few years back. He didn't have any kiddos and left the whole stinking pile to her."

Had she been looking for a father figure? Or was she cold enough to have calculated the odds that a much older husband—one rolling in money—would pass away well before her? I glanced over at her, relieved her back was to both the door and our conversation.

But Fred faced us. He wore a stern expression as he stared. There was no way he or the women at his table could hear our conversation. Maybe he didn't like seeing me talk to the police. *Too bad.* I turned away.

"Who else does Isabelle donate to?" I kept my voice soft.

"Still working on that," Wanda said.

She'd been forthcoming about Isabelle's past. Maybe I could learn a bit more about the case, things I doubted Harris or Octavia would tell me.

"Wanda, what do you know about alibis?" I asked. "For people like Zeke, Wendy Corbett, and Isabelle?" I laid my left hand on my right shoulder, right fist on my hip.

"Zeke and his lady love claim they were with each other. Maybe they were, maybe they weren't. Ms. Cooper lives alone. I'm afraid old Don's a problem, too. His wife was out of town. As was . . ." She glanced at the slim gold band on my ring finger.

"Yeah, as was Abe." Should I challenge her about suspecting me? No. I didn't think she was serious. I sure hoped she wasn't. "Sorry I asked."

"I'd surely like to order me a heap of lunch, Robbie," Buck said.

"Not a problem," I hurried to say, before he could launch into how hungry he was. Not that I didn't love his colorful expressions, but other customers were looking for my attention, as were my coworkers. I pointed to a table not far from where the Blounts and Isabelle sat. "That two-top is yours. Coffee?"

CHAPTER 42

Even as I served and bused, delivered checks and took money, answered questions and smiled, my brain was working on how to solve this thing.

I should think alibis would be crucial, except nobody had one, according to Wanda. A couple like Zeke and Wendy vouching for each other, especially when either might have cause to kill, might not stand up in court. Everybody else had been alone. Had Octavia or Wanda or their teams asked questions of Zeke or Wendy's neighbors? Of Isabelle's? I wondered where she lived. And then there was Don. I couldn't imagine he'd murdered Evermina, but I hoped he hadn't done anything stupid like meet her in public that night and demand she pay her debts.

What about camera footage of the parking lot or surrounding sidewalks? Security cams were ubiquitous these days. The police should already have canvassed abutting businesses about that and checked with town hall about municipal traffic cams, if they had them. Except, despite being the county seat, Nashville was a small town. They might not have funds or even cause for cameras to catch speeding scofflaws.

Maybe residents who'd been out walking dogs or going for a nighttime stroll had spotted a person skulking away from the parking lot at a late hour. Someone could have heard a conversation or a cry when the skillet first struck. I'd ask Wanda about witnesses if I got a chance.

The ding of the ready bell brought me back from my musings, as did Turner clearing his throat as he passed me, his arms full of cleared dishes.

I seemed to be rooted in place holding an empty coffee carafe. This would never do. I put thoughts of homicide out of my mind and got my rear end back to work.

Helen Blount hailed me at about two o'clock. "You can go ahead and put our meal on our room tab, Robbie."

"I prefer to keep lunch charges separate, if you don't mind. As I post on the web site, your breakfast is available down here for the mornings you stay except Monday, and it's included in the room charge. We open at seven on weekdays and eight on Sundays." It was a lot neater, account-wise, for me to keep the price of the B&B room a fixed amount, and for guests to pay as they went for other meals.

Fred frowned, but fished a credit card out of his wallet.

"We'll treat Sister Isabelle, naturally." Helen beamed at her.

Isabelle inclined her head in thanks.

"I'll run your card and be right back," I said.

"Add yourself a good twenty percent on that, hon," Helen said.

I thanked her and ignored Fred's dour expression. I was grateful on behalf of Danna and Turner—the tip recipients—for generous souls like Helen, even if Fred didn't approve.

"Can my husband and I check into our room now?" Helen asked.

"No, ma'am. Check-in is in an hour, at three o'clock, but you're welcome to leave your bags here until then." I turned away to the adjacent table, whose diners had left a few minutes ago.

"Helen, you know very well when the check-in is," Fred scolded his wife.

"I'll take you folks over to the church and show you around," Isabelle said. "You can leave your car here."

I ran the card at the register on the counter where we also did retail checkout. One of these days I really needed to upgrade with a portable wifi-enabled card reader we could use table-side in the restaurant, the kind that printed out receipts on the spot.

Isabelle and company were standing as I headed back to their table. I passed where Buck and Wanda sat. Wanda seemed focused on her mostly eaten Kitchen Sink omelet, but she didn't fool me. I could tell her detective radar was trained on Isabelle.

"Robbie, come on back when you get a minute, okay?" Buck asked.

"Sure." I kept moving. I gave the Blounts their slip and said I'd see them when they got back. "Please be here by four, if you can. Otherwise, text me and I'll hook you up with the keypad code but I won't be able to show you around." I'd rather supply them with their key card. If I gave them the access code, I'd have to change it before the next guests. It was easier not to have to.

"We'll be back in time, hon," Helen said in the irrepressibly cheery voice she'd used since she arrived.

The three made their way toward the exit. I focused on clearing their plates and flatware, cloth napkins and paper place mats. A movement in my periphery made me look up.

Wanda, in a classic police stance of elbows to the sides and feet rooted, now blocked Isabelle's path to the door. Isabelle lifted her chin.

I set down my busing and hurried in that direction, throwing Buck a glare as I went. Had he known Wanda's purpose in leaving the table? Maybe.

"All I want is a minute of your time, ma'am." Wanda's voice, no longer her usual cheery, now turned low and steely. "Shall we step outside onto the porch?"

"I don't see why I should, officer," Isabelle countered. "My guests are waiting, and we have business elsewhere right now."

Wanda planted her feet slightly wider and folded her arms atop her hefty and pregnant chest. "What if I told you it was about your investment in the Miss South Lick Diner?"

What?

Isabelle's nostrils flared. She glared at Wanda. "Why would this fictional investment be your concern?"

"Two minutes of your time, please." Wanda didn't glare back, but she clearly wasn't taking no for an answer. She extended a straight arm toward the door. "After you."

CHAPTER 43

"Did you know Wanda was going to confront Isabelle?" I asked Buck at his table a minute after Wanda followed the Blounts and Isabelle outside.

"Might shoulda had an inkling, but she didn't tell me nothing specific. You remember I'm not on this case, Robbie, right?"

"So you came in only for a fun cousins' lunch." *As if.*

"Kinda sorta." He had the grace to look sheepish. "Sorry if old Wanda disrupted business for you."

"At least she took it outside, and Isabelle was leaving, anyway." It was my turn to fold my arms. "Wanda said Isabelle had invested in Evermina's café."

"Is that what Wanda took and told her?" His brows knit. "I couldn't rightly make it out from here."

"It is."

"I can't say I was aware, hon, and that's the gospel truth."

"I'd like to know more about the deal. A lot more, but for now, excuse me." I returned to what I'd been doing, clearing the threesome's table.

By two thirty, Buck was the only customer left, and he'd finished eating long ago. I hadn't cleared Wanda's plate, in case she wanted to finish her meal. If she ever came back. Danna scoured pots at the sink, while Turner scrubbed the grill.

I was heading for the door to turn the sign to CLOSED when Wanda came back through it. She'd been out there a lot longer than two minutes.

"Did she talk to you?" I asked.

"Kinda had to, didn't she?" Wanda wrinkled her nose. "But getting anything out of her was like pulling teeth from a fighting cock with one hand tied behind your back."

Did roosters even have teeth? I ignored the image. "What's this investment of hers you mentioned?"

"You heard that, did you?"

"Yes." I flipped the sign and released the fire bar, so people could get out but no one without a key could come in.

"I'll tell you, it was more suspicion than fact. She didn't exactly confess to being a silent investor in the Miss South Lick, but she surely did get her back up when I asked."

"What made you think Isabelle had put money into the diner?"

"Just a couple few things I learned. The lady's loaded, money-wise, but she also has a temper like nobody's business."

"From the little I've seen of her, she seems to be a woman who's determined to get what she wants," I said.

"That, too."

"How did Isabelle even know Evermina?"

"Welp, I suspect it's through that big honking church of theirs. Now I'd best head back and finish my lunch before Buck gets his hands on it." She bustled away.

That they'd met through the church made sense. Those women on Sunday had referred to Sister Martin, as if Evermina was a regular attendee at services. Should I have pressed Wanda on Isabelle's finances? No, not right now. As I pointed myself toward the kitchen area, I did wonder why, if Evermina had an investor, she still hadn't been able to pay what she owed to Don.

"Any thoughts for specials for tomorrow, gang?" I asked my crew.

Danna dried her hands and worked her phone for a minute. "Tomorrow is National Coq au Vin Day. We could do a simple version for lunch."

"We have mushrooms and boneless chicken thighs," Turner said. "Even though it should be made with bone-in chicken."

"Sure, but simple is the key," I said. "I know we have thyme in the pot out back." During the warmer half of the year, I always had a couple of planters of perennial herbs ready to harvest behind the apartment attached to the store where I'd lived until a year ago, when Abe and I combined households in his American Craftsman-style cottage. "Let's do it. How about breakfast?"

"We could call it Spring in Paris Day and do

crepes," Turner suggested. "We haven't offered them in a while."

I nodded. "I like it." Crepes were fast and easy, plus their fillings could be savory or sweet.

"Great idea," Danna said. "And we can all wear berets, plus scarves tied European-style."

"You two can wear berets." I smiled. "Mine is wool and would be way too hot, but I do have a light silk scarf I can knot around my neck."

"I'll go check the mushroom supply, because they're perfect with crepes, too." Danna made her way to the walk-in.

"See if we have enough Gruyere or Swiss cheese, too," Turner called after her.

Danna did a thumbs-up and pulled open the heavy door.

I caught sight of Buck standing. He laid money on the table. Wanda also pushed up to her feet. I could head over and try to learn more. Or I could stay right here, on task, prepping for tomorrow. I needed to figure out food to bring to Don, and I had a business to run.

After I gave the cousins a little wave, I turned my back to scrub my hands. I measured flour and salt and butter for tomorrow's biscuits into a big mixing bowl, waiting for the bell on the door to jangle indicating Buck and Wanda's exit.

I realized I hadn't heard the bell when someone cleared their throat behind me as I cut butter into the flour mix. I twisted my head.

"Excuse me, Robbie," Wanda said. "Can we talk for a little small minute?"

I pointed my chin to hands covered with flour. "Only if it's right here. I'm busy, as you can see."

She glanced at Turner, who was slicing mushrooms, and at Danna grating cheese.

"They can hear whatever you need to tell me, Wanda," I said.

"I hear nothing," Danna muttered in a fake Russian accent.

Turner brought his hands to cover his ears, still holding the sharp vegetable knife.

"Careful, my friend," I said to him. "You don't want to channel van Gogh."

I continued with my big pastry cutter, chopping the butter into the flour. Wanda stood silent. Buck hovered by the door.

"What's up, Wanda?" I finally asked.

She cleared her throat. "I know as how we normally ask you to keep out of our investigations, Robbie. And we don't never want you to be in danger. But I would like to ask you the favor of keeping your eyes and ears open and passing along any intel you pick up. I have to admit, this case is tougher than the back of a armadillo crossed with a tortoise."

"I'm always happy to pass along information. And I promise I have no plans to endanger myself or anyone else." Especially not the tiny Abe-Robbie cross I carried inside me.

CHAPTER 44

"Robbie?" Don asked when he opened his front door an hour later, his worried brow further furrowing. "What are you doing here?"

"Abe said Georgia was out of town. I brought you a few biscuits." I held up the paper sack I held.

"That's good of you." He stared at the ground. "I haven't been very hungry though."

Slate-colored clouds had blown in, bringing a temperature drop with them, and a gust of wind nearly knocked me off my feet. It rustled the new, bright-green leaves on the tall maple and threatened to destroy the petals off a cluster of showy late tulips next to the door. I shivered in my store t-shirt.

"Can I come in for a minute?" I asked.

"What?" He gave his head a little shake. "Please. Excuse my manners, or lack of them, I should say." He stepped back and gestured inside.

I stepped across the threshold. After he and Georgia had married a couple of years ago, they'd each sold their houses and moved into a newer townhouse complex on the edge of town. They'd hosted a housewarming open house for family on both sides at the time, but I hadn't been here since. It was a comfortable and pleasant two-story space. Upstairs was an office, a full bath, and a guest room.

Down here featured an open design with a kitchen, dining area, and living room. Carved duck decoys seemed to occupy every niche and corner. A powder room was tucked under the stairs, and a bedroom with en suite bath led off the sitting area. The bedroom's open door revealed an unmade bed and clothes strewn on the floor.

"Come on into the kitchen," he said. "Can I get you a drink?"

A glass holding a clear liquid, ice, and a fat pimento-stuffed olive sat half full on the kitchen island.

"I'm having an early martini." His expression turned sheepish. "It's five o'clock somewhere, right?"

"It must be. But no thanks, for me." He did know I was pregnant, didn't he? I wouldn't blame him for forgetting. Being suspected of murder could make all kinds of things slip one's mind. At least he didn't act as if he'd been drowning his sorrows in drink all afternoon. His speech and eyes were clear, his manner normal.

I slid onto the stool next to his and set the sack on the island. The litter of toast crumbs, paper napkins, and empty takeout containers gave it the feel of a bachelor pad and made me itchy. The countertop hadn't been wiped clean for days, it appeared, and a skillet full of grease and bits of meat sat on the stove. Was Don a natural slob and Georgia usually kept things clean, or was this result of being investigated for murder?

I swiveled to face him. "Abe also told me about your interview at the Nashville station."

"You have to believe me, Robbie." He kneaded his hands. "I would never hurt anyone. I couldn't. But the cops seemed to believe I did."

"They kept you quite a while. They must think they have evidence, but not enough to arrest you."

"They don't." His voice rose. "They can't."

My phone vibrated in my back pocket. "Hang on a minute, okay?" I glanced at the ID. It was none other than Nashville chief of police Harris. A groan escaped me. I'd said I would meet her at four, which had been fifteen minutes ago. I let the call finish without connecting, then thumbed a text to her.

Sorry, something came up. Will let you know when I'm free.

Which preferably would be never. And I wasn't a bit sorry. I stashed the phone and focused on Don again.

"What kinds of questions did they ask you?" I kept my voice gentle.

He didn't speak for a moment. "It began with Wanda barging into my store on Sunday. When you were there, in fact. She was all up in my face about my finances. My dealings with poor Evermina. My whereabouts. Robbie, she was relentless."

"But it's her job, Don."

"I know." He took a big swig of his drink. "Look,

I made the mistake of kind of threatening Evermina while we were standing on the sidewalk, and people heard."

"What did you say?"

"I told her I would have to take measures if she didn't pay what she owed me." He swallowed and swabbed his brow with a wrinkled handkerchief. "Or something to that effect."

"Did you say you would harm her physically?"

"No, never! Except I might have said things couldn't go on like they were, and that she'd better watch out." He raised his gaze to meet mine, finally. "Robbie, I was so mad. Her not paying was affecting my own bottom line, which isn't that strong right now."

"But Shamrock Hardware does so well. You always have customers in there." How far should I pry? "Is the business suffering?"

"No." He stared into his drink again. "But my personal checkbook is."

I waited, my gaze on his disappearing martini. Now that my morning sickness had passed, the thought of an adult beverage at the end of the day seemed more appealing, especially in a fraught situation like this one. Except I wouldn't indulge. Nothing was going to harm my baby's development if I could help it.

"It's like this. I kind of have a weakness." He pointed with his chin to the sitting area. "Those decoys don't come cheap. I've been buying them on eBay, each more expensive than the last. My wife isn't happy about it, so I've been hiding the purchases."

I waited a bit longer. Maybe he and Georgia had

argued about his habit and that was why she'd gone on a trip. Abe had mentioned they'd been having marital issues.

"I paid upward of twelve hundred dollars for one," Don murmured. "But they can go for over six grand, often more."

What? I peered at him in disbelief. "How can a carved duck cost that much?"

His laugh was rueful. "You can find them for ten times more than what I paid, or double that, even. These are artisanal pieces, Robbie. Rare and antique works of art."

I whistled. "They'd better be."

"In addition, I've been giving my stepdaughter money."

"Isabelle?" Wealthy Isabelle?

"Yes. When she asks, I'm too weak to say no."

"I thought she was rich," I said.

"She has funds at her disposal, yes." He let out a noisy breath. "I've always wanted her affection."

"Are you getting it now?" I doubted it.

"Not a bit. And I'm afraid both outlays of money have come between my dear Georgia and me."

"Don." I reached out and laid my hand on his arm, keeping my tone gentle. "I think you need to get help. Counseling, a financial advisor, or both. You already have all these lovely pieces." I swiveled and gestured around the living room. "You can enjoy their beauty, or even sell a few."

He nodded, but his eyes drooped at the corners more than they usually did.

"And I think you know Isabelle isn't going to start caring about you just because you're padding her bank account," I added.

He gave another slow nod.

"Abe and I can help you find a therapist," I went on.

"No." He brought his palm down flat on the island top with more force than he needed. "Please don't bring him into this. He's my little brother, Robbie. He's always looked up to me. I can't show him what a wreck I am."

I didn't tell him Abe already knew Don was in bad shape. My husband would do anything to help his big brother regain his mental health and financial stability. Right now, removing Don from the Persons of Interest list was even more important.

CHAPTER 45

I mused about our conversation as I drove from Don's over to Nashville. I felt pretty confident that he hadn't killed Evermina. Not a hundred percent, but I was maybe ninety percent sure. His unease when I'd spied his open laptop on Sunday had been that I'd discovered his own debts, not that he was emailing a co-murderer or anything.

At least I hoped I was right. And he would be in jail right now if Wanda or Octavia had any actual evidence against him. But if Don wasn't the murderer, who was left? Wendy. Zeke. Camilla. Isabelle. Jim? *Nah.* He was way down on the list.

I'd give this murder business one more hour of my day. I planned to head the four miles over to Gnaw Bone and pick up three juicy, crispy, pork tenderloin sandwiches at the Gnaw Mart for our family dinner, as I'd promised Abe.

In Nashville, I found a parking space two doors down from Wendy's gift shop. I stayed seated in

the car for a minute. The last time I'd gone in, she'd
seemed suspicious of me. I needed to convince
her to talk with me. What could I do differently
today? I'd already asked her about Zeke's divorce
status, and . . .

I clapped my hand to my forehead. Where had
my brain gone? She'd refused to tell me whether
Zeke and Evermina had been officially divorced,
and I'd wanted to look into that. I glanced at my
phone. If I hustled, I could make it over to the
country courthouse before five thirty, when it
probably closed.

But when I got there, the big door was locked
up tight, and the posted hours said they were open
from eight to four. *Rats.* Well, I'd tried.

I'd probably missed Camilla, too. I thought she,
like me, closed after lunch service, but I headed
that way in case she was still finishing up in her
restaurant.

My pace slowed, but not because of the gusting
wind. Wendy and Zeke emerged from a shop, him
holding the door for her. I stepped back into an
inset entranceway and cautiously peered around
the corner, hoping the couple turned in the other
direction.

Wendy raised her left hand, palm out and gazed
at it. The late-day light glinted off what looked like
a stone set into a ring. She tucked her arm through
his and off they strolled, the two nearly the same
height.

I might have found my first destination. I conjured up a story as I waited until they turned down
a side street. Making my way to the shop, I slid my

wedding band off my finger and into a pocket. My engagement ring was safely at home. I never wore it while working at the restaurant.

Sure enough, the place was a jewelry store. Inside, a woman behind a glass counter greeted me.

"I passed a woman on the sidewalk a minute ago," I said. "She was wearing the prettiest engagement ring, and it looked like she had come out of your shop."

"She had, and that's a very special ring." The clerk raised her eyebrows. "Are you looking?"

"Yes." I gave her shy smile. "I mean, my boyfriend is, but I know he's about to pop the question. Do you have another ring like hers?"

"Not exactly, but let me show you a few in that range." She drew out several black-felted trays holding pairs of engagement rings and wedding bands and set them on the counter.

I perused, seeing only sets that were too flashy for my taste. None were as lovely as the engagement ring Abe had surprised me with over a year ago.

"I recognized the man she was with," I murmured as I examined the display. "I thought I'd heard that Zeke Martin had remarried. Was his wife getting her wedding band resized?"

"No, not at all." She glanced around, then peered at me over the top of rhinestone-studded reading glasses. "He was still in the process of getting divorced when his poor wife was killed." She nearly whispered. "Murdered, right here in Nashville last Saturday. Can you even?"

"That's shocking. I hope the criminal is behind bars."

"Not that we've heard." She made a *tsking* sound. "What's the world coming to?"

I shook my head in what I hope looked like agreement at the state of society. I stepped back and smiled. "Thank you so much. I'll drop a few heavy hints to my future hubby about where to shop." I cringed that I'd even uttered the word "hubby." I hated when women referred to their husbands that way, as if they were a kind of mascot.

"You do that, hon. Have a good day, and be careful out there."

Back on the street, I stood still for a moment. Evermina and Zeke hadn't been divorced. He and Wendy would be married soon. All useful information.

Now where?

CHAPTER 46

"For a Tuesday, the Gnaw Mart was packed," I said to Abe and Sean. "And they had live music going on in that back room with the tables and chairs." After my Nashville jewelry store foray, I'd decided my sleuthing was over for the day and had shifted gears toward food and home.

We sat around the dining table, having come up for air after initial bites of the generous, thick-cut hunk of breaded and fried pork tenderloin. The meat was tucked into a basic white-bread bun, along with lettuce and slices of onion and pickle.

"Were the musicians a trio?" Abe asked.

"Yes, with two guitars, and they all sang in harmony," I said. "You know, folky ballads, traditional music. We'll have to go and eat there one of these days." After my arteries recovered from this dinner.

"My banjo buddies and I are angling to get a gig there." Abe dug into his dinner again.

"Mmm," Sean mumbled. After he swallowed the

mouthful, he went on. "Crisp. Crunchy. Meaty. Juicy. How do they do it?" Sean had grown accomplished at cooking a range of dishes, a hobby Abe and I both encouraged.

"For one, they don't pound the tenderloin into a pancake so all you get is the breading," Abe replied.

"Speaking of frying, did you get your deep fryer yet?" Sean asked me.

"This morning, but we haven't had a chance to set it up yet," I said. "Maybe after school one day or on the weekend you can come in and help."

"You got it, Mombie."

I loved the name Sean had come up with for me. "Oh, by the way, I might have a summer job for you."

"Like cooking in your restaurant?"

Cocoa lifted his head from his bed in the corner, as if he'd picked up on his boy's mood. Maceo, who had a habit of sleeping next to the dog, cracked an eyelid but otherwise didn't move.

"We're pretty set for regular cooking, but maybe you could do a shift now and then."

Sean's excited expression slid away. I hurried to continue.

"Hang on. Phil told me he's moving away, that he got an opera job in Wisconsin. He's leaving in three weeks, and I'm going to need a new baker."

"You want me to bake the desserts for the store?" Sean's eyes sparkled.

Abe, mouth full, gave an approving nod.

"It wouldn't be full time," I said. "So you'd be able to do other stuff, even another part-time job if you wanted. But I pay well, and Phil said he'd share his recipes if you want them. Having you fill in until I can find a baker for the long term would be a big help."

"You're on." Sean grinned. "Thank you." He cleared his throat. "I have news, too." He gave an inquisitive glance toward Abe, who bobbed his head.

My own mouth now full of deliciousness, I waited.

"I've been accepted for AFS."

"You have?" I covered my mouth as I asked. "That's great news, honey. I'm so happy for you." My father's country had been the teen's first choice for where to live as an exchange student, and he'd been studying Italian with an app, but the organization had made it clear that requests weren't always honored. "Did you get Italy?"

"No. They're sending me to Greece, though. I wonder if I can find a crash course Greek app."

"Are you too disappointed?" Abe asked.

"Greece isn't that far from Italy," he said. "It's all good."

"We'll miss you," I said. "But hey, it's a vacation destination."

"In the spring, maybe." Abe gave a pointed look at my stomach.

Oh, right. I wouldn't be flying this fall, and neither would a newborn for the first couple of months.

"Except that's the bad part. They totally discourage parents coming to visit." Sean frowned. "Plus, I'll miss my little sister's birth and the first part of her life. I'm thinking of saying I can't go, after all."

My throat thickened with how caring he was. "Sean, you have to go. You've wanted this for a long time. Babies are lumps their first few months."

Abe snorted.

"Seriously," I said. "We'll get on video calls with you as often as you want. You'll see every bit of this kiddo, who might be a boy, you realize."

"We can even do an on-camera diaper change so you see what you're missing," Abe added.

"That's funny, Dad. Poop, live and in color." Sean's mood lightened again. "I still want to think about it a little more."

"You do that," Abe said gently. "Remember, she or he will be your sibling for your whole life, but this is your one chance to live abroad with a family as a young person, which is the best way to get really good at a language. And you'll meet the baby the minute you land in Indy."

Sean popped in his last bite of dinner. As he chewed, his phone rang with the tone reserved for his brainy—and cute—girlfriend, Maeve.

"Go," Abe said.

Sean hurried into his room. We usually had a dinnertime no-cellphone policy, but he was finished eating, and this seemed like a special occasion.

"Do you think he's also worried about leaving his sweetie?" I asked.

"Maybe." Abe sipped his beer.

"He is a remarkably sweet and sensitive person, Abe. Especially for a teenage boy."

"It boggles the mind, doesn't it? I'm not sure how that happened."

"The explanation is easy." I smiled at him. "That's how you are, and that's how you raised him."

Sean sauntered back out. "Maeve got her first choice. She's going to Finland."

"Good news, right?" I asked.

"Yeah, but I'm going to miss her wicked bad."

"Does that mean a lot?" Abe's mouth quirked.

"We have a classmate who moved here from Cape Cod last month," Sean said. "Wicked's kind of a favorite word with him."

"Maybe you can start a Hoosier trend," I said.

"I plan on it. You both done eating?" Sean picked up his plate and glass. "I have, like, mountains of homework before the end of the year."

"I'm finished, thanks," I said.

Abe nodded. Sean cleared the table, depositing dishes in the kitchen, and disappeared back into his room, Cocoa and Maceo trotting after him. Sean popped his head out for a second.

"Thanks for dinner."

I smiled and waved him away.

"Yes, thank you," Abe said. "Not exactly a heart-healthy meal, but a great occasional treat."

I fiddled with my unused fork for a moment. I glanced up. "Abe, I brought a half dozen biscuits by Don's today and had a little chat."

"How did he seem?"

"A little worse for the wear. I mean, the kitchen island was a mess with crumbs and trash, and he seemed kind of a mess, too." I didn't mention Don's afternoon martini.

"That's kind of his normal state, at least when he's alone," Abe said. "I don't know why I got the gene that likes things basically clean, and he didn't, but that's how it is."

"You mentioned marital issues between him and Georgia."

"Don hinted that they'd been having more than one difference of opinion. Why?"

"I hope you don't mind, but I got him to open up a little about what's going on." I explained about Don's finances suffering because of the buying sprees, and how his habit was affecting his marriage. "He needs therapy, Abe, and I think they both could benefit from marriage counseling."

"Thank you for doing that, sugar. He's never opened up to me much. Maybe it's a guy thing."

"He was horrified I might tell you. But how could I not?"

Abe drained his beer.

I continued. "I think his stress about his personal checkbook made his blowing up at Evermina about what she owed him that much worse. And unfortunately, I'll bet that's what the police are operating on." I had my mouth open to ask him more about Don's detention with the Nashville PD and what the next steps would be when Abe stood.

"Banjo practice," he said. "Gotta run."

"Don't you have your exam tomorrow?"

"Yes, but playing music will clear my head and relax me. If I don't know the material by now, a few hours of staring at my notes isn't going to help. I won't be late." He leaned down and planted a kiss on my lips.

"Have fun."

Me, I was going to sit right here, or on the couch, preferably, and do my own relaxing.

CHAPTER 47

My evening relaxation somehow turned into working on the murder. After I rinsed and slid the dishes into the dishwasher, I fixed myself a mug of chamomile-ginger tea and retired to the couch to put up my feet, snuggle with a cat or two, and work a puzzle.

Except that respite didn't last long. I turned to the next page in my *New York Times* Sunday puzzle book. A clue about detectives only made me think about how I still hadn't created a crime-solving puzzle for the current homicide. My head wasn't a bit cleared, and only one solution could fix that.

"Sorry, Birdman." I dislodged Birdy from his nap spot next to me and took my sharpened pencil to the table. A pad of graph paper and a ruler later, I was ready, except I had to organize my thoughts before I began with clues and solutions, grids of blank squares and black ones.

I first jotted down the usual headings across the top. Motive. Opportunity. Method seemed pretty

clear—a whack on the head with a cast-iron pan—
and last I'd heard, nobody had an alibi. I added
the names on my Persons-of-Interest list down the
left side.

> *Wendy*
> *Zeke*
> *Camilla*
> *Isabelle*
> *Don*

My hand dragged on the final name, but I had
to add it.

I moved to the first heading, Motive. Was it all
about money? Or did jealousy, spite, or revenge
play a part?

Sitting back, I considered what I knew. The jeweler hadn't thought Zeke was officially divorced.
He, Wendy, or the two of them could have killed
Evermina to remove any possibility that she would
claim a share of his assets, including alimony. But I
still hadn't found out anything concrete about his
finances or divorce proceedings, and I wasn't sure
how to accomplish that.

Wait. Who had said Wendy lived in South Lick?
It had been either Adele or Corrine, I thought. I
hit the Adele speed-dial button on my phone's
home page, but she didn't pick up. I'd leave that
for another time.

I jotted down Money next to both Wendy and
Zeke's names and moved on to Camilla. She'd said
she'd told Evermina to back off the libelous ads.
Did the Cammie's Kitchen owner have a history of
violence, of overreacting? I had so many questions

and so few answers. I could have wandered onto the internet to look for answers.

Instead, I decided to keep plugging away, and leave all the research until after I'd finished this initial pass.

Isabelle was the last real potential suspect, if I excluded Don. She'd been a silent investor in the Miss South Lick. She had temper issues. From the way Don had described her, she sounded vindictive, maybe emotionally unstable.

Truly, Evermina seemed like the person with issues. Mismanaging her fledging business. Not paying Don. Coming on to married Jim. Disparaging her competitors. If she'd discovered Zeke's infidelity, she might have threatened him with financial ruin, with exposure, or with another kind of harm.

But Evermina Martin was dead. Right now the real question was her killer's identity, and how to make sure nobody else was murdered. I tapped the pencil on the pad.

And dropped it when my phone jangled. Adele calling back? I checked the display and groaned. No such luck. But this was a call I had to answer.

"Good evening, Chief Harris."

"We had an appointment earlier, Ms. Jordan, and we still have questions for you. If you continue to evade us, we'll have no choice but to bring you into the Nashville station."

Ooh, somebody was upset with me—and rightly so.

"Yes, ma'am." I tried to use a level tone. Not flip, but not overly contrite.

"Detective Sergeant Slade will contact you in the morning. That is all." She disconnected with an abruptness that came close to slamming down the receiver.

It wasn't Harris's fault, but I found Octavia easier to deal with than the Nashville chief. If Detective Sergeant Slade wanted to carve out a time to speak with me, I wouldn't weasel out of it.

I yawned. Right now I planned to extract myself from thoughts of murder. I simply didn't have enough information to create this puzzle, and definitely not to solve it.

Stopping my efforts wasn't chickening out, exactly, but I needed my beauty sleep, and so did my little chickadee.

CHAPTER 48

I stuck my key in the lock of my store's service door at five thirty the next morning, as usual. The first glimmers of dawn glowed in the east, but the whiplash weather of late spring made me shiver in my long-sleeved store tee. One day it was warm, the following day cold. One day fair, the next rainy. Or windy. Or any combination of all of them, possibly in one day.

Today's chilly temps appeared to have been brought in by a stiff wind. A rustle behind me made me whirl. But the motion-detector light didn't reveal any human-caused noise, only branches rubbing. Leaves fluttered and an abandoned box skittered along the pavement. Still, I hurried inside and locked up behind me.

My nerves stayed on edge as I prepared pots of coffee. As I carried food out from the walk-in, bringing breakfast meats, prepped biscuit dough and pancake mix, fruit, and so much more. As I broke three dozen eggs into the big bowl. As I whisked them into readiness for omelets and scrambled egg orders. While I worked, I mused about why I was feeling nervous.

I wasn't usually a scaredy-cat type. I'd been brave, standing up to attackers in the past. But if a homicidal person was out there looking for me, I had to think about more than myself. I'd tried to be extra careful in this case not to act like I was conducting my own private investigation, at least not in public.

I scattered flour on the counter and rolled out flattened balls of biscuit dough while the oven preheated. I cut out biscuit after biscuit. Soon enough, two big pans of fat disks were baking.

Maybe I hadn't concealed my poking around as much as I should have. Maybe one of those persons of interest was onto me and was already plotting how to get me permanently out of the way before I revealed what I'd learned to the authorities.

Except I didn't have much of anything to reveal. Which Octavia was going to find out if she tracked me down this morning. Make that *when* she did, according to Haley Harris.

I jumped when the doorbell for the service door buzzed. Turning to stare at it, I couldn't imagine who was out there. Six was way too early for a delivery. It was even early for Danna to show up. Was a killer trying to lure me outside? The service door, which was along the driveway, didn't have glass in it, and it wasn't visible from the street. Which was exactly why I'd installed a security cam out there last month.

Right. I jabbed at my phone, trying to find the

camera app. My nerves—and my flour-covered hands—made me drop the device. My breath came fast, and my neck prickled. Maybe I should go around and shut off the lights. An attacker could head to the front of the store and peer in to see where I was.

Instead, I dusted off my hands on the apron and grabbed the phone off the floor. The buzzer sounded again. At the same time, a text came in. My eyes widened. It was from Danna.

Can you let me in? Forgot my key.

I swallowed. What if the killer had a gun to Danna's head or a knife to her throat and had forced her to text that? I thought quickly.

What's T's secret biscuit ingredient?

A murderer would never know about the curry flavoring Turner had slid into the biscuits a few years ago. My phone dinged again.

Curry

She'd passed the test . . . unless the bad guy made her. I had to check the camera app to be sure Danna was alone.

One sec.

After more fumbling, I made it into the app and saw a clear picture of my co-chef. Nobody was grabbing her arm or throat. No weapon was in sight. I hurried over, unlocked the door, and pulled her inside.

"Whoa, Robbie," Danna said. "I'm not late or anything."

I quickly locked up again.

"What's with the mysterious code word and the big hurry, boss?" Danna asked. "It's like you're in a noir movie or something."

"I'm sorry. I guess I'm feeling on edge." I let my shoulders drop the tension they'd been holding. "You're early, and I wasn't sure that was you, or if a really bad person had nabbed you and was coming in with you."

She gave me a sympathetic look. "I get it. The whole equation has shifted, right? You're not only eating for two, you have to be careful for two, as well."

"Exactly." My hand strayed to my stomach. What would it feel like when I had three or five or seven pounds of baby in there? When my skin was stretched over a full uterus, when the baby kicked and flipped half the time, when my breasts were getting ready to feed a hungry little one? I wouldn't know until I got here. I did know I'd have to be even more careful than I was now. "Thank goodness for the security cam out there."

Danna sniffed. "Did somebody forget to set a timer?" She grabbed a dish towel and pulled out one pan of biscuits, then the other.

Rats. "That would be me."

"They don't look too bad," she said.

The puffy biscuits, which had doubled in height, were tan on top instead of the golden brown we usually aimed for. I flipped one over.

"Brown but not burnt. They'll do."

"They're fine." Danna shivered.

She wore a short-sleeved vintage rayon dress in a blue print. The garment looked like one my grandmother might have worn, although Grandma never would have paired it with red socks and combat boots, nor with a purple beret over dread-locks.

"How'd it get so cold out there?" she asked.

"I don't know. The weather is getting super crazy lately." I took another look at her. She'd evidently dressed for our Spring in Paris theme. "Nice beret. I completely forgot my silk scarf."

"I thought you might have." She dug in her cross-body bag. "Here. I brought you one."

The blue scarf was printed with stylized white Eiffel towers. I let her tie it around my neck.

"I'll have to keep it tucked into the bib of my apron," I said.

"Which is perfectly French. Did you mix up the crepe batter?"

"No."

"I'm on it. That's why I came in early." She headed for the walk-in.

"Can you grab the cheeses and mushrooms, too?"

She threw a thumbs-up over her shoulder and let the heavy door clunk shut behind her.

I felt better now that she was here. A lot better. Danna had a cheerful attitude toward life that could lift anyone up, especially a pregnant anyone who'd had a fictional fright.

CHAPTER 49

Even in the first thirty minutes we were open, the crepes had already proved popular. After the first time we'd offered them, when Turner had brought in his own crepe pan, I'd acquired a fabulous vintage—and well-seasoned—version to keep at the ready.

On-the-spot cooking of a sufficient number of crepes to satisfy our customers, along with all the other demands of a busy restaurant, might get tricky later in the hour with only two of us on the job. But I thought Danna and I had pre-cooked enough before seven o'clock to last us until close to the time when Turner would arrive. We'd layered the thin pancakes in parchment paper and kept them warm.

Adele and Samuel bustled in at about seven forty. Samuel, moving with a cane, made his way to an empty two-top. He'd been having an issue with his hip lately, and Adele had said he was seeing a physical therapist.

My aunt, on the other hand, headed straight for the sink. Hands scrubbed and apron tied, she asked, "Where do you want me?"

"Good morning to you, too." I smiled at her not even asking if we could use an extra hand. "Coffee and orders, plus busing when people start finishing would be great, and thank you."

"I saw you called last evening." She lifted both coffee carafes. "After young Turner comes in, let's us two put our noggins together."

"It's a deal."

I was passing the front door a few minutes later when Zeke pushed through. My arms loaded with plates full of ham and cheese crepes, omelets and bacon, biscuits and gravy, all I could do was signal I'd seen him.

"Be right with you," I called.

I delivered the hot food to hungry diners, then made my way back to him. He stood alone, jingling keys in his pants pocket.

"Good morning, Zeke." The only time he'd been in before, he and Wendy had left before they'd ordered. Maybe she'd been the instigator of the departure more than he had. "Breakfast for one?"

"Yes, ma'am."

"Follow me." I led him to Buck's preferred table near the back wall. Buck wasn't here, and he'd never asked me to keep the two-top reserved for him. "Coffee?"

"Please." He tilted his head, regarding me, but he didn't say anything else.

"I'll be back. The menu is there on your place mat, and specials are on the whiteboard. I'll take your order when I come back."

I headed toward Adele. "I'll take care of Zeke, okay?"

"Sure thing, hon. Need this?" She handed me a full coffee carafe.

"I do, thanks." I reversed my steps and poured for Zeke. "What can I get you to eat?"

"I think I need a heartier breakfast than crepes, even though I certainly ate my share of them in Paris as a young man."

"You were in Paris when you were young?"

"You bet. Studying art, of course." His voice took on a wistful tone. "That career didn't come to much."

Huh. Art. "I saw several of Evermina's paintings in a Nashville art gallery. Well, the one I was leaving when I literally ran into you the other day. Did you meet her through art?"

"Yes." His voice was low and sad. "She had way more talent than I ever will. Such a loss."

"Then why did she open a restaurant?"

A customer two tables over signaled she'd like more coffee, and Danna hit the ready bell. Still, I really wanted to hear his answer.

"It's superhard to make a living as an artist," he said.

"Restaurants aren't an easy life, either. Just saying."

"No. But Evie always wanted to recreate the place she grew up in, a diner in Martinsville. Thing is, she didn't have a clue how to cook and was the worst with money management." He wagged his head.

Danna signaled for me to get moving. She was right.

"What can I get you to eat?" I asked.

"I'd like a western omelet with bacon, wheat toast, and biscuits with sausage gravy, please."

"You got it."

He lifted his mug with his left hand and sipped the black coffee. *Interesting.* I hadn't noticed hand-edness of any of the other persons of interest, which was a mistake on my part. Now that I thought about it, Don was also left-handed. Had Evermina's wound showed evidence of her attacker being right- or left-handed? Maybe Octavia would tell me what the autopsy had showed.

I decided to ask a different question, even though I needed to get back to work.

"Zeke, is there going to be a wake or a funeral service for Evermina?"

He cocked his head again. "Why? Would you want to be there? I didn't know you two were close."

"We weren't. I'd like to pay my respects, though."

He made a little sound in his throat as if he didn't believe me.

"Or maybe the police haven't released her re-mains yet," I added.

He winced at the word "remains," but it was too late for me to take it back.

"It doesn't matter," he said. "Her sister is com-ing to handle everything. She made it quite clear I was not to be involved." His eyes welled. "Evie was still my wife. Shouldn't I have some kind of say in bidding her farewell and putting her to rest?"

Those damp eyes were the first sign I'd seen that he was sad about her death. Except . . . he could easily have a background in acting I didn't know about. Either way, a very bad person had already put Evermina to rest.

CHAPTER 50

"Nice scarf," Adele commented as I cleared Samuel's and her dishes at about eight thirty.

"You should tell Danna," I said. "I forgot to bring one. Yesterday we decided on a Spring in Paris theme for the day. And who fell down on the job?" I raised my hand. "The restaurant owner."

"Scarf or no scarf, the crepes were delicious, Robbie," Samuel said.

"Thank you."

"They sure as shooting were." Adele beckoned me closer.

I glanced around. We were in an early mini-lull, with nobody waiting for a table or demanding my attention. I leaned in.

"What was you wanting to know when you called, hon?" she asked.

"I was trying to organize my thoughts about the, uh, recent incident." I checked with her.

Samuel cocked an eyebrow before lifting the *In-*

dianapolis Star in front of his face. He wasn't one to enter into either gossip or discussion of homicide suspects.

"I believe I might know what you're talking about." Adele said. "Go on."

"If you know anything about Camilla, Isabelle, Wendy, or—" I glanced at the table where Zeke had sat, but he'd eaten and left. "Or Zeke, please share."

"That's a pretty big range, Roberta," Adele said. "But lemme give a think on it, now."

"For example, was it you who told me Wendy lived here in South Lick?"

"No, wasn't me. Maybe old Corrine had the scoop on that?"

I snapped my fingers. "That's who it was. I'll ask her if there's a way to find the address."

"Hold up now, sugar pie," my aunt said. "You're not to be going and knocking on folks' doors anymore. You have to consider your delicate condition, don't you know?"

I was about to protest when I saw the twinkle in her eye and switched tactics. "Why yes, Auntie. Good heavens, I declare I feel a faint coming on."

She guffawed.

"But seriously, Adele," I went on. "I am taking my condition into account. I was curious why Wendy lives in South Lick when the rest of her life seems to be in Nashville."

"I hear tell prices are up over to the county seat. Could be South Lick is more affordable for a lady like her."

"I'll give you that. Okay, what about Camilla Kalb?" I asked. "Evermina had been mounting the same kind of smear campaign against Cammie's Kitchen as she did against my place."

Samuel lowered the paper. "Her late husband was a faithful member of my church, may the good Lord keep his soul."

"Camilla herself didn't attend services?" I asked.

"Not that I knew of," Samuel said. "Serving Sunday breakfasts at her restaurant appeared to take priority. I do not judge, but we always made sure she knew she'd be welcomed into our fold."

Adele's beau was the least judgmental person I'd ever met. I didn't attend church, either. Like Camilla, my Sunday service was serving food to others on the day of rest. My mom hadn't been a churchgoer when I was growing up, and I'd never seen a reason to do things differently. In the flipside version of Samuel's attitude, I didn't judge those who did participate in organized religion.

Which brought church stalwarts Isabelle and my B&B guests to mind. "Do either of you know much about Covenant Hope church?"

"That one we drove past a couple few days ago," Adele said.

"Yes."

Samuel gave a somber nod. "What in particular are you interested in knowing about, Robbie?"

I had my mouth open to answer when the Blounts themselves came down the interior stairs from the B&B area. I let out a sigh, instead.

"I have to get back to work. Thanks, both of you. Keep your ears open for me, please, and give me a call later if you think of anything?"

"Certainly." Samuel returned to his newspaper.

"It's a promise," Adele said. "You get along now, hon."

"Thanks for helping out earlier," I told her.

"It's what family does."

I bustled away to seat the B&B guests. Before I could reach them, a stream of older men came in—and kept coming. Most sported silver hair or balding pates, although several had dark hair that was either natural or courtesy of a hairdresser. It must be a kind of senior men's tour group.

First, I made my way to the Blounts, who stood hesitantly at the foot of the stairs. "Good morning. Let's get you seated, quickly, since it looks like a bus full of customers just unloaded."

"Thank you," Helen said.

The table Zeke had vacated was empty, clean, and reset. I led them to it. "I hope your night was comfortable."

Fred pressed his lips together.

"It was dandy, Robbie," Helen said.

"Good. One of us will be back in a moment to take your orders. Coffee first?"

"No, thank you, hon." She beamed. "We don't indulge."

I wasn't currently indulging myself, as a matter of fact. I hurried over to the gentlemen now milling around the entry area. One man with a full head of snowy white hair and a Van Dyke beard stepped forward. He had smile wrinkles at the edges of his eyes and wore a lilac polo shirt with a logo reading, CSGMC.

"Welcome to Pans 'N Pancakes, gentlemen," I began. "I'm owner Robbie Jordan." All the other men were wearing shirts bearing the same logo, with shirt colors that spanned the rainbow.

"We've heard so much about your place, Robbie," Snowy Hair said. "I know there's a lot of us, but we'd love to eat, and a few of our members can't wait to check out the cookware, too."

"You can do both. How many of you in total?"

"Eighteen, I'm afraid."

"That's fine." I glanced around the restaurant. "It might take a little while to seat everyone, but you'll be ahead of anyone who comes in after you. What's the logo?" I gestured with my chin.

"We're part of the Chicago Senior Gay Men's Chorus."

Thus the rainbow hues of the shirts. And the two fellows holding hands as they waited. I liked it. I'd heard of choruses featuring younger gay men, but why shouldn't they keep enjoying singing choral music as they aged?

"The guys elected me ad hoc leader on this trip, even though we have a travel agent doing the actual arrangements for our tour," he went on. "We had a concert last night in Bloomington. Tonight's is in Cincinnati."

"I'm sorry I missed last night's." I pointed to a table by the door. "You can check out menus there while you wait."

"Thanks." His focus moved into the restaurant area, and his eyes widened.

I turned to see whom he'd spotted. His gaze seemed to be on the Blounts. Could he possibly know them?

"Well, would you look at that? That's my baby sister, sitting right there across the room." He waved at my B&B guests and hurried toward them. "Yoo-hoo, Helen."

Fred stood and crossed his arms across his chest. *Uh-oh.* Helen rose and edged around her husband as the tour leader approached. She held out her arms to Snowy Hair. Fred turned his back as they embraced.

Danna hit the ready bell. A load of dishes slipped out of Turner's arms with a crash of crockery and a clatter of flatware. Life called. Work called. I didn't have time for cranky husbands apparently disapproving of gay brothers-in-law. I had people to feed.

CHAPTER 51

By nine o'clock we had the whole tour group seated. Fred Blount had not blown up at his wife's brother, although every time I checked, Fred and Helen were eating in silence. The restaurant was full, with a dozen hungry diners waiting, and my staff and I were operating at high efficiency. We'd done this before.

As I circulated on my rounds of coffee pouring, order taking, and check delivering, Samuel stopped me.

"I have a piece of information you might want to know," he murmured. "Any chance of a moment in private with you?"

"You're going to want to hear this." Adele waggled her eyebrows.

"I'm sorry, Samuel," I said. "I'd love to listen, but we're way too busy right now. Can you text me? Or I could call you later."

"I'm not a practitioner of the texting option on

my telephone," he said. "And I wouldn't want to put this information in writing, in any case."

"I'm sorry." What was I thinking? I knew that about him and his flip phone. "I forgot. I'll call you when I get a couple of minutes free."

"Please." His gaze went across the room, where the Blounts had risen. "It might concern a guest of yours."

Ooh. Too bad I had to wait. Did that glance mean Samuel thought Fred was connected with Evermina's murder? Or maybe he knew something about Helen.

"I, on the other hand, am the Texting Queen, as you know," Adele announced. She lowered her voice to a whisper. "My feeble brain finally came up with a tidbit about old Cammie I want to tell you."

"Feeble brain?" I scoffed. "As if. But do text me anything. As soon as you can."

"Will do." She pulled a handful of crumpled bills out of her pants pocket and laid it on the table. "Give my love to that handsome husband of yours. Come on along, sugar buns," she said to Samuel. "We got to get us to the feed store."

He gave me a helpless but happy smile and allowed himself to be propelled toward the door in Adele's persuasive wake.

It felt like I'd barely seen my handsome husband lately. We'd passed like ships in the night last evening, me being asleep when he got home and him sweetly snoring when I'd left early this morning. We had a date this afternoon, though, which made me smile.

I made my way to the Blounts' now-empty table. I'd told them breakfast was included with their room, and that my staff always appreciated tips. No cash obviously graced the table, but from under Helen's plate peeked the corner of a five-dollar bill. I left the money for Danna, who was busing, and continued on my rounds.

It was another forty-five minutes before any of us could come up for air. We'd finally zeroed out the waiting-to-eat list, and at least three tables were now empty, clean, and ready for new diners. The chorus members were finishing up.

The CSGMC diners at one four-top began crooning "Under the Boardwalk" in harmony, like our own personal barbershop quartet. The conversation at other tables quieted, and when the song finished, applause broke out. The other members of the group stood, and all began to sing a few bars of "That's What Friends Are For."

I smiled. "We should comp their meals for the entertainment, don't you think?" I asked Danna at the grill.

"Nah," she said. "They clearly love it. Is it break time?"

"Go. I'll cook." I washed my hands and inspected the waiting tickets.

Turner hit *Start* on the dishwasher.

"You go on break next." I poured the last of the crepe batter into the hot pan. "What do you think, Turner? Should we make more batter or call it quits?"

"Quits, for sure. We have to get the Coq cooking, and fast. I'll go erase the crepe special."

"Sounds good." I was no sooner deep into pour-

ing, flipping, and serving up when my phone dinged
with a text. And again. And another one. Whoever
was trying to reach me was going to have to wait.

Twenty minutes later I finally had time to check
my phone. Multiple messages had come in from
both Adele and Octavia. I grimaced, but I opened
the detective's texts before Adele's. The first one
was polite.

**Need to speak with you this AM. I can come to
store or meet downtown S Lick. Pls advise.**

The messages grew more insistent, with the last
being a borderline threat.

**Meet me ten thirty bench near gazebo or I'll be at
PandP.**

At least she didn't say she'd arrest me. I
thumbed a reply.

Will be there. Sorry.

I erased the "Sorry" and sent the message. I didn't
have anything to apologize for.

It was after ten now, and the chorus had departed, having left generous tips and made several
big cookware purchases. Only a few tables were occupied, and Turner was busy assembling the lunch
stew, which already smelled great. I could wander
downtown in a few minutes and not worry about
stranding my coworkers.

I fixed a quick cheese sandwich and read
Adele's text next. To say it was intriguing would be
an understatement.

**Cam a suspect in her late hub's death from blow
to head. Apparently from falling. Cops first thought C
hit him upside the head. Repeat with Ev?**

I gave a little whistle and wondered if Octavia
knew about that. I was about to find out.

CHAPTER 52

I slid on my sunglasses as I set out from Pans 'N Pancakes. Even though my store was situated at the edge of town, the square with the Jupiter Springs gazebo in beautiful downtown South Lick was only a few blocks away. The air continued to be brisk, with late tulips shivering in the breeze, but the full morning sun made it clear we were only a few weeks from the summer solstice.

The word "lick" in the town's name indicated a place where mineral salts were abundant in the soil and water. South Lick had been famous a hundred years ago for its healing mineral baths and recuperative water, and the gazebo marked the spot of the original spring. The more well-known city of French Lick in Orange County to our south had a similar history.

As I headed over, I realized I probably should have brought the bank bag with the weekend's and yesterday's cash and made a stop at the bank, but I hadn't taken the time to extract it from the safe in the apartment.

Anyway, the envelope had room to spare. These days the use of cash was growing more and more rare. What was increasingly common was the growing time necessary to take credit cards to our reader next to the cash register, run them, and bring slips back to customers to sign. When this case was solved, acquiring a portable card reader would be my first priority. After setting up the deep fryer, which still hadn't happened.

What Samuel had mentioned popped into my brain. I could take a second to call him about this mysterious piece of information which shouldn't be put in writing.

I paused in front of the Art Deco building housing the First Savings Bank, which was across from the Carnegie-built library and the Depot, a co-op natural foods store in the former train station. I loved that these antique structures still stood and had been repurposed over the years. They gave the downtown so much more character than various Indiana towns where the old was either torn down or had never been there in the first place.

Samuel's phone rang for so long I'd almost disconnected when his voice mail kicked in. I asked him to phone me and ended the call. It was time to face Octavia.

I found her pacing to the ornate gazebo and back.

"I seriously wasn't avoiding you," I began. "We were totally slammed at the restaurant this morning."

She gave me a look over the top of her glasses. "You're here now. Have a seat." She gestured at a wooden bench chained to the pavement. She perched on another one that sat at a right angle and pulled out her tablet, the cover of which became a flat keyboard.

"You were avoiding Chief Harris yesterday, I hear," she began.

"Kind of."

She kept giving me the look.

"All right, I admit it. I was."

"This is an official homicide investigation, Robbie. You can't just not show up for a scheduled interview."

"I'm here now." I shut my mouth before I got myself into more hot water.

"Please tell me what you've learned in the process of your amateur sleuthing." She stressed the word "amateur."

I ignored the dig. "I expect you know that Isabelle Cooper is heavily involved in the Covenant Hope church. Yesterday Wanda confirmed Isabelle was also a silent investor in Evermina's diner, and that she has a temper issue. My B&B guests, Fred and Helen Blount, are in town for a gathering at the church and seem to know Isabelle, or at least Fred does. He's a stern man who doesn't like Helen's brother, a gay man from Chicago." I stopped to take a breath.

I expected the detective to stop me or challenge what I'd told her. She didn't.

"My aunt said Camilla Kalb was suspected of murdering her husband a few years ago. By hitting him on the head."

Octavia gave a slow nod.

"Evermina had tried to malign her business." I almost added that it had been in the same way she'd cast aspersions on my restaurant, but I shut my mouth in time. I didn't want to put ideas in the detective's head about my own motive for murder. "Do you think Camilla might have killed her?"

"They didn't find sufficient evidence to charge her in her husband's death."

Which didn't answer my question. I pushed on.

"Zeke and Evermina weren't officially divorced. I saw Zeke and Wendy come out of a Nashville jeweler. Zeke had bought her an engagement ring."

Octavia raised an eyebrow. "Which she paid for."

If Wendy paid for the ring, she must have deeper pockets than Zeke, also interesting. And it was the first thing Octavia had actually shared with me.

"So that wasn't news to you," I murmured.

"No," she said. "Please continue."

I cast around for what else I knew. A too-big pickup truck bumped over a pothole. A crow atop the gazebo uttered its rattling mating call, and the wind made the American flag flap furiously, clanking its carabiner against the pole.

"This isn't hard fact, but a couple of people have mentioned they don't trust Wendy Corbett," I said. "A young customer who was in the restaurant recently said she worked for Wendy in the gift shop and was badly treated. The customer is a Black woman, a player on the IU basketball team."

"Noted." Octavia waited.

"And apparently Wendy lives in South Lick, for whatever that's worth."

"We're aware of that."

None of what I was telling her seemed to be news, but I kept going. "Did you know Zeke is left-handed? Do you know anything about how the blow was struck? Have you looked into the other suspects' handedness?"

She blinked at my barrage of questions. "Thank you. What do you know about Don O'Neill?"

Ouch. I was hoping we wouldn't have to go there.

"Begin with which hand he uses to handwrite," she said.

"His left." I knew I had to fill her in on his debts, even though my reluctance dragged like a knife through overcooked fudge. "He's also been spending money he doesn't have on collectible items like duck decoys. Like, a lot of money. He needed Evermina to pay her debts to kind of rescue his personal finances."

Octavia tapped away on the keyboard.

"But seriously, Octavia, Don didn't kill her. You have to believe me." If she went straight from here to haul in Don—again—Abe would be devastated.

"Thank you. What I have to believe is the evidence." She glanced up. "When did your current B&B guests arrive?"

"Yesterday." I tilted my head. Why was she asking that?

"Do you know anything about Fred Blount?"

"Not a thing. He has a valid credit card, and I have their address in my registration software. That's it."

"Thank you." She focused on the tablet again.

"Why do you want to know about Fred?"

The detective cleared her throat. "Do you have anything else to share?"

Did I? "I don't think so." If whatever Samuel knew was about Fred, I would pass it along. I didn't want Octavia harassing him about it.

"Very well." She closed the tablet and slid it into her black leather shoulder bag. "I appreciate your assistance."

"Sure. How's the case going, anyway?"

Octavia opened her mouth but shut it before speaking.

"Did you ever find camera footage from Friday night?" I asked, fingers crossed she'd tell me.

I was met with more silence. Her gaze rested on the ornate metal gazebo, a structure as complex as the facts surrounding Evermina's death.

"Do you think you're getting close?" I couldn't help asking. "There must be DNA evidence, right? On the skillet, I mean."

She stood. "I'll be in touch." She strode off across the square and around the corner.

All-righty, then. So much for the peaceful exchange of information. That had been more of a one-way road than a boat ride across the River Styx, one of Buck's favorite mixed metaphors.

CHAPTER 53

On my brisk walk back to the restaurant, I once again paused. I wanted to dig into Camilla's husband's death. If I waited until I arrived at Pans 'N Pancakes, I knew I'd be too busy to be poking around on the internet. I leaned against the facade of Paco's Tacos and thumbed in a search.

A couple of minutes later, all I knew was that there had been speculation about Camilla's involvement but nothing had come of it. Exactly as Octavia had said.

A church bell chimed eleven times. Danna texted two question marks and three exclamation points. My bladder insisted I attend to it.

Before I could move on, a text arrived that sent chills through me. It was from Fred Blount.

It has come to our attention that a murder was committed in the very room where you put my wife and I. Have you no sense of decency, Ms. Jordan? We have removed our belongings and will expect not

only a full refund but also damages for emotional distress.

I swallowed. *Yikes.* It was true, but who told them? Was I obliged to have let them know about the murder in March? It wasn't as if the room bore bloodstains. There hadn't even been blood. I wondered if the Blounts—Fred in particular—actually planned to sue me. This talk of damages could be a bluff to make me cough up a pile of money.

I considered replying on the spot, and quickly decided not to. I had to get back to work, and this situation merited calm thought, an activity I didn't have time for right now.

When I arrived at Pans 'N Pancakes, the lull had disappeared. Danna and Turner were working at high-speed cooking, seating the crowd waiting for tables, taking orders. After a quick visit to the facilities, I hurried to scrub my hands and tie on an apron.

"Sorry," I murmured to Turner at the grill.

"No worries." He flipped two beef burgers and sprinkled cheese on a disk of beaten egg. "But the lady at Buck's table really wants to talk to you. You can take her meal to her." He used his chin to point at a plate holding a grilled ham and cheese on sourdough, nicely cut on the diagonal, with a fat pickle spear alongside.

"Got it."

The woman at Buck's table was none other than Camilla Kalb, and she didn't look happy. What was she doing here during her own restaurant's busy lunch hour?

"Welcome, Camilla." I set down her plate. "Can I get you anything else?"

"What you can get is out of my freaking business. What do you think you're doing, going around accusing me of murdering my husband?" she hissed.

Whoa. How did she know I'd been talking about that? I cast around in my brain—fast—for how to respond.

"I'm sorry you think that," I began. "I did hear about your husband's passing. But I understand you weren't charged in his death. Right?"

She nodded, but her nostrils still flared, and her gaze was sharp.

"So he must have died of natural causes," I said in a soft voice.

"He did."

"I'm glad to hear violence wasn't involved." A diner waved at me. Danna signaled a table that needed clearing. The bell on the door kept jangling as new customers filed in. "Enjoy your lunch."

As I waded into the fray, I wondered if Camilla was protesting too much. Maybe she had killed her husband, and Evermina, too.

But I didn't have time to think about that. While Turner cooked, Danna and I had our hands full with orders, busing, cleaning, delivering food and checks, and starting the cycle anew. We got on top of the rush before too long. Three pairs of hands were definitely better in here than two at times like this.

Camilla paid Danna with a card and was near the door when Wendy breezed in. She hadn't seemed particularly happy with me last time she was in. Maybe Zeke had told her that his breakfast had gone smoothly and tasted of heaven. Or whatever.

I watched as she exchanged a hug with Camilla. The restaurateur caught sight of Wendy's new ring and seemed to admire it, except I was too far away to hear what they said to each other. I hadn't known the two were friends, but it made sense. They were both Nashville business owners and appeared more or less the same age.

A dark thought drifted into my mind. Maybe the women had worked together to kill Evermina and cover their tracks. Had Octavia considered that possibility? I gave my head a little shake. She'd never tell me even if she had.

But here came a person who might divulge, that is, if he knew anything. Buck held the door for Camilla as she left, bobbing his head to her by way of greeting. I headed his way, which was also where Wendy stood.

"Good morning." I smiled. "I think it's still morning. By some miracle we have a table open, Wendy. Sorry, Buck, it's the table you prefer but it's the last one, and Wendy was here first."

Buck might have perked up at hearing her name, but I wasn't sure.

"Please join me, sir," Wendy offered.

I was about to introduce them when he spoke.

"That's mighty kind of you, ma'am." Buck extended his hand. "Buck Bird, at your humble service." Buck wore a long-sleeve knit shirt with an SLPD embroidered patch on the arm. He also sported the uniform cargo pants I'd seen officers wear when they weren't out on patrol.

"Pleased to meet you." Wendy gave his hand a

firm shake. "I'm Wendy Corbett, owner of the Nashville Treasures gift shop in Nashville. You're with the police?"

"He's the chief of the South Lick department," I added, since he wasn't exactly attired in chief garb.

She blinked. "Is that so?"

"Yes, ma'am." Buck put on his "aw-shucks" expression.

I stepped in before Wendy changed her mind about sharing the table with a police officer—or about lunch at all. "I'll show you to the table, shall I? Please follow me." After they sat, I took their drink orders. "I didn't know you and Camilla knew each other," I said to Wendy.

She regarded me for a moment too long. "Yes, we go way back."

"That's great." This wasn't the moment to be digging into their relationship. "I'll be back after you have a chance to look at the menu. Specials are on the board."

"Why, I know what I want right now, Robbie," Buck said. "And I'm hungrier than a daddy elephant with nothing to eat but leaves."

That was a new one.

"Except I'm meeting a gaggle of folks here purt' soon and I'd best wait to order until the group shows up."

"How many are in the group?" I asked him.

"Five, six, around that."

"Thanks for letting me know." I surveyed the restaurant. A four-top would be open soon, and we could combine that with another one to handle up to eight at Buck's gathering. I glanced at Wendy. "Do you know what you'd like to eat?"

"Give me a bowl of the Coq au Vin, please," she said. "Although it seems like a rather fancy lunch offering for a place like this."

"It's a simplified version, and it's delicious. I'll go put that order in." I bustled away before she could get another dig in. *A place like this*, indeed. We were a restaurant specializing in delicious food, whether fancy or simple.

CHAPTER 54

Corrine showed up not five minutes later, followed by the fire chief, the town clerk, the head of the chamber of commerce, and Barb, the chair of the planning board, who also worked at Shamrock Hardware. The South Lick governing elite planned to eat together, apparently. This must be the group lunch Buck had arrived early for.

I hurried to the door. "Buck gave me a heads-up about your group, Corrine. We're arranging the tables now."

"Sorry, hon, I plum forgot to call and let you know." Corrine threw a hand up in a what-can-you-do gesture.

Buck left Wendy with her lunch and joined the group, and I had them all seated without delay. I took orders for coffee and sodas.

"What's the occasion?" I asked.

"Barb managed to snag us a big state grant,"

Corrine pointed at her. "I thought we should oughta celebrate."

"Congratulations." I smiled at the trim woman with the spiked silver hair.

"I even got a bottle of bubbly," Corrine added. "Can you take and bring us glasses please, Robbie?"

"You got it. You know they aren't stemmed."

"Not a problem."

At a restaurant like mine without a liquor license, the state allowed diners to bring their own alcohol as long as I opened and poured it. Normally we served water, juices, and sodas in heavy plastic pint glasses, but I'd acquired a dozen squat glass glasses for occasions like this.

Corrine followed me to the cabinet where I stored them.

"I can help carry." She glanced around and lowered her voice. "I saw Wendy over there. She hasn't been arrested yet?"

"Do you mean for the murder?" I stared up at Corrine. "What do you know?"

"Nothing much. Little bit of this, touch of that." She patted her luxurious big hair. "Considering her priors and all."

"Prior whats?" I wanted to screech but kept my voice as low as I could.

"Arrest for assault was one. Discrimination in hiring was another. Possible tax evasion, too."

"Wow. Was she convicted on any of those?"

"No. She's a weasel, that one. Plus, she's got family money, so her fancy-pants lawyer keeps getting her off."

I shifted my gaze to Wendy, trying not to be obvious. No such luck. She was shooting eye-daggers at Corrine and me.

"Let's get that bubbly open for you, shall we?" I grabbed a nearby tray and loaded it up with enough glasses for the table.

Danna appeared at Corrine's side. "Hey, Mama." She gave her mom a hip bump.

"Hey, girlie."

"Stop monopolizing my boss's time, okay?" Danna smiled. "We're wicked busy."

Sean's new favorite Massachusetts adjective must be making the rounds.

"Sure thing, sweetie-pie." Corrine leaned over to kiss Danna's cheek. She sauntered back to her gathering, greeting my customers as she went, ever the mayor.

As I delivered the glasses, popped the bubbly, and poured for the group, what was on my mind were Wendy's priors. Discrimination in hiring— was that what Janae had been talking about? And assault? Jeez. Wendy presented an attractive, respectable front. Her history sounded like anything but.

I gave the town officials a minute to toast Barb and the funded grant proposal. I headed over to take their orders.

Buck, who had covered his glass with his hand when I was pouring the sparkling wine, ordered first. "Give me a double cheeseburger, please. With a pile of them cheesy grits and an order of biscuits with gravy. The meat kind, mind you."

"Yes, Buck." We often also offered a miso gravy

for vegetarians, but I doubted miso had ever crossed Buck's lips.

I delivered his and the other orders to Turner. "Want me to sub in at the grill?"

"No, I'm good."

Danna was busy with the dishwasher. When Wendy signaled she'd like my attention, I drew the short straw, lucky or otherwise.

"Can I get you anything else?" I asked her.

"No, I'm good. Only my check."

I laid it face down on her table and picked up her soup bowl and spoon.

"What were you and Mayor Beedle talking about?" Wendy's low voice felt borderline menacing.

"Nothing much."

"I find that hard to believe."

"She's here celebrating a big grant for the town," I said. "You live in South Lick, right?"

"Yes." She clamped her lips shut, stood, and handed me a ten-dollar bill.

"The grant's a really good thing for the community."

"I'm sure it is. Keep the change."

"My staff appreciates it," I said, but she'd already gone.

She traced a great circle route toward the door, staying as far away from Corrine and Buck as she could.

I didn't know much, but one thing was clear. Wendy Corbett hadn't liked us talking about her, not one little bit.

CHAPTER 55

Buck seemed to be having a relaxed day. He lingered instead of joining his fellow town employees when they left to get back to their jobs. Corrine picked up the tab for the entire group and also left a hefty tip.

After asking whether I needed his table for other diners, to which I'd replied we didn't, Buck stretched out those long legs nearly to Michigan and worked on his phone.

Maybe he'd picked up news about the case. We'd had quite the run of what I'd been regarding as homicide suspects in the restaurant today. Zeke, Camilla, and Wendy had all eaten here. Not Don, but Don really didn't belong on the list. Would Isabelle stop in for a bite before we closed, too? She wouldn't if Fred Blount had anything to do with it, I supposed.

Next time I had the chance, I paused in my rounds at Buck's table.

"Buck, you didn't meet Fred and Helen Blount,

my B&B guests, yesterday, but I know you saw them in here."

"Along with the Cooper lady."

"Yes. She's hosting them at the megachurch."

"Covenant Hope. But what about them two?"

I glanced around, but nobody sat close enough to hear us if we kept our voices down.

"I put them in the Rose Room, because it's my nicest one. Fred apparently heard about the murder in there and got all freaked-out by it."

"That's a crying shame."

"No kidding," I said. "I mean, the room isn't haunted or anything, and you know as well as I do there weren't any stains."

"You'd be right about that."

"Fred texted a couple of hours ago that he and Helen had removed their belongings and expect a full refund," I said. "He also threatened me with damages for emotional harm."

"That seems a bit over the top, don't it?"

"I'll say. His wife's a sweetheart. My earlier interactions with him were far from pleasant, but this seems extreme."

The bell jangled with a foursome of late lunchers entering.

"What do you think, Buck? Am I obliged to tell customers about a murder in a room? What if that means I can't ever rent that room again?" I heard my voice rising but I couldn't help it. "And can he sue me for emotional distress?"

Buck gave me his full attention. "Set down a little minute here." He pointed at the chair next to his. "Those folks'll wait."

Danna was on the grill by now. Turner glanced

at me and headed over to the door to seat the new-comers. We weren't slammed at the moment. I sat.

"Listen, Robbie. You can't be getting yourself all shook up about a hypothetical situation. It might could be good in the future to caution renters about that room's history. But you know what the flip side might be?"

I shook my head. This emotional roller coaster of pregnancy was doing a number on my brain. I was the one going through emotional distress, and I had no idea what he was talking about.

"Could be guests out there who would compete to stay in a room where a murdered soul might linger, where they could indulge all the ghoul their imaginations got to offer."

"Seriously?" I stared at him.

"Surely as my name's Buckham Hamilton Bird. Folks is weird, Robbie. No two ways about it. One person's freak-out might be another's welcome fantasy. Don't you worry your head about it."

"But can Fred sue me?"

"Oh, 'course not. And you can tell him Chief Bird said so."

I doubted Buck's opinion carried much legal weight, but it was a comfort in the moment.

"How you been feeling, anyhoo?" he asked. "You know, with nurturing that bun in the oven."

I smiled at his caring. "I'm actually feeling better, physically, the last few days. And Abe and I have our first appointment with a midwife late this afternoon."

"You're going with midwives? That's good. My Melia did, too, for all three of ours."

"And she's an MD. That she trusted midwives with her births says a lot."

"Truly. The second two was born at home, in fact."

I sat back to think about that. A medical doctor who gave birth at home. Not to her first, but even that delivery was midwife-assisted. The thought of not having to make a frantic drive to a hospital while in labor sounded like it had merits. I was going to have to have another long talk with Melia Bird one of these days. And discuss everything with Abe, as well.

"Now, then." Buck interrupted my thoughts. "Full disclosure, Robbie. Old Haley over to Nashville asked me to find out what you know about the case. Out of professional courtesy and all whatnot."

Six more people pushed through the door. I had to get back to my team.

"She said you've been avoiding her," he added.

"I have." I stood. "How about you suggest that Harris ask Octavia? I told her everything I know a couple of hours ago."

Buck regarded me. He bobbed his head. "That seems fair."

"Right now I need to get back to work. Thanks for your support, Buck."

"Any time. You take good care, my friend."

"I promise. You, too."

I hadn't learned anything new about Evermina's homicide, but at least Buck had helped me settle my feelings about the Rose Room and its prospects for future rentals. A rumor about a benevolent ghost sighting might not be such a bad thing for business, after all.

CHAPTER 56

The populace of South Lick and surrounds seemed determined to keep my restaurant full right up until closing. As always, that was great for the bottom line. But by two o'clock, my crew and I were tired. We'd run out of the Coq au Vin, the grits were gone, and we were scraping the bottom of the sausage gravy pot.

I was headed for the door to turn the sign to CLOSED half an hour early when Isabelle Cooper came in. My palms grew sweaty. I totally didn't want an in-person confrontation with the Blounts right now.

Except nobody followed her inside. *Whew.* I went over to greet her—and to lock the door to incoming diners.

"Welcome back." I smiled, even though it was a pro forma version of my usual smile. "A table for one?"

"Thank you." She didn't return the smile, pro forma or otherwise. Her navy windbreaker and matching athletic pants were of a top brand, and her pristine runners didn't look like she'd ever worn them for jogging on pavement, not to mention trail running in dirt and mud.

I led her to a recently cleared two-top. "Coffee?"

"No, thank you. Water will be fine for now."

"We'll be back to get your order in a minute, unless you know what you'd like now."

"I'd like a turkey burger, no bun, with extra lettuce and tomato."

I waited.

"Please. And a non-fat milk."

"Certainly."

I gave Danna Isabelle's zero-carb, protein-rich request. "She's the last customer. I turned the sign and locked the door."

"Good." She laid a turkey patty on the grill, which was nearly full with bacon and burgers. "Did you put in a food order this morning?"

"I managed to, yes. It should be here before four."

"We're running low on all kinds of basics."

"I know." Standing here next to all these delectable savory smells gave me hunger pangs. When had I eaten last? "Can you do up a cheeseburger for me, please, Danna? I don't think I've eaten in a while."

"Sure. Want a double? You're eating for two, don't forget."

"No, thanks. This baby's only about the size and weight of a cream puff right now. A single burger will be fine, especially considering I'm going to have to scarf it down standing."

Danna lowered her voice. "That Cooper lady's got her eye on you, you know."

"I'm not surprised." I didn't turn to check. "She probably came here less to eat than to have a word with me about the Rose Room." I filled Danna in on Fred's text.

"That stinks." She wrinkled her nose. "But don't worry. Make up an Irish ghost and you won't be able to keep lodgers away."

I laughed. "Buck also advised me to do that."

A few minutes later I set Isabelle's lunch in front of her. "What else can I get you?"

"I'm all set, thanks." She picked up the milk glass with her left hand.

Was that habitual or because I'd set it down on that side?

Loud knocking came from the front door. I looked over to see Wanda's face pressed against the glass. My phone buzzed with a text. Probably from her.

"You keep strange company in here, Ms. Jordan." Isabelle pointed her chin at the door. "Just so you know, I'm not talking to that cop again. Not in here, not outside."

"Got it. Enjoy your lunch." I stepped away but didn't move toward the door. I faced Wanda and made a windshield-wiper movement with my forearm and index finger signaling "no". I swiped into her text.

Gotta talk with U. Why's the door locked? I'm hungry.

I thumbed a reply to her message that was part demanding, part plaintive.

Closed early. No time to talk, sorry.

I hated to disappoint Wanda, but I didn't have the physical or mind energy right now to deal with one more police officer of any stripe. Especially not with a customer, guilty or not, who'd already been subjected to an involuntary interrogation on my front porch twenty-four hours ago. I added one more text to Buck's cousin.

Come back at 3:30. We can talk then.

Wanda didn't respond, but she did turn away from the door.

"Excuse me, Ms. Jordan?" Isabelle hailed me. "There was one more thing."

"Yes?"

"We'd like to get a quote from you on catering an event for our church."

"I don't really do catering," I began. "But thank you."

"Please? It's for a group of important folks from out of town. Investors, to be honest. And we'll make it worth your while."

Huh. "What day are you looking at?"

"It's a luncheon this coming Monday."

"I'll have to think about it. Can I get back to you tonight?"

"Very well." She didn't look happy about having to wait. She pulled out a business card. "You can call me at that number."

"Or text?"

She gazed at the ceiling for a second. "Or text, but I'd prefer the courtesy of a phone call. This is a good opportunity for you to build your business, you know."

"Thank you." I pocketed the card and turned away.

What did she know about my business? We were already super busy, popular, and thriving financially without a minute of catering. I wasn't set up with warming trays or portable anything. Plus, now more than ever, I needed my Mondays off to rest, regroup, and get ready to be a mother in half a year's time or less.

CHAPTER 57

A few minutes later, a text came in from Abe that made my heart sink.

Don's on his way over to see you. Please talk him down if you can. I can't get away.

Talk him down from what? At the same time, I spied Don peering through the glass in the door. When he saw me, he waggled his fingers in greeting. This I did not need. Still, I trudged over there. What if he wanted to speak to Isabelle? Would she refuse to talk with him? Would he start a family fight?

I paused to send a quick text back to Abe saying nothing more than "okay". I gave a quick glance at Isabelle. Had she seen Don? She was studying her phone, but I had the feeling she'd whipped it out to make it seem as though she hadn't been studying the newcomer, one she had a long and fraught past with.

"Do you mind if we talk outside?" I asked Don at the door, trying to block both his way and his view.

His hair was mussed and his shirt misbuttoned, making one corner of the collar stick up.

"We've already closed," I added.

"Um, sure. Except it's a little brisk out here." He glanced inside. "Maybe we could . . . oh, crackers. Is that Isabelle?"

"Yes." I stepped out and shut the door behind me.

Don turned to me, looking even worse than before, if that was possible. "Should I go sit with Izzy?"

I shook my head. "Unless you've already reconciled with her, I don't think that's a good idea." The air had warmed a bit, but now a heavy blanket of gloomy clouds made the afternoon damp and chilly in a different way.

"But I haven't seen her in such a long time."

I took him by the arm and led him away from the door. "Don. Do you think she wants to see you?"

"No, but—"

"Then right now in my restaurant is not the place to have a reunion, especially if it might turn into a confrontation. Abe said you came over to talk to me, not her. Yes?"

"Yes. Except it's about her, in a way."

About Isabelle? This could be interesting. "All right. I have to get back to work in a minute. What's up?"

"Actually, it's about Bernard, her husband. Her late husband." Don blew out a long breath, picking at the cuff of his shirt. "I remembered a bit I overheard. At the time, I didn't think there was anything wrong with it. But now . . ."

I waited. He kept picking, avoiding my gaze.

"But now, what, Don?"

"Robbie, I think Isabelle might have killed Bernard."

Yikes. I sank down to sit on one of the rocking chairs. "Are you kidding?"

"Not at all." He perched on the edge of the bench next to me. "I wish I were."

"What did you overhear?" I asked. "What do you know?"

"It was one of the last times she was at the house, a few years ago. Mind you, Cooper was already pretty old when she married him, but he was still alive and apparently doing well at that time. Izzy was in the other room on the phone."

"Who was she talking to?"

"I'm positive it was their estate lawyer." His voice dropped to a whisper. "She was asking about their wills. Bernard Cooper died a month later."

"What did he die of?"

"They said it was a fall, during which he suffered a blow to the head and had a massive brain bleed. There was nothing they could do." He turned haunted eyes toward me. "What if she cracked him on the head same as she did Evermina?"

"You think Isabelle killed her?"

"I don't know," he mumbled. "I wouldn't put it past her."

"You have to tell the police what you remembered." I stood. "Please."

"But I can't, Robbie. Don't you see? They already think I'm the murderer of the week. They'll accuse me of trying to scapegoat my estranged stepdaughter."

"I appreciate you letting me know." I blew out a

breath. "I'm sorry, Don. Tell the police or don't tell them. Right now, I have to get back to work. Let's talk later, okay?" I made the thumb-and-pinky phone gesture.

He rose. "All right."

As I made my way inside, this time Isabelle didn't try to hide her stare. Not at me, but at Don on the porch behind me.

CHAPTER 58

"Hey boss, when are we going to set up the fryer?" Turner asked at three o'clock as he carried a box of just-delivered produce to the walk-in.

The store was empty of customers and quiet for the first time since seven this morning.

I groaned. "Not today, that's for sure. I'm beat, and the day isn't over yet. The box isn't too much in the way, is it?"

"It's fine," Danna chimed in from where she was scrubbing the grill. "But don't you have to get out of here for your appointment?"

"Not yet," I said. "It's not until four thirty." I wiped the last table clean and headed back to the kitchen.

"What was up with Wanda trying to get in after we were closed?" Turner, back from the cooler, hefted another box of food from the order.

"I don't know," I said. "Unfortunately, I told her to come back at three thirty."

I hoped Wanda wouldn't return. All I wanted was a stretch of peace to calm my mind as I did breakfast prep. I also hadn't given a minute of thought of questions to ask the midwife. Maybe they'd come to me on the way. Abe would probably come up with a slew, with his inquisitive mind and his caring enthusiasm about becoming a father for the second time.

I'd never asked him how Sean's birth had gone. Both Abe and his wife had been young new parents who had split up when Sean was a toddler. Had Abe been present when Sean was born? Either way, he'd certainly bonded with him and had been an involved, devoted father ever since.

As I started the dishwasher, I thought of Isabelle's request. "I didn't tell you guys about what Isabelle Cooper asked me."

"I hope she's not looking for a job," Danna said. "She seems cold to me. Sharp."

Danna's instincts were on the nose. Isabelle did seem sharp around the edges, and not a bit warm.

"No, not a job for her," I said. "She wants us to cater an important investor lunch at her church on Monday."

"Churches have investors?" Turner frowned. "Since when?"

"Maybe hers is more like a business than a place of worship," I said. "I have no idea."

"We're, like, not set up for catering at all," Danna said.

"Which is what I told her. Plus, we all need our day off, right?"

"You most of all, Madam Pregnancy." Danna smiled.

"I know. I think, as the year goes on, I'm going to need to have two days off in a week. But I'm good for now. We'll figure it out if Len doesn't want any midweek shifts."

"I might know a person who would be a good fit," Turner offered. "A woman I met in culinary class."

"Perfect," I said. "Maybe you should bring her in one day and I can see if I think she'd mesh well."

"I'll twist her arm."

"Anyway, I told Isabelle I'd get back to her. But it's going to be a firm 'no' when I do."

"Fine with us. By the way, Robbie, what did Don want?" Danna asked. "We saw you talking to him on the porch."

I opened my mouth. And closed it. I didn't need to enmesh my staff in Don's conjecture about what Isabelle did or did not do.

"He's kind of messed up right now," I said. "He hasn't been cleared in the homicide, and Abe sent him over for me to calm him down."

"He's a totally nice guy." Turner crossed his arms. "If a bit of a dweeb. He wouldn't have murdered Ms. Martin."

"Seriously," Danna agreed. "No way."

"I'm with you both a hundred percent on that," I said. "But it's a matter of convincing the authorities." And figuring out if Don's suggestion about Bernard Cooper's death would hold up under the close scrutiny of the law.

I glanced around the room. The food order was put away. The dishwasher hummed, the floor was swept, and the tables were clean.

"Clear out, you two." I smiled. "I'll finish up."

Danna and Turner exchanged a quick look. I didn't miss it, but I couldn't interpret what it meant.

"I have an idea for a couple of specials for to-morrow," Turner said.

"Yeah, we'll handle them." Danna slid her apron over her head.

"Perfect. Thanks, and see you in the morning."

A minute later I was alone. I took a necessary break and drank down a full glass of water. I slid the now-cooled cheeseburger onto a plate and sat to eat before I tackled prep. If Wanda showed up again, so be it.

But she didn't, which left my mind free to pick over what Don had said as I prepped biscuit dough, mixed up pancake ingredients, and chopped veg-etables for the morning omelets.

Don was suspicious of Isabelle's call to their es-tate lawyer a month before her husband died. It could have been totally innocent, her simply want-ing to make sure all their ducks were in a row. Bernard had been much older than she, after all.

Still, Don's suspicions might be valid. Had he contacted the police after he left here? I doubted it. Should I butt in? I didn't picture that going over well with any of them. Not Harris, not Octavia, not even Wanda. He was probably right. They'd think he was trying to transfer blame onto anyone but himself.

I wished I'd asked him what Isabelle's husband had hit his head on. Or, rather, what Don thought Isabelle had employed to crack over the poor man's skull. Unless . . . had the old man been found in the kitchen? If his wife had used a skillet to kill him with, she might have grabbed one again off of Camilla's outhouse to use on Evermina's head. For all I knew, she might be plotting how to hit a snoopy amateur sleuth on the noggin, as well.

The thought raised goose bumps on my arms. I glanced at the front door. Yes, it was locked. I'd done it myself. My gaze flew to the service door. Had Turner slid a wedge into the gap when he was bringing in boxes from the delivery truck and forgotten to remove it? No, it looked securely closed. Like the front door, the side entrance had a fire bar on the inside that we kept locked to prevent anyone from entering from the outside. But it let folks—like me, right here, right now—get out with nothing more than an elbow's pressure, if necessary.

My hands were covered with flour. I couldn't stop to internet search for "Bernard Cooper cause of death." I promised myself I would the minute the prep was done.

CHAPTER 59

I never got a chance to run that search.
By four o'clock I'd finished the next day's food
prep and tidying up after it. My hands were clean,
and I had about ten minutes before I needed to
leave for our midwifery appointment in Bloomington. I wished we'd found a care provider who practiced closer to South Lick, but this midwife had
received enthusiastic endorsements from a couple
of friends. She'd assured me the fifteen miles
wouldn't be a problem.

Abe was already in Bloomington taking his last
exam, and we'd arranged to meet at the midwife's
office and grab a bite to eat at one of our favorite
restaurants after the appointment.

I was about to sit down with my phone when a
text buzzed in from Don.

**Come by the house ASAP. Thought of something
to tell you.**

That sounded interesting. I still had those ten

minutes, and his place was on my route toward Bloomington. Why not? I didn't bother answering.

With work behind me for the day, I'd rather have my mind on my baby and Abe. I'd rather be focusing my mental and emotional energy on the person we were about to meet, by all reports a warm and welcoming expert in prenatal care and the process of labor and delivery. But if a few minutes of hearing out Abe's brother would help clear him of the murder, taking the time was worth it.

Before I could leave the store, my phone rang with a call from Samuel. I connected and greeted him.

"Robbie, you need to be very careful around Isabelle Cooper." His voice was low, as if he didn't want anyone to hear. "She's not what she seems and can be dangerous."

My brows came together. "What do you mean?" What exactly did he know?

"I can specify later."

"Samuel, please call the county sheriff's number and tell them, or the Nashville police. Please?"

He let out a sigh. "I suppose I must. I hate to malign one of God's children."

"If it's true, it's not maligning, and you could help keep others of God's flock safe." I hoped using his kind of language would convince him.

He agreed and hung up. I stared at the phone. Then gave my head a shake. I knew Samuel would make the call. I needed to get going, or else I'd lose my brief window of free time before Abe's and my appointment.

As I drove, though, a vaguely formed thought

about Don's message pecked at my consciousness. Something had been off about his text. But what? It wasn't until I was a block away from his house that the answer came to me. He hadn't used "please" in the text. Don was nothing if not always polite to the point of groveling. No, he wasn't that extreme, but he took Midwestern deferential to new heights.

Except his text had been nearly an order. I shrugged. He was stressed. Worrying about his future could have overcome his normal polite habits.

I turned the corner. *Oh, no.* I slowed and pulled to the curb across from and a few homes short of Don's.

A silver SUV sat in Don's driveway blocking his old Jeep Wrangler. A big silver SUV, exactly like the one Isabelle had driven too fast and too close behind me out near her church a few days ago.

"Izzy," Don's stepdaughter who refused to reconcile with him. Isabelle, the silent investor in Evermina's financially mismanaged diner. Sister Cooper, heavily involved in a church that apparently needed new investors. Mrs. Cooper, the young wife who might have killed her much older—and rich—husband. Isabelle with the temper issues.

CHAPTER 60

I had a very bad feeling about all this. It got worse when I spotted the duck decoy on Don's front stoop. What was that doing there?

I brought out my phone and zoomed in on the carved waterfowl, trying to keep my hand from shaking. As I suspected, it was the gorgeous wood duck, the one he'd said was worth a ton of bucks. I snapped a photo, zoomed out again, and got one of the house, decoy, and SUV. I zoomed in on the vehicle's license plate and snapped that photo, too.

Rain began spitting onto my windshield, that gray blanket of moisture now wringing itself out onto the world.

Don would never, ever put an expensive decoy outside to be ruined by the weather. Had Isabelle wrested it from him, maybe to take home for herself or to sell?

Or had Don placed it there as a kind of SOS?

My heart pounding, I put my little car in park. I

didn't have a speck of doubt that Isabelle had forced him to send that text to me. More likely, she'd taken his phone and sent it herself, thus the imperious, non-deferential tone. I was also a hundred percent positive she thought I would storm the door and try to rescue my husband's meek older brother.

On that count, she would be wrong. I might have tried to pull off a rescue in the past. Not anymore.

I hoped Don was still alive. I prayed she didn't have a gun. And I could only assume she'd held off on wielding her favorite weapon—a heavy object—until I got there. I was the snoop getting close to her crime, not Don.

What I was a hundred-percent sure of was that I was staying right here, safe in my car, doors locked. I had other weapons at my disposal, primary among them the phone in my hand.

I tried Buck's number. No luck. Octavia didn't pick up, either. I would have to call 911.

I raced through telling the regional dispatcher Don's name and address. "His stepdaughter Isabelle Cooper is in his house. She's very dangerous and has killed before." I didn't even hedge that with a *might have.* I gave my name, and said I was in my car across the street and didn't currently feel in danger. "Isabelle's silver SUV is in the driveway."

"Can you see the plate number?"

"I took a picture of it."

She gave me a number where I could text the shot.

"But you need to contact Detective Slade of the state police as soon as you can," I urged the dispatcher. "Or South Lick's Chief Bird, or Nashville's Chief Harris. Or all of them. Please hurry. This has to do with the recent homicide in Nashville."

"Hang on." I heard her speak away from the phone. She spoke to me again. "Ma'am, you need to leave the area if you can do so safely. Keep this call open, but drive away from the house."

I wanted to stay and make sure Don was all right. I also didn't want to put my baby in harm's way.

"Yes, ma'am. I'll be around the corner." I texted the plate number photo and laid the phone on the passenger seat. I put the car in gear and wrestled the steering wheel into a U-turn. I glanced back at the house. I wasn't sure, but I thought one of the drapes twitched in the front window.

The sound of a siren in the distance had never sounded so good.

CHAPTER 61

I didn't exactly go around the corner. I made another U-turn at the intersection and parked so I could see Don's house. From my position, I had a good view when two South Lick cruisers tore past me. A state vehicle and a brown-and-tan SUV from the Brown County Sheriff's department followed.

The cruisers parked at angles blocking the street in both directions. Two SLPD officers crept out and slipped around the left side of the house. Two others guarded the other corner.

Octavia slid out of the statey car passenger side. She wore a bulky police vest and an unzipped state police jacket, one of the few times I'd seen her out of a blazer. A county sheriff pulled out a weapon to cover her as Octavia strode to the front door.

She rang the doorbell and waited. Nothing happened. She tried the handle. The door didn't open. She retreated to behind the state vehicle.

I jumped at a knock on my passenger window. Wanda stood there making a downward pointing gesture. I turned on the engine and lowered the window. She peered in.

"You all right, Robbie?"

"Yes. Thanks."

"You haven't seen Ms. Cooper, I gather. You didn't go inside."

"No. I mean, correct, on both counts."

"So you don't know if she's holding him hostage, or if they're only having themselves a little chat, friendly like."

"I don't. Not for sure."

She began to turn away.

"Wanda," I called, waiting until I had her attention again. "Listen, there's an expensive duck decoy on the front stoop. Don collects them, to the detriment of his bank account. That's his most costly one. He never would have left it out in the rain."

She tilted her head as if she didn't believe me.

"I think he found a way to put it there as a distress signal," I said. "Like an SOS. You," I waved in the direction of the house and the assembled law enforcement types. "You all have to rescue him. Please."

Wanda nodded. This time I didn't stop her when she turned away to speak into the mike in her shirt.

"Copy that, ma'am," my phone said.

I'd forgotten about the dispatcher listening in.

"Your doors and windows are locked, correct?" she asked.

"Yes, ma'am." I raised the passenger window all the way up. I left the engine on, in case I had to get away fast.

"Please continue to keep this call open."

What, in case Isabelle got out and snuck up behind my car? That wasn't going to happen. But it might. My throat thickened at the thought.

"I will."

Behind me, another cruiser pulled across the road sideways, blocking it. Beyond the house at the far corner another panda car did the same. A man in an apron appeared on the front porch of the house to my right, craning his neck to see what was happening. Other neighbors peered out of doors and windows.

Sounds from Don's house got my attention. Despite my promise, I cracked my window two inches so I could hear better.

"This is the police." Octavia spoke through a bullhorn, her voice low and forceful. "Isabelle Cooper, we need you to come outside with your hands up."

Nothing happened.

Octavia raised the bullhorn again. "Don O'Neill, please open the front door of your home and come out, if you are able."

Still nothing. My phone vibrated with a text. I looked down and brought my hand to my mouth. It was from Don. Or Don's number.

"I'm getting a text ostensibly from Don," I told the dispatcher.

"Please open it and tell me what it says."

I tapped open the message. My breath rushed in, but I read the words aloud.

I will kill him unless you personally come into the house.

"Under no circumstances should you leave your vehicle, ma'am," the dispatcher said. "The officers at the scene have been made aware of the message."

In fact, Octavia turned toward my car. I could see her frown from here. She pointed at me and shook her head, slowly, firmly. Left. Right. Left. Right.

"I won't." I whispered to the dispatcher. I swallowed down a sob. I tucked my cold, numb hands in my armpits. I rocked forward and back.

When were they going to act? Didn't they have a SWAT team to storm the house? They had to save Don, I thought. They had to.

Buck's unmistakable form appeared next to Octavia. And was that shorter officer Chief Harris? Octavia turned away from the house and the three appeared to confer. I didn't know where Wanda had gone. For the sake of her baby, I hoped she was staying as far away from the danger as I was.

Isabelle didn't have a chance. I wished with all my might that Don would.

A big, dark, tanklike vehicle crept past the nearest cruiser and down the street past me. It stopped in the middle of the road short of Don's house. Out climbed, finally, the special weapons and tactics team, each with SWAT labeling their back. Dark gray helmets with visors pulled down. Shields in hand. Weapons held loosely. They slid behind the vehicles in front of the house.

A quiet ambulance followed the SWAT conveyance. It idled on the street next to me.

Octavia stepped closer to the building and raised

the bullhorn again. "Ms. Cooper, I'd like to speak with you. Please answer your phone or Mr. O'Neill's, as you wish."

As she spoke, the SWAT officers split up, two jogging to each side of Don's house, two surrounding the front door. One of those held what had to be an assault rifle in front of her, the other a thick rod.

What if they stormed the house? Isabelle could panic and kill Don. I kept rocking. Watching. Waiting. Worrying.

Octavia gave the bullhorn one more try. "Isabelle Cooper, we need you to come outside now. With or without Don."

When the door didn't open, she gave the two SWAT officers a nod. The one on the right had raised the battering ram when the door opened. Don stumbled out.

I held my breath. Would Isabelle follow with her own weapon? But she didn't.

An officer hurried up and helped Don down the steps and to the safety of a cruiser. The two on the landing rushed inside, weapons up, bumping the decoy into the shrubs as they went.

All I cared about was that Don was alive. He was upright and mobile. Whatever else happened, he'd survived.

CHAPTER 62

After a few minutes of me itching to get out of my car and go talk to Don, to Buck, to anyone, the ambulance pulled up in front of the house. One EMT hurried inside with his red bag, while the other bumped the wheels of a folded stretcher up the steps. Either Don had hurt Isabelle, or she'd hurt herself.

"I'm going to disconnect the call now, ma'am," my buddy the dispatcher said, her first communication since before Don's appearance.

"Thank you for keeping me safe," I told her.

"You're welcome. Glad you followed orders. All's well that ends well." Her voice smiled before she ended the call.

She must field plenty of calls that don't end as well as this one, at least for the good guys. I grabbed the phone and stepped out of the car.

As I hurried toward the cluster of cruisers and official SUVs, the EMTs carried the stretcher down the front steps. It was now loaded with a blanket-clad, strapped-on, and fully conscious Isabelle. One of the SWAT officers followed, weapon lowered but at the ready.

A bulky bandage over one eye and around her head, Isabelle raised her voice. "He attacked me first, I tell you. My own stepfather!" She tried to lift her head but winced and abandoned the movement.

I waited until the rear doors of the ambulance shut behind her before moving closer. Buck ambled to my side.

"Is Don okay?" I asked.

"Sure ''nuff, thanks to you. Want to see him?"

"Please."

Buck took my arm and led me to the cruiser. The front passenger door was open, and Don sat sideways in the front seat, his feet on the ground. He gripped a paper cup, but his hand shook. Good thing it had a lid. The coffee or whatever the cup held would have been all over him.

"Robbie." His voice was tremulous. "You saved my life."

I leaned in for a gentle hug. "It looked to me like you saved your own, Don."

"You folks excuse me, now." Buck stepped away.

Haley Harris approached. "It was your call that made all the difference, Robbie," she said.

"Thank you." I looked at Don. "Isabelle sent that text to me, not you, right?"

"She forced me to," he murmured. "I'm so sorry Robbie."

"Don't be." I smiled. "The thing is, you didn't include 'please.' The wording was so not you."

Harris peered at me. "That's how you knew?"

"Yep." I didn't elaborate about my insecure brother-in-law habitually going overboard on deferring to others. I addressed Don again. "Did Isabelle come over pretending to want to reconcile with you?"

"Exactly."

"And you pretended you were about to put the wood duck outside as a spring decoration. I figured it had to be a sign that you were in trouble."

"You figured that out?" he asked.

"It was easy." Realizing the significance of the decoy's placement made me feel almost Sherlockian. "You'd never leave that expensive carving out in the weather."

"Never," Don agreed. "Anyway, once I let her in, I could tell she didn't mean to make up, to be family again. She wanted a way to get to you, Robbie. She said you knew she'd killed Evermina." He swallowed as he glanced at Chief Harris.

"You asserted your innocence to us, sir, and rightly so," Harris said. "But we had to follow up all leads."

Don gazed at me, not at Harris, as he continued. "Izzy asked me to make tea, but once we were in the kitchen . . ."

"She grabbed the skillet, right?" I remembered Abe had told me his brother liked to leave his cast-iron frying pan on the stove top. I'd seen it when I visited him.

"She did."

"What did you do to disable her?" I kept my voice gentle. "I mean, if you don't mind talking about it."

"She'd forced me to come back into the front

room. Asking for tea was a ruse, and I guess she wanted to keep an eye on the street. After the cops showed up in force, she got distracted when it looked like the SWATs were about to break in with guns firing. I didn't want to do it, but I stabbed her in the face with the bill of the red-breasted merganser. It slipped and went into her eye." His voice broke.

"That was so hard for you." I touched his shoulder. "You'd been as good as her father."

"My family, that part of my family, is in the past now." He straightened his back. "After I attacked Izzy, she fell down, and I opened the door."

"A courageous move, Mr. O'Neill," Chief Harris said.

"It was self-preservation, ma'am," Don said. "I didn't want to get shot, and that merganser's bill is one of the sharpest of all waterfowl. Robbie, you were brilliant to stay away from the house."

"That was an act of double self-preservation," I said softly.

"Saving yourself and my future niece or nephew." Don mustered a weak smile.

Harris did a double take, staring at me. "You're pregnant?"

I smiled. "Yes, but only a few months along." I knew I wasn't showing yet. "And . . ." My eyes widened. I clapped my palm to my forehead. I swore. My phone buzzed with a text from Abe. "And I just missed my very first midwife appointment."

CHAPTER 63

"Paco knows what he's doing when it comes to food, doesn't he?" Abe asked as the four of us finished last bites of our takeout.

I'd insisted Don come home with me. Plus, his house was now a crime scene. Abe had rescheduled the midwife after I called him to explain why I was AWOL. Sean had ordered a Paco's Tacos dinner for four, set the table, and picked up the order by the time we all convened on the house.

"Totally." Sean swiped one last piece of tortilla around his plate. He stood and held out his hands, gesturing for our plates. He deposited the lot in the kitchen, then came back. "I'll do those later, Dads."

"Sounds good," Abe said.

Sean stepped over to Don and wrapped his arms around him. "I'm glad you're okay, Uncle Don."

When Don's eyes filled, mine did, too. I glanced at Abe swiping his own eyes.

Sean straightened, glancing around at us. "Hey, now, oldsters, don't go getting all sappy on me."

"Who me?" Don sniffed, grinned, and held up his palm for a high five. "I'm thinking favorite nephew and I need to get into a session of baking this weekend. Am I right?"

Sean returned the grin. "Sourdough or cake?"

"Why not both?" Don asked.

"I like the way you think, favorite uncle."

I winced a little, thinking of Sean's mom's brother, his other uncle, who hadn't ended up earning anyone's favor about a year ago. Sean didn't seem to notice, but Abe squeezed my hand.

"You might have to accept two favorite nephews come fall, you know," Sean said to Don.

"You're my family, kid, you and your little sibling-to-be." Don slipped me a glance.

Isabelle had lost family status with Don, and rightly so. Still, I was sure it still hurt.

"Don't I know it, but right now I have a date with some brutal end-of-term homework," the teen said.

"Thanks for getting dinner, sweetie." I smiled up at him.

His hug was quick and fierce, and his message whispered. "Thanks for staying safe, Mombie."

He hurried away to his room, but I saw the surreptitious drag of his hand over his eyes.

It hadn't been completely smooth sailing, becoming stepmother to a teen as part of falling in love with and marrying Abe. I couldn't have imagined a better package deal, as it turned out. Sean was responsible, fun, and caring while still acting his age. And he loved to cook, always a plus in my book.

"You did manage to stay safe, both of you." Abe gazed from me to Don and back.

"Barely, on my part," Don said.

"Did your wood duck decoy survive?" I asked. "I saw one of the officers knock it into the shrubs. I know it seems minor, but it is a lovely piece of art."

Don gave a sad shrug. "If I never see another duck decoy, I'll be just as happy. I'm going to sell the lot and mend my ways. I only hope I still have a wife."

My phone rang, then buzzed, then rang. "Sorry," I said to the men before I pulled it out to see Don's wife's name. I connected the call. "Georgia?"

"Robbie, I'm sorry to bother you, but I've been trying to reach Don for a while now, and it's like his phone is off. Have you seen him lately? I'm worried."

I smiled. "He's fine and happens to be right here at our dinner table." I extended the phone to Don. "Here you go. She couldn't reach you on your phone."

"The police took it." Don swallowed and accepted my device. "Honey, I have so much to tell you."

Abe stood and gently pushed Don out the sliders onto the patio, closing the doors behind him. Meanwhile, I'd moved to the sofa. I extended my hand for Abe to join me. He snuggled in close.

"Are you sure you and the baby weren't in danger?" he asked.

"I am. After I got a text from Don's number asking me to come over, I went but stayed clear of the house and called in my suspicion about the message not being from Don."

Birdy jumped up with that little chirping sound that gave him his name. He curled up in the narrow space between me and the sofa's cushioned arm.

"Believe me, I was a total good doobie," I went on. "The dispatcher told me to stay in my car with the doors locked. I did exactly that, Abe."

"Did Isabelle ever admit she'd killed Evermina Martin?"

I nodded. "Don said she did. She told him she knew I knew she had. Not exactly true, but I had my ideas about her. What I'd like to find out is what the police knew before I called."

"If they were on her trail, you mean?" Abe asked.

"Right."

The doorbell rang as Don came back in. He recoiled as his face took on a panicked expression. He gave quick glances around as if searching for a place to hide.

Isabelle was in custody. What if Fred Blount had been helping her and was here to, what? Attack all of us? My gut turned to ice.

CHAPTER 64

"You're okay," Abe soothed his brother. "You're safe. It's a post-traumatic reaction. Here, sit down. I'll see who it is."

Don let Abe lead him to an easy chair. Abe had been a medic in the military. He recognized what Don was going through. I let Abe's calm manner soothe me, as well. An accomplice to murder wouldn't ring the doorbell. I hoped.

A minute later Abe brought Buck into the room.

Whew. The lanky officer—and friend—was always welcome. He presented no threat at all.

"Buck, please join us," I said.

"Much obliged, Robbie. I want to begin by congratulating Don, here, on his fortitude. You put that lady away, but good, sir." He held out his hand to Don.

"After a fashion, I suppose." Don's shoulders and face had relaxed when he saw Buck. He stood and shook hands. "Thank you, Chief."

"Let's not truck with titles, now." Buck sank onto the other easy chair. "You've always called me Buck or Bird. That'll be plenty."

Cocoa trotted in and surveyed the room, then made a beeline for Buck.

"Hey, buddy." Buck stroked his head. Cocoa curled up at his feet. Buck gazed at me. "I expected y'all might have a couple few questions about, well, everything. At least Robbie surely will."

"I do have questions." I hadn't had time to dwell on the complicated web. But if Buck was offering information, I'd take it. "This puts Zeke, Wendy, and Camilla in the clear, I guess." I ticked their names off on my fingers.

"It does. They might not be the nicest folks out there, but they ain't killers, even though they each had their own run-ins with the deceased."

"Like I did." Don sat up straight as he acknowledged his dealings with Evermina.

"But you didn't murder her, O'Neill," Buck said. "That's what's important."

"Was Octavia getting close to arresting Isabelle?" I asked Buck.

"Yes, ma'am. It appears a new witness came forward, a lady from that big old church Ms. Cooper is part of. This lady seen Cooper leaving that Nashville parking lot Friday night. With the church lady's testimony, plus a stretch of camera footage, an arrest was imminent."

"I wonder if Isabelle sensed that and panicked," I mused.

"Could be," Buck said.

I sat there thinking about the why of it all. "Isabelle had invested in Evermina's diner." My words came out slowly as my thoughts formed. "And Evermina was mismanaging the finances, big time."

"Which meant she was squandering Cooper's money, big time," Buck murmured.

"Isabelle must have arranged to meet with Evermina that evening and just lost it," I said.

"My stepdaughter's always had temper issues," Don added. "And she keeps her money close, no matter how much she has, doling it out with an eagle eye on where it lands."

"So she would have been furious at Evermina wasting the investment." I gazed at Buck. "Do they think Isabelle planned the murder?"

"Octavia's team's going through her text messages as we speak," Buck said. "Cooper might could cough up that info herself, by and by, if she decides to confess. Whether or not she planned the homicide, they're tracking down a partial fingerprint from the skillet, which my clever cousin Wanda uncovered in a Nashville dumpster. Octavia's still waiting on the DNA analysis. If either piece of evidence matches to Isabelle, that, along with the witness and the camera footage, means they got theirselves a airtight case, confession or no confession, text or no text."

"Buck, what about Fred Blount?" I asked. "Any idea if he helped Isabelle?"

"It don't look like it. Him and his missus was at a different church fundraiser way the heck over in Champaign, Illinois, Friday evening, and they spent the night there. He never coulda gotten to Nashville and back. No, he might be an unpleasant sort, as you pointed out, but he's no murderer. Leastwise, not this time."

Abe stood. "Buck, we didn't offer you anything. I'm going to have a celebratory beer. Can I get you gentlemen one?"

"Why, that would hit the spot, O'Neill," Buck said. "I thank you kindly."

"I'll help." Don rose, too. "Robbie, anything?"

"Thanks, Don. I'll take one of the NAs. Abe knows." I would probably drink only half of the non-alcoholic brew. But putting a homicide behind us didn't come along often, thank goodness. My loved ones were safe. I was, too. All of that merited a toast.

A text came in from Danna.

Mom hrd about arrest. Glad yr safe. Me & Turner R opening. Don't come til 8.

I smiled. The gift of a weekday sleep in? I'd take it. My phone began playing "All You Need is Love" by the Beatles—Adele's ringtone.

"You and yours all safe now?" my aunt asked with no preamble, having obviously monitored her police scanner the same as Corrine had.

"We are. All of us, including Don, whom I brought home."

"Sounded like it was quite the afternoon."

"It was," I murmured.

"You fill me in tomorrow, hon," Adele added. "I gotta run."

"Love you," I said, but she was already gone.

"Robbie, you done good today," Buck murmured. "Staying out of harm's way, most particularly."

I covered my belly with both hands. "I plan to keep this child out of harm's way for as long as I can."

He smiled. "You got maybe fifteen years for that. Eighteen if you're lucky."

Abe and Don returned and passed around glasses of beer.

Abe raised his. "Here's to good news."

"And survival." I clinked my glass with his and took a cool, bubbly sip. It wasn't alcoholic, but it would do. I cocked my head, remembering an important event not connected with homicide.

"Abe, did you get your results?" I couldn't believe I hadn't asked him about his exams.

A blush stole over his cheeks. "I did. You are looking at a freshly certified Wildlife Educator. I passed the exams and the course with high honors."

"Of course you did." I leaned my head on his shoulder.

"Bravo, brother." Don looked proud.

Buck clapped. Cocoa yipped. Birdy streaked away. I sat there feeling happy.

CHAPTER 65

I sniffed as I let myself into the store by the service door. Amid the familiar aromas of bacon, biscuits, and burbling coffee was another that seemed out of place here.

Danna worked the grill, and Turner was busy taking an order across the room. Every table wasn't full, but the place was busy.

"Morning, Danna," I said.

"Enjoy sleeping in?"

"You bet. Thanks to you both."

After I stashed my bag and scrubbed my hands, I tied on an apron. Adele bustled in the front door and waved. Turner stuck two orders up on the carousel.

"Where do you guys want me?" I asked.

They exchanged a glance I couldn't interpret.

"You can take over seating and orders," Turner said. "I'll bus."

"You got it." I headed over to Adele. "Good morning. Samuel's not with you?"

"No. Said he got a bit of inspiration and he wanted to write a poem." She shook her head. "That man never ceases to amaze."

"He's pretty awesome. You can have that empty four-top over there if you want." I led her to the table, not that I needed to. She knew her way around. "I'll grab the coffeepot."

"Hang on a little minute, hon. You all right this morning, you and that great-baby of mine?"

"We're both fine." I smiled. "Let me go get the coffee." I grabbed both caf and decaf pots and hurried back, pouring for a few customers on my way, but making sure the caffeinated pot still held a cup for Adele.

"Appears you got your new fryer up and running." She gave a wave to the specials board.

"No, we haven't had a . . ." My voice trailed off as I read the words.

Gotcha Day to Robbie's New Deep Fryer!
Breakfast Specials:
Apple Fritters
Cheese Fritters

"Whoa." I looked over at the kitchen area. Turner and Danna both faced me, grinning and gesturing with two thumbs up, each. "Those rascals. They must have set it up last night." I blew them a kiss. That was the extra smell I'd picked up. I didn't expect the scent of hot fat and batter frying, so I hadn't understood what it was.

"Well, I'll take me a plate of each," Adele said. "Plus two over easy and a mess of links, when you have time, hon."

The next time I was back in the kitchen, I saw what I should have noticed when I came in. On the far side of the grill, the stainless structure on legs with two boxes for hot oil, two frying baskets, and LED electrical controls. We'd left it there after we'd unpacked it, but now the lights were on and the system was up and running. One basket was mostly submerged in bubbling oil. The other, resting on supports above the oil, held crispy, golden patties of yummy about the size of a flattened golf ball.

"You guys researched the oil and temperatures and everything?" I asked.

"Everything." Danna handed me a small plate from the warming lights. "Here, sample."

I bit into the first fritter, which was savory and soft, with stretchy cheese inside and a crisp outside. The other had been dusted with cinnamon and sugar. I swallowed.

"Perfection. This the apple?" I pointed to the other one. I bit into it and confirmed the apple deliciousness.

"Yep." When the fryer emitted a series of low beeps, Danna pulled up the other basket to drain and slid the lid on the box closed. The contents of the first basket she dumped on a paper-towel lined tray and slid it under the lights.

"We still have a few logistics to work out," Turner chimed in. "But we wanted to surprise you. Fried catfish for lunch."

"What a great surprise," I said. "I wasn't sure when I'd ever get around to setting it up. I'll save my hugs for later."

"Hey, boss, Danna said Don's stepdaughter was the bad guy." Turner's smile turned to a frown. "You and Don are okay, right?"

"She is. And we're all fine on our end."

"That's a relief." Danna flipped three pancakes and turned rashers. She plated an omelet and dished up grits. "These are ready, Turn."

Turner loaded up. "We'll give you a fryer tutorial after we close today, Robbie."

"Sounds like a plan." I waded back into taking orders, clearing tables, making coffee. Doing all the things. When Adele's order was ready, I carried it over to her.

"Tell me, Roberta, is Don all right?" she asked.

"He is."

"I heared old Georgia left him for a bit. Men can get into trouble when they're alone."

I smiled. "They talked last night. Later he told me he apologized and asked her to come home. She'll be back later today."

"Glad to hear it."

"Enjoy your meal, Adele." I turned away.

The bell on the door set to jangling and didn't stop. Two of the basketball players who had been in a few days ago were first, including the one who'd said Wendy Corbett had mistreated her. A party of six hikers followed, trailed by a couple of locals.

I was on my way to greet and seat when a woman at the two-top with the painted chess board stopped me. She and the friend she played chess with were regulars here.

"Everybody's talking about the murderer being

caught, and how you had a hand in it." The woman, who always wore her silver hair wound in a knot atop her head, extended her fist. "Nice job."

I fist-bumped. "I didn't really do anything, but thanks. All I did was phone in a slightly suspicious text I got. It's a relief the police solved the case and made an arrest."

"Right, Robbie," the partner said as if she didn't believe me. "Congratulations go to you. Also, we're chuffed about the new deep fryer. Love me some fried food." Her round face and comfortable body might have indicated the truth in those words.

I smiled and moved on. When I told the hikers they'd have to wait a few minutes for a table big enough to seat them, most of them headed into the cookware aisles. Hoosier player Janae was shifting from foot to foot, scanning the tables.

"She's not here, Jannie," Ellie said. "Right, Robbie? I don't see Wendy anywhere."

"That's right. Wendy hasn't been in. Thanks for coming back. You two can have that last open table." I pointed to Buck's usual spot.

"We heard about what went down yesterday," Janae whispered, now looking more at ease. "We wouldn't have been surprised if they arrested someone else."

Ellie nodded her agreement.

"I hear you." I wouldn't have been shocked, either, if Wendy had been the killer. "Go ahead and seat yourselves. I'll be over in a minute to take your order."

The door swung open again. Octavia and Jim

stood in the entrance. Not who I expected to see, but, hey, the sign said OPEN.

"Come on in," I said. "It'll be a little wait for a table."

Octavia stepped forward. "That's not a problem. Robbie, I want to commend you for staying out of danger yesterday. And for the information you relayed to us all along."

"Staying out of danger is my new hobby." I kept my tone light.

"Mr. O'Neill didn't manage to do so, but his bravery is also to be commended."

"As my aunt would say, all's well that ends well," I murmured. "Buck told me you'd gotten in new evidence about Isabelle."

"Yes."

The door opened once more. "Looks like a party." Chief Harris strode in smiling. wearing a swingy dress and leggings, her hair loose and soft.

I almost didn't recognize her. It was the smile as much as the outfit.

"Chief Harris," I said.

"Oh, call me Haley, would you, Robbie?" Haley looked from me to Octavia. "Good job yesterday, both of you."

Octavia inclined her head.

"All I did was call in a suspicion, ma'am, I mean, Haley." I was about to repeat my mantra about how Harris would have to wait to be seated when Adele stood.

"Yoo-hoo." Adele waved. "Got me three empty chairs here. Octavia, Jim, Haley. Come on over and set with me."

I shrugged with a helpless smile. The two law enforcement officers headed for Adele's table.

Jim paused next to me. "Glad you're okay, Robbie."

"Thanks."

I was okay. Way more than okay. A murderer was behind bars. I was safe and financially stable, healthy, and loved. What more could a woman want?

Recipes

Apple Dumplings

This tasty recipe is from the late Rosemary Carter, a Hoosier farmer, via her daughter-in-law, Jane Deichler Carter. The pie crust recipe is the no-fail one I've been using for years from the Julia Child cookbook, *From Julia Child's Kitchen*.

Ingredients

Dumplings:
Butter
6 apples, cored and quartered
2 tablespoons cinnamon
1 teaspoon nutmeg
1 cup sugar
Pie crust dough, commercial or homemade

Pie dough:
1 teaspoon salt
1¾ cup unbleached flour
¾ cup cold butter (1½ sticks) cut into ½-inch
  cubes
¼–⅓ cup ice water

Directions

Pie dough (if using homemade):
Combine salt and flour in a food processor. Add butter and pulse until pea-sized. Through top feeder tube, add water until dough just starts to clump.

Turn out onto a floured surface. Gently smear together a bit at a time until it is a coherent mass. Shape into a disk, wrap, and refrigerate for at least half an hour.

Dumplings:

Preheat oven to 350. Grease a 9" x 13" baking dish with butter.

In a bowl, toss the apples with the cinnamon and nutmeg.

In a small saucepan, dissolve sugar in two cups water and stir until dissolved. Bring to simmer, then turn off the heat and cover to keep warm.

Roll out pie dough to an ⅛-inch thickness. Cut into 4-inch squares.

Place an apple quarter in a square. Gently stretch the edges up around it and pinch them shut. If the dough tears a little, it doesn't matter. Place the dumpling in the baking dish. Repeat. Makes 24 dumplings.

Pour the hot syrup over the top. Bake for about 50–60 minutes or until the syrup bubbles up and becomes thick and gooey and the tops are slightly brown.

Enjoy warm with vanilla ice cream or whipped cream.

Cheese Fritters

Robbie deep-fries these yummy morsels, but you can bake them if you like. They are delicious dipped in a honey mustard sauce or enjoyed plain.

Ingredients

Fritters:
1¼ cups flour (self-rising might help them puff more)
1 tablespoon garlic powder
1 teaspoon salt
Pinch cayenne pepper
2 eggs
⅓ cup sour cream
1½ cups cheddar cheese, shredded
1 cup mozzarella cheese, shredded
½ cup Swiss cheese, shredded
½ cup green onions, diced
1½ cups Panko breadcrumbs (I use seasoned)

Sweet honey mustard sauce:
3 tablespoons honey
3 tablespoons Dijon mustard
2 tablespoons spicy mustard
2 tablespoons sugar

Directions

Line a rimmed baking sheet with parchment paper.

Sauce:

Whisk together all sauce ingredients and set aside.

Fritters:

Combine dry ingredients except Panko bread-crumbs in a large bowl. Make a well in the middle and lightly whisk in the eggs. Add the rest of the ingredients and mix well.

Scoop golf ball-sized balls onto the baking sheet.

Refrigerate for at least 1 hour or freeze for half an hour.

Place Panko crumbs in a bowl. Roll a ball in your hands to firm, then roll in the crumbs and return to the baking sheet. Repeat for all the balls.

To deep-fry:

Heat oil to 350 . Lower fritters into oil with a slotted spoon and fry until golden.

Drain on brown paper on a wire rack.

To bake:

Preheat oven to 425 before you remove the balls from the refrigerator. Bake about 12 minutes, turn all, and bake about 5 more minutes, until golden and crisp.

Transfer parchment paper to a wire rack to cool.

Either way you cook the fritters, enjoy warm with soup or as an appetizer with the sauce.

Creamy Catfish Chowder

Robbie samples this chowder at Cammie's Kitchen.

Ingredients

1 pound catfish fillets, cut into 1-inch pieces
4 thick-cut bacon strips
1 large onion, chopped
1 garlic clove, minced
1 pound Yukon Gold potatoes, peeled and cubed
1 pound frozen or canned sweet corn
1 bottle (8 ounces) clam juice
1 cup chicken stock
½ teaspoon white pepper
¼ teaspoon dried thyme
2 cups heavy cream or half-and-half, divided
⅓ cup all-purpose flour

Directions

Pat the catfish fillets dry, then cut them into 1-inch pieces.

In a Dutch oven, cook bacon over medium heat until crisp. Remove to paper towels to drain and set aside. Sauté the onion in the bacon drippings until tender. Add garlic and cook 1 minute longer. Stir in the potatoes, corn, clam juice, chicken stock, pepper, and thyme. Bring to a boil and cook for 5–10 minutes.

Reduce the heat to a simmer and add the catfish and 1 cup of the cream or half-and-half. Continue cooking at a simmer, uncovered, until potatoes are tender and the fish is cooked through, about 15–20 minutes.

Whisk the flour into the remaining cup of cream or half-and-half and slowly stir into the chowder. Turn up heat and bring the mixture to a light boil for 5–10 minutes longer to cook the flour and allow the chowder to thicken.

Top the chowder with the reserved bacon and serve with hot sauce and crackers.

Strawberry Coffee Cake

This is best with fresh local strawberries.

Ingredients

Cake:
⅓ cup unsalted butter, room temperature
½ cup granulated sugar
1 large egg
2 teaspoons vanilla
1 cup all-purpose flour
½ teaspoon salt
½ teaspoon baking powder
¼ teaspoon baking soda
½ cup sour cream, room temperature
1½ cups strawberries, sliced

Crumble Topping:
¾ cups all-purpose flour
¼ cup granulated sugar
1 tablespoon brown sugar
¼ teaspoon salt
½ teaspoon ground cinnamon
¼ cup butter melted

Directions

For the cake:
Preheat oven to 350 and butter an 8" square baking dish.

In the bowl of your stand mixer (or with a hand mixer), beat together butter and sugar on high speed for 4–5 minutes until light and fluffy.

Add egg and vanilla, continue to mix until combined.

Turn mixer speed to low and slowly add flour, salt, baking powder, and baking soda until just combined. Using a fork, stir in sour cream until it barely comes together without overmixing.

Evenly spread cake batter in pan then top with sliced strawberries.

For the topping:
Whisk together flour, both sugars, salt, and cinnamon until mixed.

Drizzle butter over flour mixture and, using a fork, stir together until crumbs form.

Sprinkle crumbs over strawberries.

Bake cake for 30–38 minutes OR until a toothpick inserted into the center of the cake comes out clean.

Allow cake to cool for at least 20 minutes before serving.

Coq au Vin

May 29 is National Coq au Vin Day, so that's what Robbie and the gang served up. The following is a simplified version of the famous Julia Child recipe.

Ingredients

2 pounds bone-in chicken thighs and legs
Salt
Pepper
2 tablespoons olive oil
¼ cup butter
1 onion, diced
12 ounces mushrooms, cleaned and sliced
2 cloves minced garlic
1 quart chicken stock
2 cups hearty red wine
1 tablespoon minced fresh rosemary
¼ cup minced fresh parsley, plus more for garnish

Directions

Remove skin and excess fat from chicken, then pat meat dry with paper towels. Season on both sides with salt and pepper.

Heat oil in Dutch oven until simmering.

Working in batches that don't crowd the chicken, brown on both sides and remove to a plate.

Add butter and sauté onion in same pan until it softens. Add mushrooms and continue to sauté until they wilt. Add garlic and sauté for 1 minute. Do not let garlic brown.

Add stock and bring to a boil. Reduce heat to a simmer. Return chicken to pan and add red wine.

Cover and let simmer for 1–2 hours or until chicken is tender.

Stir in herbs. Add salt and pepper to taste. Let flavors combine. Garnish with more parsley.

Serve hot over, or next to, buttered wide noodles or buttered boiled potatoes, and enjoy a salad and a glass of red wine with it.

Memorial Day Cocktail

Phil made a red, white, and blue cocktail for Adele's cookout, which turned out a bit purple.

Ingredients

For one drink:
2 ounces white rum
2 ounces sweetened cranberry juice
1 ounce blueberry syrup
Tonic water or seltzer
Fresh blueberries
Mini marshmallows

Directions

Combine rum, juice, and syrup. Pour over ice and top up with tonic water or seltzer, or more cranberry juice if you prefer. Float a half dozen fresh blueberries in the glass, and string a few mini marshmallows on a stir stick for garnish. Cheers!

Visit our website at
KensingtonBooks.com
to sign up for our newsletters, read
more from your favorite authors, see
books by series, view reading group
guides, and more!

Become a Part of Our
Between the Chapters Book Club
Community and Join the Conversation

Betweenthechapters.net

Submit your book review for a chance to win exclusive
Between the Chapters swag you can't get anywhere else!
https://www.kensingtonbooks.com/pages/review/